... But I Know What You Want:
25 Sex Tales for the Different

James, a servant of God and of the Lord Jesus Christ, to the twelve tribes which are scattered abroad, greeting.

My brethren, count it all joy when ye fall into divers temptations... that ye may be perfect and entire, wanting nothing.

— The Epistle of James, Authorized King James Version

... But I Know What You Want:
25 Sex Tales for the Different

by James Williams

greenery press

Published in the United States by Greenery Press, 3403 Piedmont Ave. #301, Oakland, CA 94611, www.greenerypress.com.

ISBN 1-890159-45-X

Contents

Hiding Behind Sweet Gwendoline: The Invisible Male Submissive
　by Patrick Califia .... *i*
Truth Is Stranger Than Non-Fiction: Introducing James Williams
　by William A. Henkin, Ph.D. .... *vii*
A Pure Fool 1
Goddess 17
Daddy 33
Bridges 39
Afternoon Delight 46
Cages: A Three-Part Invention
　Cage #1 49
　Cage #2 51
　Cage #3 53
Bear 57
The Magic Mirror 66
Ponyboy 83
Fire Island 1974: A Bedtime Story 98
Ritual Cycle
　One: April Fool 111
　Two: Occult Blood 112
　Three: The Fisher Bride 112
　Four: Sunset at Glass Beach 112
　Five: Mangoes 113
　Six: Your Simple Kiss 113
　Seven: White Roses 113
Straight Boy 114
Every Picture Tells a Story 121
I and Thou 123
My Life As a Wife 129
I Bow 161
Moon 164
Red Nails in the Sunset 166
Civilization and Its Discontents: My Justine, Part One 171
The Unconscionable Treachery of Fate: My Justine, Part Two 176
Plaisir d'Amour: My Justine, Part Three 183
Incubus 187
Jason's Cock 193
Trust 199
Light 212

Some of the stories in this collection have appeared previously in these same or in similar forms.

- A Pure Fool was first published in *International Leatherman*
- Afternoon Delight was first published anonymously in *My Biggest O*, edited by Jack Hart (Alyson Publications)
- Bear was first published in *International Leatherman*
- Bridges was first published orally by radio station KALW-FM, San Francisco, California, on its program *Final Draft*
- Cage #1, Cage #2, and Cage #3 were first published online in *Mind Caviar*
- Civilization and Its Discontents was first published in *Spectator*
- Daddy was first published in *Doing It for Daddy*, edited by Pat Califia (Alyson Publications), and subsequently in *Best American Erotica of 1995*, edited by Susie Bright (Simon & Schuster)
- Goddess was first published in *Bitch Goddess*, edited by Pat Califia and Drew Parkin (Greenery Press); an earlier version of the story appeared in *Attitude*
- Incubus was first published in *Black Sheets*
- Jason's Cock was first published in *Best S/M Erotica: Extreme Stories of Extreme Sex*, edited by M. Christian and Simon Sheppard (The Venus Book Club, 2002; Black Books, 2003)
- Light was first published in *Paramour*
- Occult Blood was first published in *Blue Food*
- Plaisir d'Amour was first published in *Spectator*
- Ponyboy was first published in *Best Gay Erotica 2002*, edited by Richard la Bronté, and subsequently in *Best American Erotica 2003*, edited by Susie Bright
- Straight Boy was first published in *Advocate Men*
- The Unconscionable Treachery of Fate was first published in *Spectator*
- Trust was first published in *SM Visions*, edited by Cecilia Tan (Circlet Press), and subsequently in *SM Futures*, also edited by Cecilia Tan (Richard Kasek Books)
- White Roses was first published in *Blue Food*

For inspiring or promoting the processes that led to this book, each in her or his own way, I am especially grateful to:

Layne Winklebleck, formerly editor of *Spectator*, who first offered to consider my writings on sex and sexuality for publication, and then actually published them;

Patrick Califia, who invited my first sex fiction and then actually published *it*, and who has provided unwavering support ever since;

Jim Hunger, formerly editor of *International Leatherman*, for grace that surpasseth my understanding;

M. Christian for generously dispensing dirty words I understand all too well;

Bill Henkin for gifts of time and tide of which I never have enough;

Katherine Ryan for believing beyond the bounds of good sense.

– JW

For Patrick Califia
il miglior fabbro

For Mistress Elle, inevitably,
trouvant le pays le plus agréable un lieu d'exil
si elle ne devait pas y être,
et ne désirant que rester toujours à Paris
tant que je pourrais la voir aux Champs-Elysées
– Marcel Proust, *Du Coté de Chez Swann*

and For Dionysus, Light of the Valley, always and forever
Die So-geliebte, dass aus einer Leier
mehr Klage kam als je aus Klagefrauen;
das eine Welt aus Klage ward, in der
alles noch einmal da war: Wald und Tal
und Weg und Ortschaft, Feld und Fluss und Tier;
und dass um diese Klage-Welt, ganz so
wie um die andre Erde, eine Sonne
und ein gestirnter stiller Himmel ging,
ein Klage-Himmel mit entstellten Sternen —:
Diese So-geliebte.
– Ranier Maria Rilke, *Orpheus. Eurydike. Hermes*

HIDING BEHIND SWEET GWENDOLINE: THE INVISIBLE MALE SUBMISSIVE

An Introduction by Patrick Califia to James Williams' ... But I Know What You Want

This is a book I've waited a long time to read. It has been my privilege to work with this writer as a magazine editor and the editor of several anthologies. Williams' work has always impressed me as being fresh and thought-provoking, never stale or predictable. Between these covers, at last, the short stories, poetry, and essays of James Williams have been brought together in one place. While some of these pieces have appeared in print before, it's a pain in the neck to track down an oeuvre that has been scattered in periodicals and books that may go out of print. I think it is hard to appreciate the entire scope of an author's career until you can readily compare a comprehensive sample of the full spectrum of his interest and abilities. Williams adds another worthy and talented voice to the renaissance of sex literature and political analysis that has been fueled largely by Bay Area writers in the last decade.

What really matters, of course, is not where Williams lives. Many of my favorite sex radical writers live in places like New York, Seattle, or even Boston. What matters is the work itself. These are intelligent, original, and pansexual pieces written with a great deal of facility and grace. If you have perhaps assumed that only women writers have anything new or interesting to say about sexuality, I suggest that you question that prejudice, and give this book a chance. In his essays and stories, Williams proves that he is a worthy colleague of Geoff Mains, Jack Fritscher, Aaron Travis, Mark Thompson, Guy Baldwin, Pat Bond, and other writers who have celebrated the erotic aspects of S/M or written social commentary about the scene.

Williams' short stories include such a wide range of characters and situations that it's hard to believe one author's erotic experience could enable him to realistically portray so many different experiences with pleasure, gender, and intimate relationships. Gay men are interspersed with straight men, both submissive and dominant, as well as female voices. All of them ring true to me, and one of the chief delights of reading this book is to wonder, on the first page of each piece, exactly what sort of realm the writer is going to open up for your vicarious and voyeuristic enjoyment.

My favorite piece in the book is also one of the shortest, and I fear it may be overlooked. I'm referring to "Every Picture Tells a Story." Before I can explain what I find so moving about it, I have to back up a couple of decades, to the point in time where I was coming out as a sadomasochist and searching for literature about or representations of my erotic interest in power exchange sex. One of the loveliest creations this search turned up is the reprinted work of erotic photographer, cartoonist, and publisher John Willie, whose "Sweet Gwendoline," a Perils-of-Pauline type story with a great deal of sophisticated bondage, had been reprinted. It seemed to me that a lot of the material I found featured a very feminine, female top being stern with a sweet female submissive.

At the time, there was a great deal of contempt for sexually explicit material featuring ostensibly lesbian sex if that material was created by men or published for a male audience. It was assumed (and often correctly so) that this kind of stuff would misrepresent lesbian sexuality, and was icky voyeuristic stuff that allowed straight men to perv on dykes under the illusion that two girls together would be happy to be interrupted by a hard dick. But "Gwendoline" and a lot of the girl-on-girl fetish porn that I began collecting from the '50s and later didn't have that fake quality or the presumption that a lesbian twosome was a heterosexual threesome just waiting to happen. For example, in the classic bondage novels of F. E. Campbell, male tops frequently attempt to challenge a female submissive's loyalty to her mistress, and they often lose this competition.

What is presented here is, to borrow the phrase of a lesbian scholar who would not approve, a female world of love and ritual. How is it that male sadomasochists would create such S/M utopias, and why would they want to look at or read about them? I believe this is because Sweet Gwen *is* the straight male submissive. Our culture equates masochism with femininity with the female gender. Fetishism seems to be a form of erotic energy that yearns for perfection, for absolutes. In a culture where male masochism or submission is a non sequitur, Gwen must represent bottoms of all sexes, and her male counterpart becomes largely invisible.

While it would be perfectly appropriate to rail about the sexism of this semiotic, I think there is more going on here than straightforward patriarchal oppression of women, forcing women to be dominated in the realm of Eros. Male self-hatred is also at work here; shame about the male form and its graphic representation. Girls are pretty on their knees, according to the predominant aesthetic, while men are not; they are merely incongruous, pathetic, and insincere. Until very recently, there was no aesthetic that celebrated the beauty of a heterosexual man in bondage to a dominant woman's erotic power. The porn that exists in this genre usually caricatures the men who are under the sway of the Bitch Goddess. Unless humiliation is your mètier, it is difficult to jack off to something that heightens your worst fears about yourself.

It's exciting to see this change, to see, for example, the intriguing and intense images that Michael Manning has created of male lust in captivity, bent to the service of another's pleasure. But it's interesting to see how often in this radically new sort of erotic art that images of femininity are associated with male submission as a way to heighten its authenticity. Manning's slave boys may have very large and very hard cocks, but they are also often corseted, their faces prettily made up, orifices dilated and plugged. Thus far, it is only in gay male leather porn that the viewer can reliably expect to find masculinity and submission co-existing comfortably in the same image. I wonder when we will see erotic art reminiscent of Tom of Finland that features dominatrices and their butch boy toys.

I'm not suggesting, of course, that there is something better about being a masculine straight guy who likes to go under instead of a crossdresser or some other variation in gender expression. It's just interesting to try to figure out why we see certain kinds of S/M representations a lot more often than others.

"Every Picture Tells a Story" comes, I think, from the cultural place where male submission and female identity have been cathected, where it seems as if to authentically experience yielding to the power of another, one must assume a female form. It is also one of the most poignant descriptions of gender dysphoria that I have ever read. The grief and yearning that the narrator experiences as he tries to imagine himself in place of the beautiful young woman who is treasured, cared for, and contained by her older female lover brought me close to tears. This is a moment of cognitive dissonance that is well-nigh invisible in our culture, and in our literature. Williams has put something rare on paper here, and done it very well.

This theme of the gender fluidity of the male bottom is picked up again in "Bridges," "My Life as a Wife," and elsewhere. Williams has shown exceptional courage in writing so explicitly about the male submissive/female dominant experience, as he also does in "Goddess."

Williams seems equally at ease writing sexy stuff about dominant heterosexual men, including "Daddy," one of the few stories about infantilism I've ever found titillating, and "Incubus." The nebulous and mysterious story "The Magic Mirror" is a richly detailed tale of time travel, the training of a female submissive, and the exchange or blurring of identities that is so often a psychic component of romantic love.

It is a little mind-wrenching to move so quickly and so often from the realm of hot heterosexual sex to the midnight realm of gay leathermen. But some of the best stories in this volume celebrate the testosterone-enriched delights of top men who wrest control from their grown-up boys. "A Pure Fool" is a well-crafted story about a grief-stricken master who decides to reenter the scene despite the loved ones he has lost. It is a picture-perfect portrayal of the scene circa 1973. "Bear," "Ponyboy," and "Straight Boy" are classic works. But my favorite piece that features an all-male cast is probably "Jason's Cock," an erotic narrative that has such a nice twist that I'll let you discover it on your own.

There are also some lovely vanillaesque sketches of gay male lust like "Afternoon Delight," in which innocence is lost when a hard cock and wet lips collide via a glory hole. In "Moon," a bout of anal sex is deliciously recounted.

There's absolutely nothing vanilla about "I and Thou." This is perhaps the riskiest piece in the entire book, and one which some readers will probably wish was not included. This "Deliverance"-style tale of kidnapping and sexual violence is pretty strong stuff. I read it in much the same spirit that I read Bret Easton Ellis's *American Psycho* – as if I was taking some bad-tasting medicine. This is a powerful and tragic story. You come away from it with the nauseating taste of terror in the back of your throat. I found it interesting in part because my response to the rape and battery in "I and Thou" was so very different from the vicarious arousal that I was able to experience in pieces about consensual S/M. If nothing else, the genuine degradation and violation depicted here makes the difference between negotiated role-playing sex and real-world battery shockingly clear.

Some critics will probably be obtuse enough to fasten on this story alone as representing everything that is pathological about leathersex or the S/M community. But I think it is clear that Williams is not writing about the scene here. He is exploring some uncomfortable questions about the exercise of force as an aspect of human nature and experience. By describing the utter devaluation of the victim in "I and Thou," he takes the reader to an unexpected place of horror and compassion. While this is not an emotional experience that the typical reader of erotica may be expecting, I think that we must expand our assumptions about the effects of sexually explicit fiction beyond mere arousal. S/M people are perhaps no better equipped to explore the Shadow than everyone else. By its very nature, it is repellent and forbidding. But I think an honest and skilled writer has to be curious about the less savory aspects of what we are too quick to call civilization.

If ...*But I Know What You Want* has an overriding theme, it is about the epiphany that takes place when the spirit appears as the living force within matter. Williams is a connoisseur of transcendence, a polytheist and sexual animist. Whether sacred or profane, the body is a vehicle that can take us on journeys of understanding, healing, and worship that would be impossible to experience if we were merely flesh. Sacred and profane, drop-dead serious and completely irreverent, this is a memorable book that deserves a second reading and will no doubt trigger a great deal of speculation and discussion.

Patrick Califia is the author of several landmark works of S/M fiction and sexual politics, including <u>Macho Sluts</u>, <u>Public Sex</u>, <u>Sensuous Magic</u>, and the forthcoming essay collection <u>Speaking Sex to Power</u>. He lives in San Francisco, where the high cost of living goads any author to be as prolific as possible. Patrick is also a therapist and a parent, so has very little time to actually do any of the kinky things that he writes about.

TRUTH IS STRANGER THAN NON-FICTION: INTRODUCING JAMES WILLIAMS

by William A. Henkin, Ph.D.

1. One Man's History

I met James Williams in the mid-1970s, as I left one of San Francisco's booming disco-era bath-houses some time after midnight. He recognized me as the man who had shared his pursuit – though not his conquest – of a particularly inspired individual, and invited me out for a commiseratory nightcap. We ended up at the old Café du Nord, which was still a Basque restaurant in those days, and sat at the long carved bar before the rose quartz mirror that was a relic from the restaurant's speakeasy days. The bartender back then so closely resembled pictures of Gurdjieff that I once accused him, only half in jest, of actually being the old master trickster himself. He laughed instead of giving me a straight reply, but he let me drink on the house that night; and when James and I walked in he was already pouring my Pernod.

The place was quiet close to closing time as James and I became acquainted. He was considerably younger than I, about six feet tall, very lean and lithe, and moved as if he balanced on his head a precious vase of great antiquity rather than the tight sort of mop of dark auburn curls that will never grow thin and possibly never go grey. We found that we shared interests in psychology and literature, as well as in sexual exploration; in Peet's coffee, then available in only one Berkeley shop; and in baseball, about which he knew far more than I: his knowledge seemed encyclopedic as Bill James's[*]. He also expressed

---

[*] *Baseball is a game rife with statistics all fans can cite, and others that only the most diligent experts know without computers. But the preservation and knowledge of statistics has always been a hallmark of the baseball fan, and without doubt Bill James is the greatest statistician in baseball's history. He is the author of Bill James's Historical Baseball Abstract, the All-Time Baseball Sourcebook, the All-Time Major League Handbook, Bill James Presents Stats: Major League 2000, Bill James Presents Stats: Minor League 2000, Bill James Presents Stats: Major League 1999, Bill James Presents Stats: Minor League 1999, and a slew of related titles.*

considerable interest in my early careers as a university English teacher and a literary magazine editor, and spoke with a humorous, exaggerated tolerance about the vagaries of the jobs he then held as a substitute teacher in a private high school on the Peninsula, a San Francisco tour-bus driver, and an occasional gigolo. As we parted a pleasant hour later I voiced the hope that we'd soon get together again, but James turned out to be fully as reclusive as he claimed to be. My next encounter with him was several years later, when he left a message on my answering machine in 1978, asking me to listen to him read a story on the radio the following day. But he left no number at which I could call him back, he was not listed with Directory Assistance, and the person who answered the phone at the radio station when I tried to find him after his reading said she had no way to reach him.

It was more than a decade before I heard from James again, when I received a typescript of the story "Straight Boy" and a note that ended, "Truth is stranger than non-fiction," reminding me of the evening we had met. A few days later he phoned, and on a stormy afternoon in the winter of 1992, while a heavy rain tattooed against the corrugated plastic roof and the dim lights made the large, thinly-warmed, fern-filled room feel like a cozy covered shelter in an outdoor garden, we met for coffee at The Patio on Castro Street.

James wanted a closer conversation about writing than we'd had before and so did I, and we chatted on all afternoon. At one point I asked how he wrote fiction and he said he didn't know. Sometimes he just sensed that a story had come to him and he sat down to write it immediately. Sometimes he was writing something else – a letter, a shopping list – and found he was writing a story, so he had to abandon whatever his first task had been in order to follow the story's thread to the end: if he didn't follow the thread right then, he said, there would be no thread to follow when he went back to look for it later. He said he never knew what a story was going to be about when he began it, he never knew where it would go except while it was going there in the writing itself, and he never knew how it would end until it actually ended, usually surprising him. He had never been able to decide to write a story and then write one. All he knew about writing – all he had ever learned, he said – was how to open himself to whatever Muse or inspiration it was that seemed to write through him.

As dinner-time approached James said he thought he should be getting home. Home where? I wondered. Home to whom, home to what? He smiled almost ruefully and shook his head. "Home," he said, and then he said good-bye. Episodically over the ensuing years I've received envelopes from him containing stories and requests for my responses to them, but until very recently I never received a reply in return when I wrote to his P.O. Box.

In 1994 or '95 James called again and asked if I would represent him. He'd had a story published in an anthology edited by the writer then known as Pat Califia, and Pat had asked him to read it at A Different Light, San Francisco's premier gaylesbitrans bookstore. He wanted to accept, but had become either agoraphobic or clandestine – it didn't matter which, he said – and just did not feel he could step that far out into the light of visibility. I agreed to appear in his place, explained his absence and my presence to the audience, and read "Daddy" for him. Our occasional correspondence resumed.

In 1998 James called to tell me Race Bannon had accepted his collection of stories for publication at Daedalus Publishing Company, and asked if I would help him select and arrange the stories. Race had published a book I wrote with Sybil Holiday, *Consensual Sadomasochism: How to Talk About It and How to Do It Safely*, and I both liked and respected him. Since I also had come to feel a personal interest in James's fiction, my answer was easy: yes: of course. James agreed to answer my queries about his manuscript and book, and for that purpose we have spoken now and again in the intervening years. When Race decided to move on from Daedalus, James asked me to represent his book to other publishers. Once more I consented, and brought it first to Janet Hardy, whose Greenery Press is a pre-eminent publisher of alternative sexuality publishing in America today. She read the manuscript and, happily for everyone concerned, gave it an appropriate home at Greenery.

Also in the intervening years I came to understand that as the nominal editor of this collection I ought to say something about the stories I was going to help select and organize. This worried me, because usually fiction speaks so well for itself and in its own language that an editor, reviewer, or other sort of commentator risks undermining its impact by saying too much, or slighting its purpose by saying too little, rather than illuminating the work's intention by saying just the right thing.

2. *The Right Thing?*

Pornography is a word coined only a couple hundred years ago, combined from two Greek words, *porne*, prostitute, and *graphein*, to write. It was originally applied to writing that depicted prostitutes and their trade, particularly in matters regarding public hygiene; later it came to mean writing and pictures intended to stimulate sexual desire. Eros, the cherubic son of Aphrodite who flies around on little wings toting his bow and quiver of arrows in generations of Romantic paintings, was the Greek God of love. He was desperately feared by all the gods, even Zeus, king of the Olympians. *Erotica*, a word derived from his name, originally denoted writing and pictures about sexual love; it still does. In literature as in real life, sexual love and sexual desire are frequently confused and frequently conflated; not always, but sometimes, they are also the very same thing.

The stories in this volume fall into a long literary tradition that celebrates sex in a wide array of aspects, and variously they bear witness to the value, honor, and power James Williams accords both sexual desire and sexual love. Rather than wade through that rich history of physically amatory fiction as a way to explain, justify, or classify this book, or as a way to set it in some sort of historical context, I prefer to turn my attention to what happens on the pages that follow. Or not actually *on* the pages but *behind* them rather, because what happens on them seems always clear to me.

At the climax of each of James Williams's stories I find an epiphany – an insight or a realization – of discovery and surrender, and every such epiphany demands a kind of transformation that changes the nature of a character's humanity. Sometimes the epiphany is concerned strictly with sexual desire, as in "Jason's Cock" or "Afternoon Delight," sometimes it is concerned with sexual love, as in "Cage #3" or "Daddy," and sometimes it is concerned with love expressed erotically, as in "Trust" or "My Life as a Wife." Sometimes the climax takes place at the very last moment, as it does in "Cage #2" or "I and Thou," and sometimes it takes place before the story has even begun, as it does in "Incubus" or "Cage #1." Frequently the epiphany takes place in the context of an erotic power dynamic, as in "Every Picture Tells a Story" or "A Pure Fool," other times erotic power is irrelevant, as in "I Bow," or it is a very understated background, as in "Bridges." Sometimes sex is explicit, as it is in "Bear," or "Fire Island 1974," but more often sex is tacit because, as in

"Goddess" and even more apparently in "The Magic Mirror," few of these stories are actually about sex at all. Instead, sex is the context in which they all take place. It is as if, for Williams, the pornographic world of Eros is an ideal realm in which we humans may find the psychological and spiritual surrender he associates with epiphany.

Perhaps because these stories are all driven by what their characters and circumstances demand, rather than by what the plot or storyline might want, they are also about discovery for me as reader: like Williams when he writes, I never know when I begin to read one of them the *direction* in which it will lead me. I sometimes feel as if I am following a chain of erotically directed associations that suddenly *resolve*, the way some free-form jazz cadenzas suddenly resolve, with a kind of sigh of recognition that is not so much a musical climax as it is a musical *ahhh* ... telling me *this* is where I was supposed to end up, *this* is what I was supposed to surrender to, *here* was home all along. Sometimes that resolution comes as a surrender of the heart, sometimes of the genitals, sometimes both, but it always comes as the surrender to a uniquely human question: who – or what – am I now, in this moment? And what about now, in this one? And now, in this one, with (or without) you?

The handful of poems and expository stories included in this collection proceed the same way the other stories do, and I read them in much the same way I read any other narrative in this book: in each the author begins his riff, and plays his instrument, his alphabet piano, as if guided by the song. Nowhere do I find the tendentious moment when I feel the author had a point to get across, for even in the poems a character discovers who or what he is, or where or how he has to surrender; only now, more explicitly than when the author is disguised by characters, the epiphany belongs explicitly to Williams himself.

3. Postscript

Editing these stories and working with James Williams has been exciting for me, but it has not been without its tribulations. As I indicated above, James is not always easy to reach. He is extraordinarily jealous of his time and privacy, does not like to be thwarted, readily turns peevish when something about the work distresses him, and guards his authorial prerogatives rigorously. He is perfectly willing and able to undo someone else's labors – mine, in this case – to achieve his artistic ends, so at his insistence and over my objections I have included one story in this collection that deeply unnerves me and that I would very much have preferred to leave out for reasons of my personal morality; and on occasion I have accepted punctuations and variant spellings that violate the rigors of academic style sheets. Still, the rewards of the task have always far outweighed the miseries, and in sum I am glad and proud to be associated with the author and his first collection of writings.

When he and I spoke most recently James asked me to be sure that I concluded my remarks by saying just one thing on his behalf: he asked me to end my Introduction by saying that no one in his stories is based on a real person; everyone is a fiction.

William A. Henkin, Ph.D.
San Francisco, CA
July, 2002

William A. Henkin is co-author of Consensual Sadomashochism: How to Talk About It and How to Do It Safely, and author or co-author of a dozen other books. He is a licensed psychotherapist and a board-certified sex therapist, and conducts his private practice in San Francisco.

A Pure Fool

The first time I saw him at the Eagle I came alive again, and knew this one could be important in some way. But the moment was so unexpected that I was really able to do no more than sip my tired scotch to keep myself from gawking. He was something sweet to look at in the face: clean-shaven, with the short black hair and young angel's trusting eyes that would have pleased Caravaggio so much that in my mind I named him Angelo instantly. At the same time he was also a big, statuesque man, 6'4" or so, with the broad shoulders, trim hips, and nipped-in waist that motorcycle jackets seem designed to shape – except it was one of those warm, balmy nights San Francisco gets for about a week in May and another week in September, and above his tight black jeans and seasoned, polished boots he wore only a close-fitting plain black t-shirt that made his chest and arms look as if they'd been pumped up by Industrial Light & Magic. He sent those innocent's eyes on a quick bar cruise and they didn't come to rest on me, maybe because I was wearing sunglasses and maybe for all the other reasons I was not yet ready to be seen.

I had been away for awhile and had not yet made my decision to come out again, but I had seen the boy in Angelo immediately and I knew just what he was looking for. After Sean died of that rapacious plague that stole a generation of men as if we'd been sent to war with no weapons I found that I was too angry to be fit company for anyone but wild dogs. I moved up-country, grew a beard that was greyer than I'd expected it to be, and lived by my wits in the Mendocino hills for a few months. I went to the original Billy Club gathering just because I was lonely, and by winter I was holed up outside Ukiah in a little old Airstream trailer with a boy I'd met there who said he was 18 but hadn't yet learned to read or write having grown up as a hobo on the road with his illiterate backwoods Pappy. But if he couldn't read words he could surely read deer tracks and run down rabbit, and we ate all right till spring, when he lit out for Alaska to work on a fishing boat. With the boy gone and the days getting long I found myself bored with everything and my own company most of all, so I came back to town and became a suit in one of the money buildings downtown. I don't remember anything that matters from all that time until the day I looked at someone else's calendar and realized Sean had been dead for half as many years as we'd been together and if I was going to honor what we'd had I couldn't write myself off as just as dead, so I started thinking about what I wanted to do with my life now that I was going to be a grown-up all over again. I began to come to the Eagle on weekend nights to do my thinking because it was public, there was space on the patio to dawdle under the city's meager skyful of wan stars, it was comfortable to a man of my persuasions, and the other men who patronized the bar were willing to leave a quiet man alone.

I was still thinking the evening Angelo walked in, and though I hadn't yet decided to haul out my old leathers he made me notice that it could be a good idea. Waving and nodding without stealing all the light, he seemed familiar enough with the bar and its patrons that I knew he was a regular. That meant I could find him when I wanted to, so I decided to let him go while I thought some more. As I say, I hadn't even decided yet to come out again, and if anything had made me a good Top in my day it had been patience and the ability to choose my moves.

The more I thought about the boy the more I thought a little coming out – at least privately — would be a good thing in my life. I didn't mind the fact that I had surely aged enough to be his father, so the next weekend as I swizzled my drink I let myself be talked to by a couple of the men I'd seen him spend time with that first evening. I didn't say anything about my interest, but I didn't derail any conversations that seemed they might go in his direction either, and eventually one came around to him just as fully as their visions of Jesus must have come upon the saints. They said his name was Michael, but I never changed my mind. After my years of despair I feet presenting the dry leash and my drink, both of which he held until my boots had been spit-shined. He always performed in ways that earned my respect. Scott had trained him to be one fine boy, but while a good bottom can be trained up out of nearly anyone, a great bottom has to be born to it. I knew Keith had brought Scott a lot to begin with.

Sometimes I wished it was Keith I wanted rather than Angelo, because he was *such* a good boy. But the heart is a funny kind of Master, always running ahead of the brain, and I had learned long ago that the heart would not be denied however foolish the brain might think its desires.

All in all my first new evening out was uneventful. Angelo didn't show up and I didn't hear anything about him, and when the beer bust turned into an amateur-hour auction I took Keith home directly. But a couple of the regulars did notice my dress, my pins, and the diligence with which Keith served me. I kept going to the Eagle on weekends and people looked at me differently from that night on. Apparently the scene had changed in my absence, and confident, knowledgeable Masters with graceful, well-trained boys were not as common as they once had been. The third time I brought Keith along we were easily accepted regulars, even treated with occasional deference, though several erstwhile Tops seemed confused when Keith politely declined to serve them and referred them on to me. Then Angelo appeared and I knew what the Old Man felt when the marlin hit his albacore one hundred fathoms down.

I was seated at the far corner of the front bar so I could see the doorway, with Keith at my boots so he would be seen from it. Angelo couldn't miss the slave and then he wouldn't miss the Master. The way his whole head hitched I knew it took some effort for him to hold his eyes in front as he made his way to the people who were greeting him. I would have bet anything his dick was hard already: I was the life that he'd been looking for with his Stand and Model crowd, and even if he'd been beating off to that tune since he was a pup he had never really known it till that moment. *Good*, I thought: *take the bait*. He pulled himself together to greet his young familiars and I didn't do a thing. My whole recent career at the Eagle had been composed of doing nothing with intention, and I saw no reason to change. I sent Keith to fetch a glass of water just so I could watch him kneel and kiss my boot. He presented the glass held high above his head in both his hands and didn't spill a drop; the water hardly even quivered as I took the glass. I let Keith kneel up and rubbed the nape of his bowed neck. I didn't pay any mind to Angelo just then. I didn't have to. *Good boy*, my gestures said to Keith; *good Master*, I meant for Angelo to read. A few minutes later I led Keith into the night.

✦✦

I once wanted to write a book called *How to Pick Up Leathermen*, but after a week of work it seemed to me that all I'd put down on paper was a collection of platitudes no one could possibly need in order to get laid, so I went out to practice what otherwise I would have preached, and in the practice I realized that all the clichés are true but that they argue with each other: just as absence makes the heart grow fonder, so also out of sight is out of mind. All the clichés may be true, in other words, but their truth is worthless: you can't live by any of them unless you're constantly figuring out which one applies and when.

For the next few weeks I varied my visits to the Eagle. Sometimes I'd go on Friday, sometimes on Saturday, sometimes both; sometimes I'd take Keith, sometimes I'd go alone; sometimes I'd go early, sometimes I'd stay late; sometimes I'd be in full leathers, sometimes I'd dress down; sometimes I'd talk to people, sometimes I'd sit in the shadows with my sunglasses on. I always behaved according to my whim, and with my intention clear before me: to secure a place for myself in Angelo's mind.

Consequently, as the weeks went by, Angelo was always searching for me in the bar. The first thing he did when he walked in was to look the whole place over until he found me and then, whatever else he did, he never did not know where I was. If he got there before I did his eyes were always just twitching away from the door when I entered, and then, again, he was never unaware of me.

Just before he should have gotten bored with our cat and mouse game I decided it was time for me to make my move. Like an old cliché artist, I took the bit in my teeth, took the bull by the horns, bit the bullet, took aim for the prize, reached for the brass ring, and went for the gold.

It was one of those ordinary San Francisco summer nights so cool with waves of fog sweeping the streets that shorts-clad tourists were wondering aloud how to get to California. At the Eagle a few of the fashionable boys had trotted out their uptown leathers knowing they wouldn't get all sweated up as long as they undressed by noon, and the smell of body-warmed hide and dye gave the place a nice, old-fashioned, friendly feeling.

I was sitting a little off to one side, alone and peaceful in full dress with an empty collar and leash on the seat beside me when my prey arrived. I didn't let him settle in at all: as soon as he spotted me I pointed one gloved finger straight at his heart. He stopped like a buck caught in headlights and I let my finger describe a curve like a noose, pointing to the floor beside my boots. I suppose he might have blown me off and left me feeling foolish as a cupcake but the possibility, frankly, never crossed my mind. Nor, I think, did it ever cross his. He came, instead, as I must have known he would, and knelt before me as he had seen Keith kneel a dozen times, though not, I must acknowledge, with Keith's natural panache. He clasped his hands behind his back, bowed his head, and waited.

The bar was as quiet as I'd ever heard it. Angelo was quite well known, and though no one really knew me there I had become something of a figure because of my demeanor during my studied comings and goings. Our meeting could not have been seen by the gentry as anything but auspicious, which was as I meant it to be. I longed to take that noble, sculpted head in my hands, turn his face to the light, and kiss his meaty lips, but I knew better what protocol demanded. I slid one foot between his legs and kicked his thighs a little farther apart. I raised my foot and pressed the toe of my boot more and more snugly against his basket, pleased that he still held his position even after there was moisture on his forehead. I picked up the collar and studied him over its rim, letting every man in the place have a look at what I was about to do, then wordlessly brought the leather band down to his mouth. Someone must have even turned the DJ off because I could hear his dry lips part, hear bones crackle in his neck. He leaned forward the missing inch as delicately as a girl in some neo-Victorian bodice-buster and kissed the collar as long as I held it out, leaving his head more fully bowed than before when I took it away from him. Slowly, deliberately, I wrapped the band around his neck, took a padlock from the coils of chain leash, and secured it with my fist. I snapped the leash onto the d-ring at his throat and touched his head. He bent obediently to kiss my boots until I stood and told him, "Up, boy." Then, without raising his eyes, he followed me out of the bar and home.

✦✦

You probably want to know what went on that night – I certainly would if I were you – but even in the fetish world a man's entitled to some privacy, and other people's privacy is often the only excuse we have to exercise our own imaginations. Besides, what went on *after* we left the bar could not be nearly as entrancing as what went on *before*, so as far as that's concerned you've already read the good stuff.

The next few months were basic training for my new young slave. Their only claim to interest for anyone apart from those of us who lived them was the way Keith managed the relationship between the boys so that Angelo could learn from him without ever feeling he was second class and Keith himself never felt less special than Angelo, while I could have the pleasure of watching the best slave I'd ever known train my boy in his special skills for me. It wasn't that Angelo didn't already know *what* to do: he was bright, reasonably experienced for his age, and had bottomed as well as Topped before. He was about the best the young crop had to offer, as well as being pretty. But because submission came so naturally to Keith, he could show Angelo *how* to do what would otherwise have been inexplicable: how to stay alert to his Master's touch so that all his little nerve endings were almost constantly erect, and the merest suggestion that I *might* touch his skin made his body tremble with anticipation; how to feel proud of his humility and humble in his pride so that he knew how rare a privilege it was to occupy the place reserved for him on the floor at or under my feet; how to let the cat and snake run *through* the muscles of his back so the sensation actually took him someplace instead of only hurting; how to be shaved so that the simple proximity of blade to skin reminded him that I *could* cut his balls off then and there, and he would not resist.

Keith could show him how, and Angelo could learn the moves. What Angelo could never learn was the easy grace with which Keith made those moves, as elegant as a flower's blooming. Keith never had to turn himself over to me: I just had to welcome him. For Angelo each move was always going to be a studied thing, an *exercise* in turning himself over to me, which is not necessarily a bad thing for a slave to have to think about almost constantly. By the time autumn came to

San Francisco – a season we could identify because the weather finally resembled California's – I was ready to take the next step.

＊＊

In the peach-grey light of later dawn, when the fog is lifting off the water, only the endless generations of gulls, rats, and feral cats populate the little cliffs above the city's old abandoned forts. On one edge of town, just beyond the most deserted of these structures where the batteries were long since sealed and even memories of fantasies have given up their ghosts, I brought the two boys one late summer morning in the last few days before leather week began. Each was blindfolded, each carried a bag of my gear, and each was on a leash I held firmly in one hand. I'd kept them up all night at a party, making them run errands for every man who wanted anything, because I intended for them to be tired. After I led them over some ice-plant-covered dunes to a cliff above the gulls that wheeled above the Pacific I had them set the bags down, commanded them both to their knees, told them to keep their eyes closed, and removed their blindfolds. I told them they could open their eyes gradually against the light, and set each one to kissing a boot. When I was satisfied with their efforts I took the leashes from their collars and instructed Keith to remove Angelo's clothing, then I told Angelo to undress Keith, yes, while they both were kneeling there in the big outdoors before Apollo and everyone and yes, right down to the socks and jock: this was not a movie, this was the real thing.

I looked over my brace of naked boys. Their hands were clasped behind their backs, their cocks and ball sacs had shriveled in the cold, their thigh muscles had begun to quiver. Angelo's finely sculpted, all but hairless body shivered slightly with chill or fear, but though he had learned to keep his eyes cast down, still he kept his head held high. Even on their knees Keith was several inches shorter than Angelo, wiry where Angelo was bulked out, a little furry on the chest and back, and starting to go bald. Where Angelo still had to maintain his ego's pride to keep from feeling humiliated, Keith's deeper pride shone through his profound humility. He was seasoned, deep, a man of enormous value in himself. Each of the two was as open and defenseless as he knew how to be; each had placed his trust in me, and I found the two of them in their very different states of surrender the most beautiful sight that had touched my heart since Sean. I wanted to kneel with them and embrace them both and love them till the sun came up and went down and came up again.

Instead, while they knelt naked, facing me, I made a single knotted pile of both their clothes and hurled the lot over the cliff toward the distant ocean. Angelo made a sound, but he stanched it quickly. He didn't know what he was in for when he agreed to play, but he was game and he would stay. I opened the first of my gear bags and took out several lengths of rope, and tied Angelo's wrists securely to his legs, padding the insides of his thighs to protect the femoral arteries. I tied his ankles together as well, and took his balls in my hand and suddenly crushed them like a pair of pitted plums. He shouted and gritted his teeth and turned red as the cords in his neck stood out, and when he finally stopped fighting I let him go gently and kissed him till he kissed me back. Then I smiled at him. "Wait here," I said, and let him, panting, kiss my hand.

I secured Keith's limbs in the very same ways, cradled his head to my abdomen, and petted his face. "Scott would have been very proud of you," I told him. "He always knew that you were real." I felt his head nod once. "Thank you, Sir," he whispered.

I had the boys move closer to each other till their knees and thighs were touching. I bound them together at their waists, at their chests with ropes around their backs and under their arms, and at their thighs under their butts. I made the ropes so tight their cocks, tits, and bellies were rubbing and they could not help but look into each other's eyes unless they leaned their heads on one another's shoulders. "Kneel and you kneel together," I said, "fall and you fall – together."

I brought out some whips and for nearly an hour I warmed them up, working back and forth between them, reddening their backs and asses with suede and well-oiled latigo. Keith surrendered right away of course, breathing into every stroke and making melting butter of his muscles. Long before I'd worked my way up to any sort of heavy flogger he was rushing on the energy we shared, opening for the endorphins that would soon take over, offering in his wordless way to carry Angelo along. But despite his training Angelo was still set in his desire to be stoic. He clamped his jaw and made his body stony so that every time the whip hit him he had to absorb its impact all at once. I continued to whip Keith not only because the men were bound together, but because his task was also his reward: I wasn't Scott, but one way or another he'd come home again. Tears were drifting down his face, and though his mouth was open while he breathed, he smiled silently and drifted high above his body, his spirit soaring freely as the gulls. Angelo I had to beat, bringing all my weight to bear and working with my wrist at every stroke. Somewhere in the second hour, as I brought the flogger down again and again on Angelo's bloody back, he finally began to cry for me. At first he just mewed in little staccato spits, like a baby's surprising hiccoughs; then he started to moan, then wail, then he roared in rage and shook his head, and then sobs wracked his body one after another and his great chest heaved, his shoulders shook like boulders in an earthquake rocking dreamy Keith along, and finally he shouted to the ships at sea one long shriek that tore through his body as if some ancient soul was wrenching free. Catching the rays of early morning sunlight slanting to us over the humps of hills to the east, his tears ran down his cheeks toward the ocean like liquid gold. I hit him harder and harder, over and over again, using both hands to bring the big whip down. His blood spattered over Keith and me, the whiptails, and the sand. I beat him till he started to laugh, then Keith, surprised, began to laugh as well, and I shouted in my own little pissant leather Master's glory while I beat them both and the sun took me full in the face and we *all* laughed and laughed and laughed.

※

I had brought peroxide for their wounds and flannel sheets to wrap them up in, but otherwise I took them home just as they were and put them both to bed before I took a nap myself. By evening we all had our clocks turned around and we were all a little numb. I took their collars off them and sent them to bathe and shave; when they were finished I brought them naked to the living room on their knees. Beside me I had two leather gear bags. The boys had been through a real ritual, and I reached into first one bag and then the other, bringing out for each of them new jeans, t-shirts, and socks to replace the ones I'd given to the sea. Then I brought out belts, boots, and vests for each of them, and had them dress themselves.

"You are leathermen in a whole new way today, and insofar as I have taken you across that threshold, to that extent you belong to me; so I've bought these new clothes for you. But, of course, there's more. There always is. Angelo," I looked at him, "you came when I called, and you've worked hard to learn the rudiments of belonging specifically to me. You've been my slave in training for several months, and now is the time to choose: Do you want to become my slave and wear my collar?"

"Yes, Sir."

"Ask."

"Sir." He looked up into my eyes as if he were spreading his chest open for me to touch his heart. "Sir, will you please allow me to become your slave, to wear your collar, and to serve you in the manners you desire?"

I grinned a little since the question hardly needed any answer. I gestured and he crawled toward me, knelt up. I brought out a brand new collar from one bag, crisp and sturdy, and as I had done those months before at the Eagle I held it out for him to kiss. He showed no hesitation but leaned forward so I could embrace him into the life he'd been preparing for. I locked the collar around his neck, let him kiss my boots and kissed him on the mouth, and kept him on the floor beside my chair.

"Keith, in truth you've never been my slave. You've been my bottom in a process of my own, and you've helped me bring my boy to where he is today, for which I am grateful as a man and as his Master. But what would you say *you've* gotten in the course of our work together?"

Keith smiled gently. He never raised his eyes to mine, yet he knew where I was looking. "I've forgiven Master Scott for dying, Sir. I told you I was on my own, the night you took me into your service, and I believed I was, Sir. But now I see that I was simply Masterless, which is a very different thing, Sir. Now I *am* on my own: now I'm a free man, Sir."

From the second bag I withdrew three packages, spread them out on the floor before me, and pointed to the one on my far left. "Angelo: bring this package to Keith. In your mouth. Don't get it wet." As Angelo complied I spoke to Keith again. "In what remains of this little leather netherworld you both have earned your belts and boots from me. I've given you your vests as gifts to acknowledge your hard work and accomplishments over the past few months. I cut Angelo out of the herd because I wanted him as my slave, and he has earned the right to please me by asking for my collar and by doing so. You began in a different place and you've earned my gratitude, as I said, for which this gift is intended as a token. You may open it."

Angelo had returned to his place at my feet. I laid one hand on his head, and as Keith unwrapped his new leather gloves I watched Angelo's face for signs of jealousy; I was as pleased to see none as I was pleased with the surprised and happy look Keith gave me.

"Thank you, Sir," he said directly to me. He knew enough not to hand me a plate of false modesty. "May I put them on, Sir?"

"In a minute, maybe. I'm not through. You've earned not only my thanks, but my respect and admiration as well, and so I offer you an unusual choice. It's not quite the Lady and the Tiger because I'll show you what's in both packages before you choose. But although you could take neither, you can't have both: you *must* choose. Do you understand?"

"Yes, Sir," Keith answered, clearly mystified.

I opened the package on my right, disclosing a pair of leather pants: an item of apparel that in Keith's world and mine no slave, no bottom, could ever wear, and that acknowledged how greatly I respected his mastery as my co-trainer. He stared at them, and then at me as I opened the package directly before me to display another leather collar. I hadn't realized till Keith dropped his shoulders that he'd been tense during these last couple of minutes, but now he was relaxed. Tears filled his eyes, and he bowed his head. When he looked back up he said, "Sir, may I please have the honor and privilege to wear your collar, to attend you as your servant and slave, and to be brother to my brother Angelo, Sir?"

I think I had known Keith would choose that path, but he *was* a free man, as he'd said, and I had to offer him the option. "A very pretty speech," I said. I picked up the collar and held it out for him to kiss, which he did with profound reverence. When I withdrew it from his lips he bent his neck and laid his forehead softly on my thigh, then raised his head enough to receive the band of leather.

When both men were collared I sat back and looked at what I'd done. "Angelo, what do you think about the choice your brother made?"

Angelo regarded Keith with some combination of affection, respect, awe, and gratitude. "I'm glad he'll be around."

"What do you make of that choice, to be a slave instead of becoming a Top?"

Now Angelo was on uncertain ground. "Fools rush in where angels fear to tread?"

"Keith? What would you say if someone asked you why you did what you did?"

"Master Scott used to say it's all about awareness, Sir: that there's no difference between Top and bottom except in practice. There are always two ends to the leash."

I reached into one of the gear bags a few last times, and took out some towels, some alcohol swabs, non-stick first-aid pads, steel wool, my poker, and finally my acetylene torch. I lit the torch and set it in a stand to heat the steel initial while I attended to other matters.

"I want both of you out of those fine new jeans. Roll them around your fine new boots to make yourselves a couple of pillows. Place the pillows under your hips and put your butts in the air. I grinned at Keith. "There *are* two ends to the leash, but you know what the Hindus say about reality: it's all illusion, but *very convincing* illusion."

My thanks to Gayle Rubin, Ph.D., who generously provided me with accurate historical information pertaining both to the Folsom Street bars that were popular with leathermen in 1973, and to the origins of the Folsom Street Fair in 1984. My thanks also to Joseph Bean, who graciously gave me information pertaining to the manner and sequence in which bottoms might earn their leathers in the small, tight communities of West Coast leathermen at that time.

Goddess

remember the colors your living room featured long after dinner the April evening when we met. You lounged in the deep blue sofa facing the fireplace; I waited on the edge of a soft rose chair beside you. The yellow candles had long since guttered and our amber brandies glinted in the light of the logs' orange embers. A waning moon the color of butter presaged dawn beyond the windows at my back, and lit the bones and hollows of your face so boldly I could almost feel your flesh.

All your other guests had gone and I had begun to feel awkward, since there was obviously no excuse for me to stay. Yet I could not bring myself to stand and mouth the usual platitudes of thanks and farewell. From the moment I had seen you I had been drawn to you – to your beauty, of course, but even more to your vibrancy, your intelligence, your playfulness, and most of all to your emotional *presence*, which I felt encouraged me to be intimate with you: to know you, and allow you to know me.

More than once I took my eyes from yours because I wanted to stop the longing I felt welling up in me; wanted to stop the longing before it became too visible; before I spoke inappropriately, and said something you might not want to hear; before, in a sense, I exposed myself to you without permission. But every time I took them away I brought my eyes back to yours, because more than I wanted to stop my feelings I wanted you to feel them too: to feel the corresponding desire growing in your breast, swelling your lips and moistening your thighs; I longed for you to *want* from me what I wanted so greatly for you to take.

You still wore the plain, black, high-necked leather jerkin one guest had said made you look like an ancient diety, and on this soft skin, below your throat, a long, clear crystal pendant rested. As I stayed a minute and a minute more your fingers lit upon that pendant and lifted it up, and with an eye cocked my way you drew its narrow tip along your lips. Black curls tumbled down your tilted head and framed your eyes in a bandit's mask. Your sidelong look became a gaze that entranced me. I felt I could not escape from you, nor did I think I would ever want to.

Only the language of love as divine has devised words for the feeling I had, so the more completely I recall the night, the closer I come to the breath of passion: to saying I wanted to give you my life, to feel your teeth break my boundary of skin and your mouth suck out my very soul and make my spirit spill.

I must have spoken then because, although I felt confused, I wasn't surprised that you replied. "Goddess?" you asked: "Did you call me 'Goddess'?"

Had I? I didn't know, and you seemed to find in my dilemma a source of genuine merriment. Your voice was as clear, your laughter as musical as glass bells. "I like to be seen for the Goddess I am," you said, cautioning me with the crystal finger, "but I am a Goddess who makes demands, not one who necessarily grants favors. Are you ready to worship, and serve, and supplicate? Is that what you have in mind?"

I stared at your dark eyes, and the mischievous smile in your lovely human face. I fell into whatever the play was that I seemed to have begun myself. "Yes, Goddess," I replied, "I am ready for that; that is exactly what I have in mind."

You leaned on one elbow with your chin in your hand and looked me over as if we'd never met before; then "Down," you said, pointing to the floor before you. I came off the chair and dropped to my knees in a single movement, torn between my urge to prostrate myself before you and my equally strong desire to remain on my knees looking into your eyes so I could see the heat of erotic power rising up in you. Showing the tiny pink tip of your tongue, you sat up on the couch and raised one booted foot to rest upon my shoulder. I wanted to bury my face in the flesh you bared, startling white beneath your black skirt, but you let the weight of your foot impose, and I bowed my neck to your command.

I pressed my lips to the top of your other boot as the pressure of your foot demanded, kissing in the valley between your toes and the bone that rose above the arch. I did not aim my kiss at the supple leather my mouth met but at your foot beneath it, which was part of you. I sought to let you feel how deeply I wanted to submit my will to yours, to serve your desires, to follow you to the edge of my self until I lost all sense of me and begged you to let me vanish into you. My body shook for the first few times that night and I felt the tears of my first small passionate release. You removed your foot from my neck. "Up," you said. I rose on my knees and spread my arms to you.

"Thank you, thank you, yes oh yes oh please," I prayed, all but certain you could hear my thoughts, willing my hopes across the wordless air that tingled now like hot slapped skin. You gazed at me intensely, as if envisioning my surrender. You pushed the toe of your boot into my crotch, pushing my legs apart. I was hard and you pressed on my erection. My body responded, pressing back, and you kicked me from beneath, lightly but with no mistake. I stopped for a moment, imagining I was sobered, and took this first pain you had ever given me as if it were a gift and a promise. You nodded once. "That's right."

You leaned back and crossed your legs. I could see the curve of your calf within your boot, the angle of your hip, the small swell of your breast, the waves and curls of flesh that made your mouth. "You may proceed," you said, gesturing at my jacket, "but do not stand up."

As quickly as I could from my position on the floor I undressed, folding my clothes and piling them beneath the chair I'd sat in. When I was naked and kneeling quietly once more you turned me toward the silvery window to give yourself a better view of what was being offered. You smiled at me kindly and stroked my hair, stroked my cheek. I could smell the different parts of you. Erotic tension charged me with desire. My penis swelled and ebbed, swelled and ebbed like a live thing breathing on its own. The air around you seemed to glow. I closed my eyes and nuzzled your palm feeling elated, feeling devoted, restraining my need to kiss and lick and suck and bite and take your hand your arm your body self into me my mouth was dry when you slapped me across the face. My eyes jerked open and I awakened to the shame of my lost control.

"You kiss on command, not on your own initiative." You raised your brows, asking if I understood.

"Yes, Ma'am. I – "

"Do you wish to speak?"

"Please, Ma'am."

"Do you wish to apologize?"

"Yes, Ma'am."

"Don't."

You moved your hands across my chest, tugging a little at the hairs now and then, and let one come to rest massaging my breast. You began to pinch me between your nails, alerting my flesh and taking my attention where you wanted it to go. You pinched harder. I breathed more deeply, feeling cut, till suddenly you let me go, let the blood rush back, and slapped my breast. You held the hand that had hurt me to my lips until I kissed it. "Good boy," you smiled.

Your hands began their wanderings again, over my sides and belly and hips and ass. You came to my cock, which was wet and partly hard, and ran your nails along the shaft. I thought by the tension in your jaw that you resisted some desire in yourself to scratch long reminders of your passing in my blood. You slid your hand down, wrapped one finger and thumb around the neck of my scrotum, and slowly started to tighten your grip on my balls. My breathing quickened and my eyes widened; you grinned and squeezed me harder.

"You like this," you mused. I tried to answer but the truth was so extremely Yes and No, and the pressure was taking me down so far and so fast, I only gasped and stammered. The pain itself was a doorway I did not want to go through, but I knew that it would let me give myself up and make of myself a gift to you, and I did want that. You kept your eyes on mine as I began to whimper, making sounds I did not mean to make. You reached up through me and sought my heart, sought to carry us both deeper. I wanted you to have it; I wanted you to feel that you could own me. I forced my breathing down, and down, slowing the rush of sensation, enriching my response to you.

"Turn around," you ordered. Panting and aching all the way up my abdomen, light-headed and in awe to feel controlled by my balls in your surprisingly strong hand that neither softened nor let go, I managed the awkward move and straddled your arm.

"Bend over and put your face on the floor. Spread your cheeks. Use your hands. Push out. Pull in. Push out. Pull in. Again. Again." You slapped my cheeks beside my hands, first on one side then the other, lightly at first then harder and harder. Abruptly you slapped directly on the tender inner skin I'd opened for you. I tightened up, and when I relaxed you slapped again and again, stinging me repeatedly until I stopped fleeing and eased myself onto the gentle probing of your finger. You came inside me, moved around, moved in and out, probed some more, pressed and pulled and opened me farther. Pushing up against me with one hand and bearing down with the other, suddenly you broke through me. I cried out, let go, fell sobbing on your arm and pushed myself deeper into your tightly balled fist, relieved to live as if forever beneath your will, taken, surrendered, turned over, possessed, your human property at last; you let go and I screamed as the pain of release rose snaking to my brain.

"Now," you murmured, listening to me cry, "now we can begin."

Slowly you withdrew your hands from me. I shook as I wept before you and wept for you on the floor. I reached devoutly for your feet but you just pulled away. "Ask," you said. "No: *beg.*"

Joyful, despairing, proud to give this up to you, I started to obey but lost myself in the meaning behind my words. "Oh Goddess, Goddess," I began, "please please please please please may I hold you, please may I hold your legs, please may I kiss you, please may I" please may I please you, please may I live for you, please may I die for you, please will you use me, abuse me, hurt me, humble me, amuse yourself with me, take me beyond myself, let me stay with you, let me live in you, let me disappear upon your hands and hold this holy moment in your eyes with mine –

"Yes, you may."

I grasped your legs and pressed myself as far as I could to merge with you from the floor. As my shuddering subsided and peace took me over you prodded me onto my back and rested your feet on me. Through my fading psychic haze of pain I heard you move in your seat; later you shook me with a foot against my face. "Time to serve, my pet. Kneel up."

✦✦

"There are some things to do before we get fully started," you said. You sent me scuttling to a chest beside your desk, and had me bring back a zippered bag you opened slowly, watching me watch your hands. You took out a plain black collar with a D-ring opposite the buckle and put it to my lips to kiss. I agreed – eagerly, gratefully – to be your slave until you took it off: to obey and serve you as you commanded me to do, to honor and worship you in the ways you directed, to accept without question whatever punishments and rewards you might mete out.

After I agreed you told me to bow my head, and when I felt you wrap your collar around my neck all the tension of the night drained from my body and I felt free. You buckled and locked the collar in place and lifted my chin; I looked up at you with a growing sense of veneration. You brought out a much smaller collar with a smaller D-ring and had me kiss that as well. One side of your mouth turned up as you wrapped it around my scrotum where your finger and thumb had captured me, and snapped its lock shut as well. The little metal sound reverberated in my skull like the echo of a heavy prison door banging closed. You took out a chain with a black leather handle and clipped it to the collar at my neck. How happy I was, how near to ecstasy, on my knees, in your collars, and in your thrall.

"Down," you said, "on your hands and knees. When I say 'heel' you are to follow me. Stay out from under my feet so I don't have to trip over you, and pay attention to the leash so that you stop when I do, without my having to speak to you. Do you understand?"

"Yes, Goddess," I replied.

"Good. Then 'heel'."

Every movement I made took me farther out of the deep place I had been, yet each was also a sign of my obedience, and a step along the road of my submission to you. You stood and walked me up and down your living room, turning figure eights until I stumbled; then you shortened the leash to hold my face against your knee. I followed you through the hallways of your house from room to room, keeping my eyes on your moving feet, dancing backwards and to the sides, learning to match your rhythm as you changed speed and directions. When you stopped we were on the cool apricot tiles of your bathroom floor. "Not bad," you said as you sat in a wicker chaise against a mirrored wall and draped the leash across my shoulders; I caught my breath and presented myself before you. "Draw me a bath, warm, not hot."

I plugged the tub and turned the water on, testing it with my hand as the pastel basin filled.

"Undress me, starting at the top. Do not remove my pendant."

When you signaled that you were ready I removed your clothing piece by piece, and as I exposed your body I worshipped it in my heart, shoulder to back to arm to breast to belly to cheeks to lips to legs and feet. At first you held yourself a bit apart from me, testing the bounds of this physical intimacy, testing the trust we were building between us, but I did not touch you more than necessary to unbutton and undrape because you had not yet been pleased to tell me to touch you anywhere at all.

You sat in your bath, closed your eyes, and sighed, luxuriating in the water's warmth while I knelt beside the tub. After awhile you said, "My sponge is on the shelf behind me. Use the lilac gel. Do my face first, only with your hands, then use the sponge starting at my shoulders and work your way down to my feet."

I set the sponge in the bath to soften while I coated my hands with gel, and as I gently bathed your face, kissing it with my fingertips, I watched your jaw relax, and your eyelids relax, and some of your life's cares ease. After I rinsed your face I filled the sponge with gel and bathed your shoulders, your arms, your back, your breasts.

You stood in the tub for me to wash your belly and – gradually, leaving you plenty of time to stop me if I was wrong – your pubic mound and vulva; then you turned around so I could wash your buttocks and, delicately as you bent forward, your anus. You sat again to cover yourself with water, and let me lift first one leg then the other so I could sponge each one from thigh to toe.

"Another time I'll teach you to wash my hair," you said as you stepped from the tub and wrapped yourself in the towel I handed up to you. "For now, I think, you can simply – soak in my bath."

You unclipped the leash and set it on the chaise. You snapped your fingers and I almost leapt into the pale gray water that was still warm and smelled of you and lilac soap. "Down. All the way down. Put your face in it." You placed your foot on my head and held me under water for a few long seconds, then let me up to breathe again. "Now I am on you outside," you said. "I want to be inside you as well." You stepped into the tub again, positioning yourself immediately above me. You gripped my hair and tilted my head back. "Open wide." When I opened my mouth you started to let your urine flow, first a little dribble down your leg, then a full stream flushing my face. Using my hair as a hand-hold you pulled my mouth to you. "Swallow," you commanded. "Drink it all."

I didn't know I had anything more to give you but I reached and did as I was told. When you were through I was gasping for air. The smell of you filled my nose and the taste of you filled me from my stomach to my lips. I saw your eyes, amused and satisfied. I wanted to weep when you smiled at me. You pulled my head forward and let me lick you clean in silence, stepped from the tub and pointed at the floor again. I clambered out and knelt beside you. You dropped your towel on me and told me to rinse my face and dry myself. You filled a glass with water and handed it to me.

"Wash your mouth out," you said. "Even a Goddess's piss is acid. It's not good for your teeth."

After I had rinsed my face and mouth and swallowed the water as you told me to do, you reattached the leash to my wet collar. "Heel."

You walked me to your bedroom and took a large clean sheet from a dresser drawer. You handed me the sheet and showed me a tray of unguents. You told me to spread the sheet over the bed, and said you wanted a massage. You said I could stand and walk around as necessary in order to perform these tasks. You looped the leash around my neck, put on some simple music whose soft rhythms made the room seem like a temple, and after I had stood and covered the bed with the sheet you lay face down upon it.

I stretched my own tired limbs and consulted the tray full of bottles. I selected a delicately scented floral lotion, poured some into my hand and put the bottle down, then warmed the lotion between my palms. Finally I touched your neck and shoulders and gradually rubbed lotion down into your back and buttocks and the backs of your legs .I soothed your flesh from your thighs down toward your ankles, smoothed the tight webs of muscle from the heel forward, pressed lotion into your feet through the outsteps and around the balls, through the insteps and under the toes, spread the bones and stretched the ligaments, opening your soles to the earth. Finally I brought your feet together, wiped them down with the towel, and wiped my hands.

I stood beside the bed and waited. Across the room your mirror reflected back to me the image of a middle-aged man in respectful service: naked and open, idle hands held out of the way behind his back, collared at the neck and genitals with a leash draping off one shoulder down his chest, owned and available for – for you. Feeling myself under a Goddess's control filled me with joy and made me want to laugh. Beside my image in your mirror I could see your image stir. You rolled over onto your back and said, "Continue."

Again I started with warm lotion at your chest and shoulders where your pendant glittered on its chain like ice. I smoothed the lotion up along your throat and down your ribs, stretching your arms, pulling and pressing on your breasts and yielding belly, working toward your feet. When I was done I stood at your head and wiped your brow, and spread stray wisps of hair off your face. After a few minutes you opened your eyes and stretched. "In the kitchen, in the refrigerator, you will find an open bottle of wine," you said. "Beside the refrigerator you will find a crystal goblet. Fill the goblet with wine and bring it to me."

I went off to do as I was told. When I returned I knelt and proffered the goblet as if it were a sacrament. You took the goblet from my hands and set it down beside you, then held my face with one hand and slapped me smartly with the other.

"Who told you to?" you demanded.

"Goddess?" I cried, stung.

You slapped me again. "Who told you you could walk when you went to fetch my wine?"

My heart fell. "No one, Goddess."

"Do you decide these things for yourself?"

"No, Goddess."

"Why did you?"

"I made a mistake, Goddess, and I am deeply sorry."

"As well you might be. You shall be punished later. Do you understand?"

"Yes, Goddess."

"Good. Then you may entertain me now. Stand up – " I stood "– and do some jumping jacks."

"Excuse me, Goddess?"

"Jumping jacks. You don't know what those are? You jump in place, and as you do so you spread your legs and clap your hands over your head. Then you jump again and bring your legs together and clap your hands to your sides. That's a jumping jack. Then you repeat the movement until I say to stop. Do some jumping jacks for me."

Feeling foolish and older than I wanted to be I started doing jumping jacks. Each time I jumped my genitals bounced up and down. Leaning against the headboard of your bed sipping your wine, you began to smile.

"Stop," you said, and I stopped. "Down," and I knelt. "Come," and I crawled to you. You released the leash from the collar at my neck and reattached it to the collar at my balls. "Stand," you said. "Jump." You gradually shortened the leash until each time I jumped the collar tightened, making me my own tormentor.

"You're slowing down," you said, slapping at my flopping cock with a riding crop you'd taken from your bedside table. "Don't do that. Jump. Jump higher."

The doorbell rang and I thought I might be saved, but you had another plan. "Stop." You attached the leash to the collar at my neck again, and hung the leash around my neck. "Jump." I started jumping. "Keep jumping until I return." And with that you left, trailing the scent of the lotion I'd massaged you with, that smelled like the last spring flowers in the first summer rain.

I was tired and sweating, my thighs and calves were quivering from exertion, my knees were sore from kneeling and crawling, my balls hurt from being squeezed and pulled, my cock hurt where you had cropped me, my mouth and breath tasted of your urine, and I hadn't pissed in hours. Left all by myself with this inane instruction to jump until who knew when I thought that maybe I had come to the wrong place, was doing the wrong thing, was playing the wrong game. Why did I want so deeply to please a woman I had never met before? Why didn't I just want to please myself? What kind of idiot was I, anyway? Why didn't I at least just chill till I could hear you returning? Then I could resume this jumping – you'd never know the difference.

But I saw myself in the mirror again, and instead of seeing the tired man, I saw the collars that belonged to you and with which you had claimed me, and I knew I couldn't fake it: I knew if you were really able to hold me, I had to let myself be held by you. Sighing then, I jumped, and I jumped, and I jumped.

After only a few minutes you returned, wearing a loose robe and accompanied by another woman who cast a brief glance at me, then turned her attention to the tray of lotions, oils, and powders.

"Stop," you said. You pointed to the floor beside you and I knelt on the spot, breathing hard.

"Are you tired?"

"Yes, Goddess," I replied.

"You may rest." You pointed to your feet, where I lay my forehead. I felt so grateful for this little respite I wanted to cry.

"Do you need to drink?"

"Yes, Goddess."

"Do you need to urinate?"

"Yes, Goddess."

"Come. Heel."

On hands and knees I followed the leash as you led me from the bedroom, down the hall and over the white living room carpet, past the blue couch and the rose chair, past the cold fireplace, past memories of last night's dinner party, and through a sliding glass door into your back yard and the full daylight of a late spring morning. In a far corner, upon a patch of bare earth, lay a rusty trowel.

"This is where you may relieve yourself," you said, pointing to the spot. "Dig a deeper, wider hole than you plan to use, and after you're through fill it up with dirt."

I dug the hole, then realized I had never tried to piss while kneeling – or while a woman held my balls on a leash. Time passed.

"Come on," you said. "You're going to have to get over it or you'll burst your bladder."

Just as I felt myself about to let go you squatted down and grinned and took my cock in your hand. I began to get a little hard. More time passed and now you seemed infinitely patient, enjoying the sun and my discomfort. Your friend came out of the house and the two of you chatted. You gave the handle of the leash to her and she played with the chain, pulling me back and forth and jiggling me around. She laughed, not unkindly, and you laughed with her. I tried to tune the two of you out. Finally I pissed, my urine frothing and disappearing in the hole I'd dug.

"It feels so funny," you said to your friend as you shook the last drops from my penis for me, and then stood up. "The whole thing sort of vibrates. It must be odd to have your genitals hanging out in the wind like that." You and she continued to talk while I shoveled dirt into the hole, then you led me to a garden hose. You put the leash around my shoulders and turned the water on. You let me drink, and when I had had enough you hosed me down all over. The water was cold, and when I gasped you laughed.

You led me to a bush with long, smooth, flexible branches, and snapped a thick one off. You whipped it through the air and it whistled its greeting. You stripped the branch of leaves and touched it to my flank. "Do you remember why I am going to punish you?"

"Yes, Goddess."

"Why?"

"For walking without permission, Goddess."

"Will you disobey again?"

"I hope not, Goddess."

"You hope not?"

"Yes, Goddess."

"What does that mean?"

"I do not wish to disobey, Goddess; I did not mean to disobey the first time. But since I made one error I fear the possibility exists that someday I may make another despite my best intentions, Goddess."

You looked at me through a very long silence. You might have been amused or you might have been irritated: I could not tell from your face. "That may be true," you said at last, "but even though I value the truth I am still going to punish you three times: once for your disobedience, once because I don't like the truth you told, and once because I enjoy doing it. Turn around. Face on the ground. Are you ready?"

"Yes, Goddess."

"Ask."

"Please, Goddess, may I have my first punishment?"

You did not wait, you did not warm me up, you gave me no word or sign or warning, you just snapped your wrist down like a gate. I felt the switch and heard the wind it made, then felt the heat, and finally the pain ran along my nerves like a fire through dry leaves.

"One Ma'am," I gasped, "thank you Ma'am. Please, Goddess, may I have my second punishment?"

Again you were neither kind nor cruel, and you did not wait or tease. The switch came down and every step lit up my brain and made my body quiver.

"Two Ma'am, thank you Ma'am. Please, Goddess, may I have my third punishment?"

You brought the cane down softly to my skin and moved it in deft circles on my two fresh stripes while I grew frightened, then impatient, and finally just hungry, my twitching muscles giving me away. You scratched lightly at my welts with your fingernails. "The third punishment I shall hold in abeyance, to deliver any time I see fit. Any time. Any time we should be together – in my house, on a beach, at a party, in the back row of an airplane – any time I believe my special attention is called for I may punish you once more if I want to, and you will ask for it. Do you understand?"

"Yes, Goddess."

"And do you agree?"

"Yes, Goddess."

You bent down and laid the tip of the switch against my lips. "In that case your life is mine," you whispered in my face. "You have the heart of a slave, and I have the heart of a Mistress. I want your soul. I will cut your throat, not deep enough to endanger you, but deep and long enough for you to know I own you beyond recall. I will brand you and pierce you and lock you to my desk by your penis for weeks at a time. You will never be dressed except in clothes I've worn that smell of me, you will never be uncollared, you will never not be freshly marked. You will serve me always, and serve my friends when they come to call, and you will learn to show in front of them the humility I can see is powerful within you, covered as it is today by layers of fear and pride. You will sleep restrained beside me, or on the floor beside my bed at night. Each morning I will re-assert my rights as your owner. You will learn to love the weight of me standing on your flesh. You will learn to love to weep in pain for me. You will please me over and over without your own release until I have a purpose for your orgasm. Look at you, boy: you know I'm speaking to your heart."

I'd grown erect while listening to you, mesmerized by your voice and eyes, mesmerized by what you were saying. You *had* spoken to my heart and oh Goddess! You brought hope and joy to that heart. You took my head from behind with one hand, and brought the other up to caress my cheek. You brought your face close to mine and kissed my eyes. You smiled from deep within you to deep within me and you began to slap my face, gently at first, harder as you worked yourself up, holding my head to keep my neck from snapping, seeing that I hated being slapped, seeing that I loved to give you any gift you wanted. You shook in your own orgasms, and when you were through you took the leash from the collar at my neck and clipped it to the collar at my balls.

You pushed me onto my back and stood over me. I felt your heat descend. I saw you, I smelled you, I let my mouth fall open as you brushed against me. I tasted you, and suddenly, with a flood of blood, my cock grew so hard it ached.

Up and down my face you rubbed yourself, marking me as an animal marks her territory. You pushed yourself onto my forehead, my chin, my nose, my cheeks, my eyes, you wiped yourself in my hair, pressed yourself on my chest, and slid down my body leaving your scent everywhere, returning at last to sit astride my mouth again. "Now, use your tongue. Very slowly. Very soft. Long strokes. To the right. Up. Up. Yes. Yes. Yes."

I lost myself in pleasing you, my senses utterly submerged in you. Now and then I rolled my hips to still the numbness that kept creeping into my hands, now and then I worked a cramp from the muscles of my tongue and jaw, now and then you pulled the leash, reminding me that I belonged to you as I made myself your vehicle and drank you in as you rode me through the afternoon.

If I had had a sense of time before I lost it in the music of your sounds; if I'd had a sense of place I lost it in the pressure of your hips and thighs; if I'd had a sense of me I lost it in my passionate desire to give myself away. I held my mouth in place for you as you came and came in long, drawn-out waves. In the tensions and releases of your climaxes your breath came hard, and with it you laughed and laughed. You braced your feet against my hips, your breasts teased my face, and you stilled slowly down, settling yourself softly in my mouth again.

I wanted to kiss and caress and make love to every part of you. I thought I must be permanently erect. I was close to orgasm myself but knew I was not allowed, so I dropped down and became the sensation, became an extension of my Mistress, my owner, my Goddess, you. I rested my head against your thigh. Peaceful as though your orgasms had been my own, at last I fell into the space you were and vanished.

The sun was setting for the second time. You led me back inside. You took your goblet from the dresser in the bedroom and walked me to the living room where you reclined on the sofa as you had the night before. Your friend leaned back in the chair I'd assumed last night. She found my clothes beneath it and at a nod from you she slowly tore them all apart: pants, shirt, jacket, shorts, socks. She couldn't rend the shoes, but with hardly a glance in my direction she tossed them with the tatters I once had worn onto the ashes in the fireplace, which were grey and cold and fluttered in the breeze the torn cloth made.

You pointed to the hearth and to the brandy glasses we had shared in what seemed to me another life. "I want the fireplace brushed clean," you said, "and the rags and ashes bagged together and put out with the garbage in the garage. I also want you to wash the glasses the next time I send you out of the room."

In one part of my mind I was stunned to see my clothes destroyed, and I thought about the wallet in what had been my hip pants pocket with the money that was mine and the cards that told me who I was. I thought about the keys to what had been my car and what had been my home. I remembered people and places from the life I'd lived before this moment, or the moment before dawn when you first said *down*. I knew I was no longer free, and wondered if I would ever again be free to leave or disobey or disagree with anything you said. But in another part of my mind I also knew that none of my recollections mattered any more. As I stared into your eyes which had gone flat black, I felt I had become an object subject to your mercy or your whims, and I was thrilled.

"Yes, Goddess," I whispered for the form.

You took me by the hair and pulled me forward, then bent me back on my elbows so the front of my body was completely open from my throat down to my parted knees. You left me exposed while you got up off the couch and took the crystal pendant from your neck. You knelt beside me and stared into my eyes, and brought the pendant's point to rest at the base of my penis.

"You are my slave now, is that so?" you asked.

"Yes, Goddess," I replied in terror.

"Is there anything I don't have the right to do to you?"

"No, Goddess."

"Then you'll be happy I'm so kind." You smiled. "At least for now."

You brought the pendant to my breast and drew a sign on me with its icy point. From the corners of my eyes I could see the lines of the sign quickly fill with blood, although I felt no pain. Your eyes glittered like the pendant. You squeezed my cuts and made the blood run freely to your hand, then slapped me and smeared my face with red.

"I hereby claim you, before a woman witness. You will never be free again." You kissed the pendant and held it out for me to kiss, then put it on again. My blood slithered down its length in streaks between your breasts.

You pulled at my legs as if I were an animal, examining my bruised, raw knees. "I don't think you should crawl or kneel much more today," you said. "Soon it will be time for you to prepare dinner. My friend is staying so you will set two places. I will feed you afterwards in some – special – way. But for now you may kiss my feet while I visit with my friend. You are not to *stop* kissing them until I tell you to. Do you understand?"

"Yes, Goddess."

I settled myself on the floor in front of you as comfortably as I could, and for the next long period of time, while you and your friend visited, I made love to your feet with my hands and mouth, kissing, caressing, licking, petting, sucking, till someplace deep inside my soul I had a kind of cosmic orgasm. I didn't come, by which I mean my cock didn't shoot – I didn't have permission to do that in any case – but at another level of my being I found that as I worshipped at the feet of this Goddess in your human form I was also worshipping all the Goddesses, right up to the Great Goddess who creates all life and love and happiness of every kind, and all terror too: She who takes life and love and happiness away; She who is the Mother of the childish, warring gods we human males pretend we're like; She whose power and grandeur reign over all of us like the sky that is Her skirt and the stars that are the jewels She scatters through our mortal heavens so that we may know that She is always there to love and comfort us if only we are willing to come to Her and ask, and say as we may say to Her through all the Goddesses on Earth – through our mothers and sisters and wives and girlfriends and colleagues at the office and on the job, through the ticket takers at the movie houses and the waitresses who bring us coffee and the customers we serve in our stores and the women we leave starving on our streets in wounded countries and dying of neglect around the world – and say as we may say to Her through all the Goddesses on Earth, "I love you. I adore you. Thank you for letting me worship at your feet."

Daddy

hen I was a callow young man I was sure I'd make a good father because I was soo-o-o fond of little kids. They were inherently sweet, I often said, full of possibilities, and innocent as clouds. Some of my friends who were parents regarded me as a unique sort of loony, as if I'd just announced for the presidency; others believed I was merely infantile or uninformed. A few ignored my romantic effusions altogether. Eventually someone would remark on the economy, foreign hostilities, or reincarnation, and conversation would resume.

When one spring I finally did get married – the last of my crowd to do so by a half-dozen years – the love of my life and apple of my eye presented me with a bouncing pair of ready-made two-year-olds, one pink and one blue. This, I asserted with my cheeks flushed and my eyes aglow, was what I had been born for: *Daddy*. Somehow the word just seemed right.

Throughout the summer I rushed home from my job to be the first adult male at the local park, pushing my double stroller with my darlings freshly turned out in brand-new shirts and shorts (or coats and hats depending on the weather), bright balloons and mylar trailers streaming from their chariot's plastic fretwork, a waterproof sack of diapers, powders, unguents, and balms, and bottles full of apple juice slung across its handle bars. Women whose children *were* their work took note, and men who hated Sundays thought I was a traitor: *Chill out*, a younger one confided to me at the swings, *You're gonna get a reputation*. One day I found another man trying to let the air out of my stroller's solid rubber tires.

At home, I fed the kids, gave them their baths, wrapped them in huge terrycloth sheets with their names embroidered in contrasting colors, read them bedtime stories in the fading light, then tucked them in, whispering sweet nothings in the holy whorls of their baby ears. Finally I returned to the woman whose labors had given me so much happiness.

Carin was no stranger to the simple joys of motherhood. She'd dropped an older couple of whelps in the years before we'd met, and had sent them off to be raised by their fathers in a pair of far-off lands. She loved birthing babies so much I never knew when she'd do it again.

One evening after the kids had gone to sleep, my honey-lamb and I sat alone on the porch of our modest suburban home beneath a sky full of night-hawks.

"What is it about babies," she asked, "that makes you go gaga?"

I sighed a deep, contented sigh. I could feel that my lips made a moue of a smile, and the skin of my nipples tingled.

"Is it their tenderness? Their helplessness? Their warm and hopeful natures? Or is it their soft skin? The possibilities residing in their futures? The *tabulas rasas* that they seem to be?"

I had never had children of my own, and had always wanted to. My smile grew slightly melancholic and my lips began to fall. "It's all of that, Carin. It especially has to do with their innocence, and the trust they place in me. I love to be trusted as deeply as that, and the best way I know to receive that trust is to be a Daddy. And what is required to be a Daddy is kids."

Carin buffed one fingernail with a thumb. "*Any* kids?"

A few days later when I rushed home from work the kids were not at home – but Carin was, sitting in a largeish playpen full of dolls and bright soft plastic things. She was wearing rubber pants stuffed with diapers and a soft white cotton smock with little yellow ducklings waddling around its borders. The matching bib had yellow letters spelling out her name.

"Carin?" I asked, startled enough to leave the door ajar.

"Gaa," she answered; "goo. Daddy." And she held her arms up for me, elbows akimbo, one pudgy hand clutching the ruptured neck of an ancient Cabbage Patch doll.

Slowly I approached the playpen, bent down, and lifted her out. "Darling," I said as the doll fell away, "you're wet."

Carin cooed and burbled in my ear as I carried her to the dining table and laid her down upon its cotton cloth. She seemed entranced by the glass crystal teardrops in the chandelier above her, tinkling in the breeze from the open door. I lifted her bottom with one hand and pulled the rubber pants down with the other. The sweet pungent odor of milk-and-apple-juice urine pricked my nostrils. I unpinned the diapers and dropped them, along with the rubber pants, into a bucket someone had thoughtfully left beneath the sideboard.

Above it, on a shelf, I found a bowl of warm water; a soft, clean towel; and a pile of fresh, large diapers. I soaked the towel and wrung it out, then gently bathed Carin's closedy-shaved pink pudendum. She giggled with unashamed delight, although her eyes stayed fixed on the chandelier where sunlight shattered into all its hues.

After I dried her, and powdered her, and diapered her back up, I lifted Carin in my arms. Face to face with me she laughed and pinched my nose. I was at a loss, though. Could I take my grown-up wife to the park spilling out of a double-sized baby stroller, dressed in diapers as if she'd lost her mind?

I shrugged. War, disease, and famine were decimating the world's overblown population, but I was still a Daddy.

People gave us lots of room as I wheeled my little girl past the duck pond. She shrieked and pointed her hand excitedly at the fat birds that scurried clumsily from our path, and bounced in her seat when she heard the bells from the ice-cream cart. I bought her a little cone and watched with glee as she relished the cold concoction, smearing it on her face and hands and bib. When she finally threw the cone down I took it and tossed it in the trash, then spit on a napkin and tried to rub the worst of the stickiness from her hands and face. But Carin wrinkled her nose and scrunched up her eyes and pulled away from me, and when I forced the issue as any parent should she began to cry, so I made a quickie job of it and said, "See? All done. Okay?" For a minute or so she looked at me suspiciously, as if unsure I could be trusted, but then she seemed to forget all about the incident.

The sun had started to set and the first nip of fall was in the air, so I turned our stroller around and made for home. There I fed her, and while I drew her bath I took off Carin's stained smock, soiled diapers, and dishevelled socks, and tickled her where she lay on the dining table. Carin kicked and laughed and tried to push my hand away as it found the special places in her belly that made her jump and leap like a summer trout, but I could see that she was growing tired. I didn't want this special day to be marred by any crankiness, so I playfully lifted her up toward my shoulder and swung her back and forth as I carried her to the bath. I tested the water with my elbow and very gently set her down, splashing her limbs and stomach before settling her in the tub. After her bath I dried her with two towels, then powdered and diapered and rubber-pantsed her for the night, and carried her to the childrens' bed.

It was the middle of the night when I heard my darling cry. I leapt from between my lonely matrimonial sheets and into my slippers, and pulled on my robe as I ran across the hall.

Carin coughed as if just a little collicky, so I understood there was no need for me to be distressed. Nonetheless, I held her in my arms and rocked her for a while, singing gentle songs about soft winds and friendly, furry animals until her little snores told me she'd fallen back asleep.

As I laid Carin back in bed her nightshirt bunched up and bared the bottoms of her milk-and-honeyed breasts to my kindly, fatherly gaze. Lest she catch a chill from uneven temperatures, I pushed the shirt up so it formed a bowl beneath the tender hollow at her throat. I seemed to sense her lifeblood quicken there, and her breath almost came faster: still she slept. I let my eyes caress and linger on the pale disks of her nipples, which perked up and hardened as if my fingers had touched them. She moaned in her sleep and stretched her arms above her head.

Pale and soft in the Mickey Mouse nightlight's glow, her breasts jiggled. Mounds of cream, I thought. Thick, warm gelatin *frappé*. Merringue. For just a moment I wondered what the babies had tasted when they nursed. Then I bent my head to suckle, and she rolled back and forth and the little bed shook violently.

A wedge of moon had risen and its light lay like a finger on the window pane, along the futuristic planes and classic dolls and Legos scattered on the floor, up the footboard of the bed beside me, up her thigh the soft peach cotton blanket had uncovered as it fell. More curious than prurient, as if I had all the time in the world, I took off

Carin's rubber pants and diapers, and I marvelled. Her hairless pudendum did not look shaved at all: it looked innocently pre-pubescent, virginal, and calm.

Then the moonlight pointed out the way, reddening and widening as it occupied the window altogether, spilled bright light across the floor, and slid between her legs. Her thighs parted as if on cue. She sucked and bit and nibbled on her thumb; her little lips were glistening with dew.

I traced the moonlight with my breath, in and out and up and down, imagining my wife's body was a child's. My head felt airy, as if I'd fallen asleep. I seemed to look down upon myself and her from the corner of the room where the ceiling met the distant wall. The way I saw her she was very small; her lips were parted like her thighs. When I thought of her as baby-like she pushed her hips to meet me. First a finger; two; then three. I woke with my fist at the door of her womb.

❧

The next morning, as I was trying to feed Carin breakfast, tradespeople started ringing the bell. It never occurred to me not to answer: the newsboy came to collect his change, the gas man wanted to read the meter, Jehovah's Witnesses sought to save my soul, the mailman left a postcard from the twins' grandfather saying they were having a glorious time together. Though Carin kept behaving like a baby in most respects, and none of my visitors seemed nonplused, the presence of strangers also provoked in her a quite ungirlish, quite unsubtle display of sultry and seductive gurgling and mewing and tugging on the fibers of her clothes.

When momentarily we had peace again, between the missionaries and whatever plague the Lord next planned to send, she held out her arms all speckled with milk-besotted cornflakes to signal she was ready to be lifted from her chair. As I settled her against my hip, she started grinding hers, and making gutteral sounds low down in her throat. She pressed her baby face up to my neck and sucked on the soft hollow beside my carotid artery. I grew instantly erect, and my bathrobe sash fell open.

Carin had always been profoundly erotic. Not only did she achieve each of her three pregnancies with a separate man, she also had a lengthy history of affairs and sexual friendships with both men and women. For example, she had taken up with me while married to a different man and living in a one-bedroom home with his wife. During our pre-nuptial fling she more than once arrived at my door with any of several sexual companions in tow, and she was quite frank about the guests she occasionally entertained while I perambulated the twins about the park. Anything that shook – cars, trains, planes, motorcycles, horses, vibrators, hotel beds with magic fingers, cuisinarts, joy buzzers, ancient elevators, earthquakes – anything might set her off on an orgasmic escapade. I more than once watched her shudder to a halt in broad daylight on a city street while walking past a road crew's jackhammer.

I knew my wife was a woman of vast sexual experience who had as well a vast sexual hunger. I also knew that if I did not allay her appetite, she would make certain one or another of our next visitors did. I harbored no illusions about being able to contain or limit her erotic life, but I did not want rumors about this particular baby set loose in the streets of our little town, pulling on the grown men's pants.

I did not stop to wipe the cornflakes off her arm, therefore, or change the reality our life together had recently become. I simply carried Carin to our marriage bed and lay us down together there, and held her in the crook of my arm. As if she had cats' claws, she kneaded the skin on my belly and chest. Her hips pushed up and down on me. With an instinct that would have seemed preternatural in another child, she scuttled down my body to find the nipple of my one hard teat and started to nurse in earnest. When I could tolerate this milking no longer I slid from her mouth, knelt above her, and placed myself in her hands instead. Immediately she inserted me into herself and rocked and shook and rubbed and jumped and howled and laughed and cried at once, and her body convulsed repeatedly for several long minutes. Just before she relaxed again and settled down, for one brief shining moment my grown-up wife looked up at me. She licked her lips lasciviously and winked, and as her eyes began to flutter shut she smiled at me and whispered, "Daddy."

Bridges

orty years of being on the bum had made Bridges a pro. Even in winter he could find a drink and a place to sleep. But winter down by the docks at three in the morning when it rained was not the place for a pro. Certainly not an old pro.

It was the rain that had finally driven him to the subway. He had ducked under the turnstile and caught the first train out, uptown. He remembered as far as Times Square, then he had slept.

Now iron wheels ground along on iron tracks tucked tight between damp stone walls in the dark. The train shrieked through the tunnel like a string of huge tin cans dragged over boulders and spikes by some monster child. Bridges slumped down in his hard pink plastic seat and wrapped his arms around himself, trying to keep warm. He wondered which part of the city he was under.

The door at the far end of the car opened to a loud clatter of wheels. The torso of a man stacked up on a rolling board slid into the car. The man was dressed in a ragged red flannel shirt whose grimy ends were stuck haphazardly beneath the stump of his body. His face was streaked with dirt and a scar ran down one cheek to his scabrous lips. A dented metal cup hung from a splintered broom handle that rose crookedly up from the front of his board like a broken finger. The man leaned forward and placed his enormous hairy hands on the floor of the car and pulled himself forward. "Please," he said. "Please."

Bridges cowered. For all his years on the skids he thought the man horrid, obscene. A pretty girl, too young to be a woman, wearing a bright green coat opened her black leather purse and took out some change. When she placed the coins in the man's cup she looked him in the eyes, expecting nothing.

"Thank you. Bless you," he whimpered.

"You're welcome," she said. "Bless you too." And she smiled.

The man on the board rolled through the car collecting money in his cup. Bridges was the last person he came to. The man stopped in front of him and looked up.

"I don't have any money," Bridges said.

The man said nothing.

"I don't have any money," Bridges said again. "Look." He emptied his pockets: some dirty tissues and a pencil stub, lint, a lifesaver. The man continued to look at him.

"Hey, listen, you've got more money in your cup than I've had in years. You should be giving me something." He pulled his pockets inside out for the man to see and an unexpected quarter fell to the floor with a dull clink. Bridges watched the coin roll with the rocking of the train until it came to rest directly in front of the man's board. Bridges looked at the man, whose expression had not changed.

Bridges shrugged his shoulders. "I didn't think I had it. Go on. Take it. You can have it." He bent down and picked up the quarter. He was about to drop it in the cup when the man shook his head.

"No," he said.

"Go on," Bridges urged, "take it. I'd have given it to you right off if I knew I had it."

"Don't want it."

Bridges looked at the money and looked in the cup where several dollars worth of coins nestled together like eggs in a nest. He looked back at the man whose expression still had not changed.

"Please open the door for me," the man said. "I can't reach."

"Sure," said Bridges. "You sure you don't want the money?"

The man said nothing. Bridges put the quarter back in his coat pocket and stood up and opened the door between the cars. The noise of the train grew louder. The man looked out toward the next car, whose door was closed. He looked back at Bridges. Bridges stepped out between the cars and slid the second door open, straddling the cars and keeping the first door open with his foot.

"I can't cross between the cars," the man said. "My wheels get stuck."

"What do you want me to do?" Bridges asked.

"Pick me up."

Bridges hesitated. "Wait till the train stops."

"It's easy," the man said. "Pick me up so I can reach the cross bars. I'll hold on while you move my board. Then you just set me down on the board again."

Bridges looked past the loose chains that swayed between the cars with the rhythm of the wheels. The tunnel walls sped by. "All right," he said.

He bent down to the man. Ozone from the tracks mingled in his nose with the man's old sweat and something else vaguely medicinal. Specks of soot kicked up by the train wheels stung his cheeks and eyes. He squinted and set his lips and clenched his arms around the torso.

The man was unexpectedly heavy. Under the best conditions Bridges wasn't sure he could lift him. But standing on the lip of the moving car –

"Count to three," the man said. "When you say 'three' I'll jump."

Jump? Bridges began to strain.

"Count to three."

Bridges grunted. "One. Two. Three."

And the man did jump. Abruptly he became lighter, and Bridges lifted him off his board and turned to face the following car. Slowly, to keep his balance, but as fast as he could, he moved the man toward the cross bars flanking the opposite doorway. To reach them Bridges had to step across the empty space that slid between the cars. As he put his first foot down he felt the man begin to slip from his grasp. "No!" he shouted, and flung the man forward.

The man cried out in pain and the bottom of his shirt shook loose and for a moment Bridges could see the reddened fish-white skin that was the end of his body. But his hands gripped the bars and he clung to them while the tunnel wind whipped the red cloth about his missing hips.

Bridges grabbed the board and set it in the mouth of the car. He gripped the man under his arms from behind and half lifted, half threw him down to his board. The man gasped and his eyes watered. Gingerly he placed his hands on the floor and adjusted himself on the board. He took some quick, shallow breaths and then, without looking back, tucked his shirt tails under him and pulled himself forward and away. The door between them slid closed. Wan light filled the tunnel. The train slowed and stopped.

Bridges didn't move until the train did. Then he felt he couldn't wait. He climbed the thin chains that had just begun to sway again and leapt off the train onto the end of the station platform. He lay where he fell while the sound of the train died away. The dull click of thrown switches and the faraway rumble of other trains in other tunnels drifted up to him. He got to his knees and looked at his hands. They were covered with blood. From where he knelt he could see the door to the men's room. It was padlocked.

◆◆

Outside the rain had stopped, but the air was still wet and the streetlights seemed to emerge through a patina of frost against a black and colorless, textureless background. Bridges didn't recognize the corner. He looked down the street wondering what there was in that direction. Then he looked up the street and saw the girl in the green coat. She was standing at a bus stop watching him. He turned in the other direction.

"Wait," the girl called.

Bridges paused. He didn't want to talk to the girl. He only wanted to find a dry doorway to sleep in until it grew light enough to panhandle carfare back down to the docks. He turned and faced her anyway.

She looked down and toyed with her purse for a few seconds. When she looked back up she said, "You're a little bloody."

"Many people make that mistake," Bridges said. "Actually I'm a little drunk."

"What happened?"

"I fell."

"Where?"

"On the subway platform. I think I skinned my hand."

"You should wash the cuts."

Bridges looked at the dirty rainwater trickling down the gutter. "With what?"

"What? Water. And soap."

Bridges grinned at her. "I think I left them back at my hotel."

"Come here. Let me see your hands."

Bridges did as he was told. She took his hands in hers and examined them. Up close she wasn't quite as young as he had thought. Young, but a woman, not a girl. She looked tired, despite her careful hair and expensive coat.

"You didn't cut your hands," she said. "This isn't your blood."

Bridges looked at his hands and saw that there was blood on his shirt as well.

A bus appeared out of the mist with a ghostly hiss.

"Come back to my place," the girl said. "I have a couch you can sleep on, and you can have a wash."

Bridges peered at her. "Why?"

She shrugged. "What difference does it make?"

Suddenly Bridges felt exhausted. She was right, he decided. It didn't make any difference. A couch, a doorway, washed, not washed. He climbed on the bus and she followed, paying his fare.

◆◆

She was a prostitute, she said: a high-class escort who turned tricks by appointment with executives and diplomats. She was employed by an agency in mid-town. She said she was very well paid.

"You must be awfully," he searched for the word, "professional."

"Sometimes."

"Were you working tonight?"

She turned to the window. "Oh, yes," she said to the glass.

"You don't sound as if you liked it much."

She smiled thinly and drew a Happy Face on the foggy pane. "Sometimes yes and sometimes no. Tonight – no."

"Is it so hard?"

"The hours are short and the money is long. It isn't like walking the streets. But after a thousand strangers have come and gone you get driven down inside. Or you become the stranger, and he isn't really there at all. I used to pretend I was screwing myself. But then I started to disappear as well."

She wiped out the Happy Face with her fist, opening a hole in the steam on the window that let the night come through. "Tonight I had an old boyfriend," she said. "He didn't recognize me. He didn't know who I was."

◆◆

Her apartment was high above the Hudson, which slid like a silver worm through a crack in the earth below. He stood at her window swaddled in towels and watched the far-off water wend its way to parts of the city he knew best. Far away, on a night like this one, he'd squat beneath the West Side Highway and keep warm by holding his hands above a trash fire. Winter would go and he'd have survived again.

Light filled the room and he saw himself reflected in her window: younger than he'd looked in years, the muscles in his bare arm defined by the shadows they made. Then he saw her in the same glass standing in the bathroom doorway with the light bright all around her. She was naked. One arm was raised and her hand rested high on the door jamb. Her body looked as young as he had thought she was when he saw her on the train. He didn't know what she expected him to do, so he continued to stare at her image as if looking out the window.

"The way you live," she started, "are you lonely?"

Bridges began to sweat and cursed the rain that drove him from the docks. "I don't know," he said. "I never think about it."

"Are you lonely tonight?"

He faced her. "I want to go home," he said.

"Your clothes are all wet. I washed them. You'll have to wait until they dry."

"I've worn wet clothes before."

She let her hand fall down from the jamb, slow and white. She walked toward him like a guilty child, head down, watching her feet cross the thick beige carpet. She took a last step and placed her foot, very lightly, on his own. Her fingers climbed his chest and hooked the top of his towel. She tugged gently till it fell away, and turned her face up to his. "Please stay. We've both had hard nights."

❦

Sometime in the dark he woke and listened to her breathe beside him. She breathed more like a man than like a woman, the sounds deep and sonorous as the air left her body. Her arm, when he touched it, felt strong like a man's arm too. Bridges fell asleep again and after a long time he began to dream. He dreamed that it was morning, and that he awakened and cooked himself some eggs, and made toast, and a pot of coffee. He dreamed that he ate, and washed the dishes, and went into the bathroom where he saw his tattered clothes, dry and wrinkled, hanging on a rope above the bathtub. He dreamed that he looked at them with a kind of fondness, and that he carefully washed his face and patted it dry with a thick towel, and put on eye shadow, mascara, eyebrow pencil, rouge, and lipstick. He dreamed that he put on a pair of brightly colored underpants cut very low, and a skimpy, sheer brassiere. He dreamed that he put on a blouse of dove-grey silk, with a matching scarf he tied into a bow around his neck. He dreamed he put on a garter belt, and rolled a pair of stockings up from his toes to his thighs, and hooked them to the belt. He dreamed he put on an ivory colored skirt, and that the zipper almost snagged. He dreamed he put on a pair of dark grey shoes with short heels. He dreamed he slung a black leather purse over his shoulder, and took a bright green coat in his arm. He dreamed that as he looked out the window a brilliant day had already begun. He dreamed he looked at the bed and saw among the rumpled sheets a middle-aged man, half bald and gone mostly grey, asleep with his arms around a pillow. And he dreamed that on the street, walking to the bus, he put the green coat on and put his hands in its pockets and found, in one of them, a quarter, which he placed in the tin cup of a blind man selling pencils in the sun.

Afternoon Delight

had not yet come out to anyone about anything – I had not yet visited the bars and bath houses whose very names made me catch my breath – but when I moved to pre-AIDS San Francisco in the early 1970s I knew I was not going for the ocean view.

Soon after I settled myself in my cozy new apartment in a nondescript low-rent neighborhood I headed out for the Castro district, which was just taking over from Polkstrasse as the gay mecca of the western world. Right behind the gas station, on the triangular corner where Market, Castro, and 17th Streets intersect, I noticed a lot of foot traffic around a brown wooden building set back from the sidewalk by 10 or 15 feet. The men moving in and out were tall and short, stocky and lean, young and old, and they wore all the different uniforms of the day: leather, levis, plaid flannel shirts, and disco polyester; but they all seemed to know what they were doing, and I did not. For someone who still thought of himself as straight the sight was surprisingly exciting. Fear, hope, and a sort of eager curiosity raised the temperature of my blood and I began to feel light-headed. After walking around the block a couple of times in an effort to calm myself I took the proverbial deep breath and walked on up the stairs.

Inside the door a sweet-looking man with a fierce mustache sat in a small closet behind a dutch door. He looked me up and down as I gave him the $5 a sign said would admit me, then he nodded me through a thick velvet curtain. On the far side the silence was profound. I stood in a barn-like room where a film of men with enormous cocks sucking each other off played noiselessly against one wall. A few men sat or sprawled on benches watching the movie, but I knew this building had to be more than a porn palace. Someone rustled through the curtain behind me and I watched his back as he walked up a flight of stairs I hadn't noticed before. He vanished on a sort of balcony that hung over me from the second floor. With my heart racing I followed him.

At the top of the stairs I found what seemed to be tiers of confessional booths. Because their walls were low and they had no roofs I could peer into the little chambers easily. Many were empty in the middle of the afternoon, but in others men stood or sat or knelt, some with their bellies and others with their faces pressed up against the walls. I entered an empty booth and shut the door behind me, then I heard another door shut nearby. By the time I turned around a hand was resting on the inside of a cut-out hole a little less than waist high in the far wall. The index finger curled at me: conventional sign language for *Come here.* Fascinated, I obeyed, opening my jeans as I went as if I'd always known just what to do. When I reached the wall where the hand was poised it closed on my rigid cock and pulled me up against the hole and through it. Then a mouth closed softly over me and commenced to suck and lick and nibble at my hard-on while the hand caressed my balls as if they were my heart.

In the ten years I'd been sleeping with women, and the five I'd been fooling around with men in bath houses each time I visited a new big city, no one had ever just made love to my cock, and no one had ever kissed me so deeply its roots quivered and shuddered and made me want to cry and shout and sing all at once. My cock jerked and twitched, wanting to come immediately, but I knew enough to hold myself back. I let the man suck me for what must have been half an hour, and when I could not stop myself from coming any longer I literally left the ground, as if pulled up by my elbows as I leaned on the ledge that separated our two booths. My legs shot out, my toes curled inside my boots, my fingers stretched, and I'm sure the men who were at the glory hole that day still remember the groan I let out as I came from every deep-down sex cell in my body. My hips kept pumping long after I was dry, and the mouth kept sucking on my limper and limper dick.

Finally I was truly done. Some part of me wanted to reciprocate, and maybe I should have. But I still thought that I was straight, and

I was frightened that a man could give me so much pleasure. I packed myself away inside my pants, and as I was buckling my belt I looked over the ledge that had held me up. The man who'd taken my $5 stood and smiled at me. Impulsively I bent forward and kissed his mouth; he smelled and tasted like my come. "Thank you," I said from my heart. "Thank *you*," he answered, and he winked. "Come again."

Cages:
a Three-Part Invention

"Invention. A term of rare occurrence, but known to every musician from Bach's collection.... The usual denomination, "two-part and three-part inventions" is not authentic, but would seem to be justifiable.... Bach's reason for choosing his terms is entirely obscure.... The term invention was used by Vitali as a title for pieces involving special tricks.... Four of Bonporti's "inventions" have been reprinted as works of Bach...." – Willi Apel, Harvard Dictionary of Music, *1944*

CAGE #1

She hung from the vaulted gothic ceiling in a high white macramé cage. From a single turk's-head knot the ropes depended to a wooden platform fitted with a round white cushion she could stand or sit on. The platform was lashed to the lower third of the webbing and tied off below, where the rope-ends unraveled to dozens and dozens and dozens of floating strings and whimsical ribbons frayed and trailing away like white streamers in the breeze beneath her feet.

Her hair was so pale and her skin so translucent she almost looked like part of the cage itself. I did nothing to change the way she came to me but wrap her in a layered cloak of brightly colored feathers. When I pressed the button beside my chair she descended in an outward silence from the shadows above and I heard nothing but the thin wind as air was pressed from beneath the falling cage, and, as if it were ongoing, the glass-bell clarity of her sweet soprano that grew more present but never louder as she came closer till I could touch the cage or, sometimes, even her.

She must have sat at other times but she was always standing when the cage came down, delicate hands and loose long fingers tapering around the closest ropes without any expression on her face at all. Sometimes the cloak was wrapped around her shoulders like a shawl, sometimes draped like a toga or part of a sari, sometimes wrapped around her hips like a pareo; when it lay in a heap on the cushion she appeared more naked than any human being has a right to be before another. Once she had woven the feather fringes into the macramé, shielding herself as if behind a huge bird wing. Still she was singing, her rich lips mouthing the words to her fluid songs in a language that made no linear sense to me but that immobilized me where I sat and gently prised the casing from my helpless heart until I felt exposed from the inside out. Then her deep, sad eyes seemed to translate what I felt to her, as if I'd understood her music; as if those eyes had found me from the shadows high above long before I'd even made her out; as if she'd always meant to sing to me.

I kept her for her singing, of course, and because as the cage ascended later her voice grew fainter and fainter until I heard only its memory. Sometimes after I had sent her away her absence felt like such a piteous loss I could not bear the echoes of her silence. Once I brought the cage back only part-way down so I could hear her singing at a distance, and though I could not make myself send her up again, her false proximity made my grief seem sharper. I fell asleep to her music and woke to it at dawn, too haunted to be rid of her for days. For nights thereafter I dreamed her voice as if it were her eyes, piercing whatever shields of time or distance I placed between us, floating as if disembodied in a pool of pastel music.

Another time I thought to defeat the music. I let the cage descend until it rested on the floor. Even the old Aubusson beneath it could not muffle the tones she made, and she did not hesitate when I approached the cage and slowly opened the locks. I'd been afraid she would grow silent or try to flee, but she remained leaning as if languishing against the satin ropes, clutching at the cage that arched above her head, her eyes on mine, her song perpetual. I stepped back from the cage and still she sang. I sat down in my chair and beckoned her with a gesture of one hand. Eyes still fixed and voice still singing, she slid one leg in front of the other, flexed her foot, and took a step so quick I did not see it but she'd landed on the carpet leaning toward me on her toes, both hands clutching the ropes that were behind her now, naked breasts and shoulders still emerging from the feather cloak that settled to the cushion as if it were a single piece of down.

I pointed at my feet and she soared to me: as if she had fairy wings she stepped and knelt and bowed in a single movement curving as a fawning swan to press her lips where my finger commanded, and her song seemed to emanate from all around her as if her covering her mouth had no effect on it.

I raised her up with a touch to her neck and she brought herself full face to mine. I wanted to hold her, attend to her, touch her slight body, but notes rose from her floral breath like bubbles in sweet water. When I placed my finger against her lips they parted and softly closed around me as she nuzzled, suckled, and kept on singing.

❧

CAGE #2

Why do you keep him locked in a cage?
I don't keep him there, I just put him there sometimes.
Why?
I like to see him contained, in my control.
Can he get out?
When I let him.
Where's the key?
Keys. There are nine locks. I have keys for every one. Right now they're up there on the fireplace mantle.
Do you always keep them there?
Of course not. I just put them there today.
I guess that makes them easy to reach.
Yes. I expect to let him out before you go.
You do?
Well, someone's got to make dinner.
I guess he can't cook in there.
No. That's what the long chain is for.
Which long chain?
The one in the kitchen.

You keep him chained?

When he's not in the cage I do.

Why?

For the same reasons. See what happens when I put my foot to the bars?

He kisses it.

He *worships* it. Look at his face: rapture. He reaches for me with his fingers, as far as he can reach through the bars. Look how he presses his lips to me: reverence. Whatever I offer he worships.

He's pretty big for that small space.

Follow my foot. Kneel up. Follow my finger. Lie down. On your back. Spread your thighs.

Is that another lock?

Yes. It's how I attach the chain.

You chain him by his balls?

It makes things very clear between us, doesn't it?

I'll say.

Hands and knees. Face down. Ass up.

Does he do everything you tell him?

Everything. Would you like to see him out of the cage? Hand me those keys.

Why does he wait for you in that position?

I taught him to. I like him to show me that he knows his place. I like to remind him that he belongs to me. But sometimes I have him kneel up so he's more exposed in front and he can see my eyes.

Well, the door's open. Why doesn't he come out?

I haven't given him permission yet.

He's very obedient.

Yes. Come here. Kiss. Good boy.

Is he ever allowed to stand and walk?

When I say so.

When is that?

When I want him to do something he couldn't do from his knees.

Such as?

All right, my boy. Kill.

❦

*C*AGE #3

"We waited and waited for music that never began. Silence stretched before us like an India rubber cat awakening: licked its whiskers, licked its chest, and settled back to sleep. You had talked about the prospect of this concert almost as long as I had known you, and were plainly excited by the very notion.

" 'Sound is soft,' you said to me as I served your supper the night before, 'malleable, permeable. Anything can happen in it. You can do anything with it.'

" 'Me, Maitresse?' I asked.

" 'You goose, you know exactly what I mean.'

" 'Yes, Maitresse,' I answered, though I certainly did not."

◆◆

"The mid-December night fell early and the temperature fell with it, frosting the snowdrifts melted in the day with smooth, treacherous caps of ice. You declined to take the car, which you found unreliable in the modern streets, preferring to borrow, between the two Margeaux, one carriage, four black horses, and even one Margeau herself when she offered to drive us because she thought the night too special for her coachman's Montparnasse eyes and knew it would never occur to you to refuse. You sat bundled in your furs looking in the direction of the Bois like *noblesse oblige* herself, as if you weren't paying attention to me at all; but I knew nothing would be closer to your mind, as I sat naked on the carriage floor beneath my own pile of rugs and rubbed your feet, than the upturned nipples of my teacup breasts and the beckoning drapes and welcoming vestibule of my young, dark pudendum. Watching you peer through the isinglass at what I couldn't imagine, I sometimes brought your toes to my lips and kissed them through your stockings. If I licked hard along your right instep I knew you were likely to shudder and lose control, but I was worshipful, not in a playful mood. You turned your gaze on me.

" 'Are you warm enough, dear girl?' you asked.

"I hugged your legs to me and with my eyes closed pressed my cheek against your closer calf. 'I am warm enough, Maitresse. Thank you for inquiring.'

" 'Then remove your robes and let me look at you.'

"In motions so fluid they were as one, I slid your feet into their shoes and raised myself to a kneeling posture, emerging from the center of the resounding pelts like a mermaid shedding the depths of her bath. Your eyes took so solemnly to mine I extended my arms and struck a saucy odalisque pose, one hand behind my black curls, the other with splayed fingers obscuring but only partially these breasts you doted on. I saw your eyebrows rise a hair and softly swept that arm away and down, revealing, as if it slowly rent a curtain, all the front of me beyond my navel and past my quivering thighs which, parted as you had taught me to keep them for you, revealed me, warm and moist for you. I wanted to feel your hands on me so badly that I ached throughout my groin. My tender button was erect, my nipples reached for you as if they were fingers, hands, arms, young girls themselves in love with you, even my breath and heartbeat called to you while I, your goose, your slave, your whore, your new coquette, while I who waited on your pleasure longed to taste your tongue on mine, to feel your breath hot in the hollow of my throat, your teeth against my thinnest skin as you struggled not to wet your lips with my willing blood and ground yourself against my narrow, bruised hips until you bucked and spat and cursed exhaling like a sliced balloon. The thought of your hunger consumed me as I kept my body steady in the rocking carriage, knees toed in, so that you'd want to take me to your bed tonight as well as to the music.

"Time began to stretch so that whole worlds of meaning were born between two steps of the horses' progress. Your eyes made love to my eyes, to my cheeks and then my lips, to my shoulders and my underarms; when they caressed my breasts and nipples, pulling at them as if they were pouting mouths, I could not prevent myself from dancing the little dance, and a cry barely voiced escaped me. The horses took another step.

" 'Turn around,' you said. 'Bend over.'

"I obeyed. I always obeyed you, to the surprise and sometimes the chagrin of women my age but never those of yours. I felt your hand caress my cheeks as if they were my face, felt your fingers part my lips as if they were my mouth, felt you enter me and stroke my convoluted walls, my frantic little tongue, urging me on to lather like a manic pony, helpless and shaking with more than just desire. You rested your thumb against my other hole and said, 'Sit back,' so rolling slowly from side to side I took you into me, pursing and kissing with my small pink obedience. You were so strong and I so little, you lifted me from the floor that way, by your thumb and finger, too quickly for me to gasp before you'd set me naked on your lap to kiss and fondle like a doll. You held me tight against your soft, round, fur-wrapped breast and yes, I shook and threw my arms about your neck and pressed my face against you whimpering, but you just let it pass."

⧫⧫

"Nowhere but that place, never but that time, could you have taken me from the carriage as you did, in only brand-new pumps, one long fur, and a neckful of diamond-bedded sapphires. Margeau herself escorted us into the hall and to your couch, and smiled at me like a fond aunt. With infinite *politesse* she took the fur from my shoulders, revealing me a moment at a time, and then she took the pumps from my feet and was gone. The leash you attached to my necklace was white gold, worked in such an intricate design it took the light itself like diamonds. I knelt on the floor beside you with my hands folded modestly before me, outwardly composed but inside seething with shame and pride, fear and excitement, embarrassment and hauteur: for others' eyes, though not of course for mine, a human thing and not a person, the simple property of your display. The chamber, though it could not seat more than several dozens, was full, and no one with eyes could have failed to see us.

"The instrument glowed dull gold at the front of the room. The chair adjacent shone from the dark depths of its richly polished wood. As if another person's horses had frozen in their walk, nothing happened for so long we ceased to be the center of anybody's unacknowledged attentions. It was not just that, as in the carriage, time itself moved slower: now, here, the air itself grew gradually thicker. Though sounds could only travel shorter distances, their timbres became greatly magnified. Some less polite gentlemen coughed and I could discern the sympathetic rhythms of each uvula. I felt the impatient intake of breaths and the puffery of their exhalations. I heard a flask unscrewed before I smelled the spirits, and I knew by the way the pewter scraped and rasped which threads were worn from careless use. Shod feet shuffled on the carpet, bone joints cracked, and papers started rustling. Here and there a voice exposed itself enough for me to name its mutter, then its meaning. I heard some man stand, and turn, then walk away. A door was opened before his step, and shut again with a muffling hand. More people spoke with gentle lilting voices full of air and inspiration; some talked whose anger clicked and chipped. Couch springs sank and chair backs snapped as more people stood. The door stayed open while they left and every person's steps receded differently, each with its own cadence, each with its own heft. When the room was nearly silent I heard you breathe as if you were asleep. I looked up at you at last and saw you smiling down at me.

" 'Come up here across my lap,' you said, and lithely I obeyed. Your silk-draped thighs were firm and yielding both, and the damask rose wool couch seat smelled of hair and prickled against my face. You rested one forearm on my back, your hand gripping my far shoulder. As your other hand stroked me, roving my two mounds, my far hand, fallen, clasped your ankle, and my near hand snaked behind and underneath you. I heard the clap of skin on skin before I felt your palm strike down on me, but after that first slap you did not let up and all the hard sounds of your spanking disappeared for me in the rush of heat then pain that took me over in a flurry I did not count or time, but when it was over I was crying and panting and I knew that I had squealed and you were happily shaken in your seat. You took me up and held me to your breast again as you had done in the carriage, but smiling and contented now.

" 'Now,' you said, 'I want to take you home.'

"I looked in your eyes and pointed to the front of the room. You nodded and released me. I walked, conscious all the while of your eyes on my flesh, but after I had collected the ancient tape recorder, dull gold in the light of colored gels, I turned and knelt and bowed, then came across the floor on hands and knees to bring this offering for you to turn off in the room that had now grown completely empty."

Bear

The zoo is nearly empty on this still, hot Friday afternoon in autumn, as if the city's humans, like their furrier brothers now tucked out of sight in caves and shady roosts, have stayed away in favor of some cooler place, or else are hibernating, saving themselves for a busy weekend to come.

I like the park this way: so nearly private, it feels safe. In the solitude I grow soft and languorous. In your arms I lean back lazily against the slatted wooden bench and watch the honey sun in dappled bars fall streaming through the eucalyptus leaves, go threading through the needles of the giant evergreens, glide on motes like a thousand gentle fingers teasing through your warm black curly hair and glinting there like eyelight on the blue steel bars of a cage in the night as you bend over me, blocking out the sun, and settle your hot lips on mine. I feel your breath all over my face, close my eyes and open my mouth for you, feel your teeth and the insides of your cheeks, draw you into me, lick the rasping surface of your tongue, drink from it, suck on it as I would suck your dick right here if I could get away with it, could slide my hand between us just like this, unbuckle your wide belt, unbutton your pants, prise down the zipper with my thumb and feel you tightly sprung in your straining shorts, press my palm against your belly as I'm doing now and creep beneath your waistband, feel the wet tip of your fat cock leap and paint my fingertips, and push down into the mass of coarse damp hair to fill my hand with your huge, heavy balls whose heft always makes me moan deep in my throat.

I feel your mouth leave mine and I let my eyes open as if from a dream just as my fingers close four, three, two, one around your cock but are not quite able to meet my thumb, and I hear my voice whisper to your languid eyes, "O Dear, O Honey, O Love my love, please now please I want to taste you now, feel you fill me now now now...."

"Let go of my meat now, Baby," you smile speaking softly, tall and broad above me as the great Sequoia that holds the sun behind you so I shudder in the sight of your gentle strength, "and put my clothes back on me right. You know you can't be doing me here, and you know you never asked permission anyway. So you know what has to happen, don't you."

You make a mocking moue with your mouth but I know you are serious: I know that what you say is a reminder, not a question, and O Love, I know what you will do and no, I didn't touch you just to make you do it, didn't really want for you to chain me to the wall again and beat me for my insolence – I just couldn't help myself, I love you so, and want you as I've never wanted any man. If I had wanted anything from you of what you did to me that last time I was disobedient it would not have been the punishment but what came after: *after* you beat me and made me beg for mercy and apologize and swear like Galileo on his knees before the Inquisition that I would never disobey you again, *after* you lifted me up in your big hands and heaved me deep into the thick, unmoving cage to let me know how unhappy I had made you, *after* you bolted the relentless gate against me and locked the door to the soundproofed blackdark room so you wouldn't hear me cry all night for you: it was after that, hour and hours after, when you opened the door to let the first thin light of morning in and looked down on me huddled in the farthest corner of the cage naked, sleepless, and forlorn, shivering against the cold bars, exhausted from weeping and bruised from my shoulders to my knees from what you'd done the night before: it was then, when you unlocked the cage and opened the gate and ordered me out to press my mouth against your feet, when you hauled me upright to my knees and dragged me by my balls stumbling and screaming in pain across the floor and took my head in your firm hands and held my eyes with the sorrow in yours and slapped my face back and forth, then, then: lifted me high up in your wide, high yes in your kind, up yes in your healing arms, and carried me yes to your bed, and laid me down among the sheets that smelled of you, and yes you kissed me with your pounding kisses, laid me down beneath you, laid me down beneath your deep, great love again, forgiven.

Forgiven. Then, my love, then. That is all I ever wanted: your arms, your kisses, your bed, your love. Everything else you took from me – the chains and locks, the collars and whips, the beatings and bruises, my terror and long howls that thrill you in the night, your name burned into my ass for life – everything else is what I gave for you: a gift. Everything else is what I give *to* you. Everything else.

"I know," I say now, looking away. A pair of peacocks strut about the lawn, dipping their heads against each other in regular rhythms like ancient Egyptians of my imagination dancing in a moving fresco, fanning the overheated day with their iridescent feathers. I turn back to you and say, "But later, yes? Much later, yes? Tonight? Not now, please not now, it's still so early and I want this day with you. Please? Please? I know I misbehaved, I know I was out of line, I know you will not forgive me till you've taken what is yours, what is your right to take, but please can we just have this day? Tonight will come for you, will come for me too, all too soon enough."

Somehow I have fallen to my knees and I'm imploring you, oblivious to the day and our surroundings, pressing my face against the bulges of your crotch, fumbling to get your shirt tucked in, your zipper closed, belt buckled, to obey, to please you, when what I really want is to take you out of that well-worn cloth and bury my face in the rich chocolate smell of your thick flesh. Softly you pull me up by my elbows, bend down, and kiss my eyes, caress my cheek. You are so big my whole face disappears in your one hand. You don't say you wish you didn't have to do it – I know you do, and you wouldn't lie. And you don't say you love me – I know you do. But you let me rest my face against the broad, warm wall of your chest, and I look up at you with eyes as hopeful as a kitchen dog's as you walk us along the asphalt path past elephants and giraffes, hippos and rhinos, all the time with my head cocooned against you, underneath your shoulder, wrapped up altogether in your arm.

You take me into you this way, so different from the way I open up to take you into me. How long that is from start to finish, how deep you go unraveling me till first there is nothing in the space above me but your chest, your head, your face, your eyes, and how I try to reach my legs around you, hopelessly: to press my heels against your thighs while you spread me wide as a mouth and enter me slowly and lower yourself slowly into me, a tree is what I think every time: you plant yourself in me, a tree, and then the breath goes out of me and then your weight becomes the world and then there is nothing left in me forever then but you.

Behind us one peacock calls like a banshee loon in mourning. I must have closed my eyes and fallen into a trance listening to the beating of your heart, and that cry startles me as if from a dangerous dream. As if in a dream I see you pull open the heavy door and I am overcome by the dank, fertile smell of something remorseless, not indifferent. The house is like a hangar with other couples, other lovers, other people, kids. You move us forward. Little clutches of people stand at cages where the cats are being fed.

Big cats. The obvious lion with his sandy mane paces the concrete floor of his sterile cell, muscles flowing on like merging currents in a river beneath the surface of his tawny fur. A side of horse the size of a white shark's bite lies untouched beneath his wooden shelf. Again and again he raises his head as big as a mastiff and shakes it toward the humans crowding him. A child ducks underneath the rail that separates the species and his mother and the lion roar at once, savage warnings that stop him as nuclear blast would stop his shadow dead upon a wall, and ricochet, rebound, reverberate against the building's stone. Your heart beats calmly, twice, before the child regains himself and wails like the peacock, flees his spot, hurtles to his mother who embraces him and holds him and protects him just as you hold me.

"You ever see a tiger eat?" you ask, turning me around.

The biggest cat of all stands orange and black as an Asian sunset's autumn bamboo forest, with elbows bent back and lowered head, eyes half closed as if in ecstasy, licking his ball of dinner where it lies like a mystery between his meaty paws. I see him bent as maybe you see me in your mind's eye, bowed on hands and knees before you in the iron collar, commanded in my movements by the big chain leash that fits your hand, working my feline lips and tongue along your own meat muscled like the tiger's thigh, remembering how I learned to open my throat so I could swallow you and breathe, swallow you and breathe, so wholly your slave, utterly your animal, abject in my love, and how I came to worship your massive balls, sucking on them one by one like holy icons I could only try to honor and revere, too big to think that I could take them both into my mouth at once, and how one time, hunkered back on your haunches and riding my face like a camel, you forced them into me anyway and filled my face and pinched my nostrils closed, and how I passed out watching you watch me go, how I showed you I would die before I'd let you go.

Another cat is nursing on a joint, and yet another has tossed aside some bloody part to concentrate on a carnivore's popsicle, a dinner's worth of frozen flesh wrapped up in a rabbit's pelt. I turn my face into your indulgent chest and you, who know me better than I could hope, take me right back out the door and into the sun, which has begun to slant toward evening. Eyes closed again, I smile as if I follow you in sleep, pretending. You walk me up and down, around in circles, back again. When at last you tell me, "Open your eyes," we are standing to the side of a small lagoon. Beyond the water, on a backlit spit of land, on the broad cross-arm of a fallen tree trunk, a great bald eagle spreads its clipped or wounded eight foot wings and stares at us across its body as if it were a picture eagle looking boldly across its fictive history on a piece of American propaganda, or posing for the flag above the bar where you sometimes like to go.

Bald eagles, when they mate, I've read, meet where they soar, so high above the earth that they can dance amid the currents. They wheel in easy circles around each other, then the bird on top dives down upon the bottom, which turns on its back, upside down to meet him in the sky. They grasp each other's talons and they drop together, joined as if out of control in a bond of trust so absolute that nothing stops or interrupts it, freefalling through the heavens until just before it is too late, when they uncouple and fly free, apart, in different directions. Later they return to one another, bonded, mated in their dance.

So you circled me the day we met, walking in wide, lazy arcs around the silly picnic I had almost left because there was nothing and no one there I cared to know about. When I saw you pass me I had to keep you above me in my sight, turning too, so you would know I saw. With every pass your steps came closer and I was barely breathing in anticipation, fear, and longing. If you had snapped your fingers I'd have fallen at your feet. Instead you came toward me one small step more, and in the breadth of your shadow I stepped back to let you in. You moved one arm toward me and I turned my hips to keep my face to yours. You stepped back again, and when I stepped into the slipstream of the air your heat had warmed I found your broad hand clasping my entire waist and everybody watching our silent tango. I fell forward into your arms and kiss. You lifted me, and carried me off like prey.

A small zoo train chuffs politely past on miniature tracks, children cheering and all the outsized grown-ups on it looking embarrassed. The Casey Jones in striped bib overalls pulls twice on the steam-puff whistle and waves his cap, but only I wave back. You spin me around in mid-wave and kiss the breath from me when the riders and I expect it not at all, releasing me gasping to face the polar bears that lie like twins beside each other on their bellies on a shaded eastern slope of rock. Their feet splay out and seem to touch, as if they were holding loving hands. They rest their chins together on the granite and move their eyes only to watch the train of people passing by.

"This is what I brought you here to see," you say. Then you seat me on another long bench, stretch out on your back with your head upon my thighs and lap, shade your eyes with your big forearm, and sink off into sleep. I am surprised, but I watch you for a while and then I watch the bears; I watch you and I watch the bears. The low, black-painted fence that separates them from us is iron, but it is nothing like the cage you keep at home. The bears could easily step across these bars, and so could I. What they can't breach is the chasm maybe thirty feet deep that's cut between their rocks and a small shelf of grass on their side of the fence that runs with narrow water a few feet deep. Precipitous steps lead down to the moat from where the bears have roaming ground, but on the human side the wall is straight and flat, with nothing to grip in the concrete.

You sleep without a movement I can see except your steady breathing. The bears persist as well, as the shadows lengthen and the air cools off. Small chirpy birds come and go, squirrels chitter and fall still, people appear and then they disappear, far away another peacock cries, and after a long while evening falls like a curtain ringing down. Is it the cool that stirs you then? or is it the coming dark? All at once you swing your legs around and you are sitting up. In your next movement you grab me by the collar and throw me to the ground, literally tear off all my clothes before I can react, ripping cloth and breaking buttons, and set one booted foot on my face when I lie naked in front of you. It would be pointless for me to struggle, even if I wanted to. I kiss the bottom of your boot.

"What am I going to do with you?"

"Sir?"

"Who told you you could touch me?"

"I – "

"Don't answer that. Don't answer anything until I tell you to. You understand?"

I nod beneath your sole. You set your other boot between my legs and I part my thighs for you. You draw back your foot and on the emphasis –

"What am I going to *do* with you?" you ask again – you kick me, hard.

The few stars that had begun to come out disappear and the purpling sky turns red. I would double over but you are standing now, over and on top of me, so I can't budge. The pain moves through me and I can almost breathe but I say nothing, as you have ordered. You bend down and take my ass and balls in one hand and my shoulders in the other, lift and lug me to the fence before the bears, then drop me on the grass in their enclosure. I have seen the chasm but now I am in their land. I turn quickly to see that they have raised their snouts and lumbered up, starting to move close to me across the great but very small divide. I want to stand and climb the fence, but you have put me where I am and I will not disobey again. I turn back to you, on my knees now and wilder-eyed than I have thought you'd ever make me, to see you dropping my torn clothing in a trash container near the bench you'd slept on. Do you mean to leave me here? You shamble back to the bench and take your seat. I grip the fence bars in both hands and try to plead with you wordlessly.

"Bare with bears," you say aloud. "I wish I was a painter." You watch me for awhile from your side of the fence, and I watch you from mine. The air is cooling on my skin. Behind me I hear the bears shuffling about the rocks.

"You've got to understand me, Baby," I hear you say in the growing gloaming. "I know you love me, but when I give you an order I do not expect your loving feelings, or your horny feelings, or your feelings of any kind whatsoever to countermand what I have said. Do you understand me? You may answer."

"Yes, Sir. Yes Sir. I understand you, Sir."

"You don't act like it."

"I – "

"Shut up. The last time we had such a misunderstanding I beat the crap out of you and left you alone to think about it and I thought we understood each other better. Now I find when you get hungry what I said doesn't count. Can you see me? You can answer."

"Yes, Sir. I can see you, barely, Sir."

"Good. Catch this."

You fish something out of your pocket and toss it to me. I see it well enough to catch what turns out to be a ball of rough twine that I thought at first had come undone in flight before I realize you're holding onto the other end.

"Put that through the bars, not over it, then tie a loop around your balls. Make a knot, real tight. Real tight. Be quick. I'm going to count to five and I want you to be done. One. Two. Three. Four. Five. Done? You may answer."

"Yes, Sir. I'm done, Sir."

I wince when you pull hard on the string and slam my balls against the iron fence, then pull them through. Considering what divides the world for me, I am with the bears and my balls are with you. I hold the bars of the fence to steady myself.

"I could just pull your balls off, of course. That might change your attitude."

I say nothing, as you have told me to do.

"Take hold of your dick." You pull on the twine rhythmically and fast, bouncing my balls too hard for me, as hard as you want. I think I'm going to fall. "Jerk yourself for me. But don't even think of coming."

I do as I'm told. Of course I do. I try to forget the ruffling bears, I try to forget the zoo-keepers who must be due past here by now, I try to forget everything and concentrate on pleasing you. You want to have me naked on my knees and beating off for you without coming, and I will do that till my body dies. I only want to please you, I only want to see you pleased. My dick is hard and running wet, my balls are jouncing, my fist is flashing back and forth and up and down and I am trying to make you proud that I obey you everywhere and every time and doing everything you are my Master you are my love you are my life you have my life you own my life and I will do whatever you say I will kneel here naked in this public space behind the bars with polar bears watching my ass emblazoned with your name and jerk myself until you let me come or stop or tell me I can die I do not care I only want for you to love me take me back forgive me love me take me back forgive me love me take me back forgive –

And this is when you tell me, "Stop," and walk up to the fence. My breath is ragged and I am sweated and my knees are sore and my shoulder is tired. You tie your end of the twine to the fence so I am tethered by my aching balls to a small patch of dirty grass. You make me turn around on my hands and knees and face the pacing, staring bears, and then I hear your belt unbuckle, then I hear the smooth slash of leather through the night, and then I feel the fire, first just once on the cheek without your name, and then again on the other side, then on my thighs, and on my back, and soon I can't keep track: it's all I can do not to fall over on the grass, pitch into the chasm held back by the twine. I am so lost in the fury of your beating that I do not even recognize it's stopped until I feel your big hand opening my hole and then my God, you're on the grass behind the bars and fucking me and fucking me and fucking me. I only live to stay upright now beneath your weight I feel you ready to come in me and my mouth is bleeding from my own teeth where I will not speak and disobey you no I will not speak and disobey you, then you bend your big head massive as a bear's down to my ear and whisper hoarsely the only thing I ever want to hear you say, you say, "You know I love you, Baby, and I'll never let you be so stupid that I leave," and then you make me jerk myself and fuck me more and more and then you tell me "Come with me. Come now." And I can only cry and shout and sing, "*Yes, Sir! Thank you Sir! I love you, Sir!*"

The Magic Mirror

for S

"Fare well, stranger; in your land remember me who met and saved you. It is worth your thought." – Nausicaa to Odysseus, Homer's Odyssey *translated by Robert Fitzgerald*

ONE: THE MAGIC MIRROR

A number of years ago, and without any formal purpose, I became a collector of mirrors. I began with just two I inherited from my parents when they died, which simply for aesthetic amusement I positioned opposite one another on the side walls of my entrance hall so that to the left and right they created the visual effect of a kind of infinite regression. Later a friend broke up his house and asked if I would store a few of his more valuable belongings, among which was a mirror I liked so well I asked if I might store that piece on my wall rather than in my basement. My friend of course said Yes, and I hung his mirror also in my entrance hall, facing the door, so a visitor might be confronted first with his own image and next, if he looked to either side, by his image once again in the midst of the infinite regression which could, itself, be seen obliquely in the third mirror which, of course, he had seen first. Later, when I had my flirtation with neo-Victorian sex practices, I had a variety of mirrors installed in the bed and bath rooms, and then mirrors just seemed to proliferate throughout my house so that now, looking back over the decades during which mirrors appeared in and gradually disappeared from my life, I can't even say how I came to own the only mirror that still hangs in my bedroom today, on the far wall across from the bed itself. I don't even know why I hung it just where and as I did, since I can't see myself in it unless I'm sitting bolt upright on only one side of the bed: a position and a place I assume exclusively for reading when I don't want to fall asleep, or for writing in my journal as I do most nights before I turn out the light, or for recording my dreams as I do whenever I wake with enough memory of one to write down something of it.

But I do know the mirror holds a special sort of charm, at least for me, because on several occasions when I've looked deeply into it I've seen my own face from when I was a child, and in that way I've held protracted conversations with my history. I also fell into the mirror one time, during the month of the last important San Francisco earthquake: I was sitting in bed reading a curious volume by some quaint, forgotten author, and when I looked up either to digest a passage or to relieve a crick in my neck the mirror had gone utterly opaque and blacker than obsidian: it reflected nothing back – neither the room, nor me, nor the light itself: nothing. So I stared at it, as who would not? wondering what in the name of all the gods and goddesses was going on, when all that blackness seemed to open up and draw me in, and I seemed to fall *upwards*, the way a scuba diver might tumble from a reef through his bubbles toward the bottom of a small boat rocking upside down upon the surface of the sky; then I was *inside* the mirror looking out at my own bedroom where I saw myself reflected sitting in the bed. I put down my book and so did my image on the bed before me. I touched my face and so did he. I was fascinated to have – to *be* – my own *döppelgänger*, but then, exactly as I began to worry what my life might have become, I fell back out of the sky, as it were, and found myself safely in my bed once again, looking into the eyes of my image in the mirror. It seemed to me my reflection winked at me, but it might have been a tic in my own eye, or a trick the changing light played on me, or any number of events easily explained by circumstance. I became aware of the telephone ringing and I answered it, but as often happens in my dreams I heard only a dial tone. I hung up the phone, turned out the light, and lay awake for hours wondering what to make of this extraordinary experience before I finally fell asleep.

The mirror was just a mirror for several years after that, and I'd even begun to forget, from time to time, that it was a portal into other worlds or that it was anything, in fact, but a large, somewhat ornately framed, reasonably good quality looking glass. And then one night last April the mirror opened up to me again, except this time, rather than taking me into it, it brought something to me from within.

Again on the night in question I was sitting in my bed engrossed in someone else's writing, and again I raised my head for some innocent reason I do not remember. This time the mirror's glass had turned a roiling opalescent white, as if seas full of pearls had been melted into steam and billowed in a wind that was caught and confined by the limits of the frame. The sight so astounded me I simply stared, the book fallen shut onto my bed's coverlet. It seemed I heard the washing such a wind might leave, like large but gentle waves wallowing from shore to shore of a too-small sea; and then, as if Leviathan were breaching from the deep, the mirror screeched and tore and burst outward from its very heart, throwing foaming waves of shattered glass about itself. Too shocked and frightened to even lift the blanket to shield my face, I could do nothing but watch as what seemed to be a storm passed on amid the crystal tinkling of a last few falling shards, and the rounder sound of something rolling across the floor to rest beside my dresser.

As my heart slowed down I got up cautiously to investigate, and carefully picking my way between shreds and spikes of silvered glass I soon found an old water-tumbled, pebble-pock-marked bottle settling down from a final spin and pointing its wavy neck in my direction. I bent to take what the mirror had fetched up when I realized that all its broken splinters were now quivering somehow, liquid like little pods of mercury; and as I watched they took themselves away, sucked backwards till they all were gone and the mirror was whole again, a looking glass complete as when I'd first retired.

My mouth had gone quite dry, but after a few minutes I turned my study to the bottle because, of course, I did not know what else to do. The glass was the sort of cloudy, almost whitish-green some would-be-fancy latter-day cognac companies acid-etch their bottles to achieve, that time and tide etch quite as well in their own less uniform ways. Considering how it came to me I could hardly say that it was unremarkable, but other than that the bottle seemed like nothing any ocean might not leave on any shore. I held it to the light and saw by its interior shadows that it contained something, but the mouth was formidably well sealed with some kind of colorless substance. I took to it with a knife but could neither scrape nor prise the seal away, so I got a hammer and took it with the bottle to the little concrete stoop behind my house and began to tap away at it. After several minutes of gentle persuasion had failed, I raised the tool in frustration to smash the glass – and that is when the top fell off: the wax relaxed and rolled away, the bottle tilted toward its mouth, and a small sheaf of curling papers fell forward as if pushed, to settle on its inner lip and open like a hand unfurling. A drawing of a comely girl from a bygone era in the early flush of adolescence lay on top of numerous sheets of heavy paper yellowed with age and filled with writing. I picked up all the pieces – wax top, hammer, bottle, papers: all – and brought them back indoors and took them to my bed again. I had no expectations left of sleep this night, and so, after setting the hammer and bottle top on my nightstand, I extracted the papers, rested the bottle on the coverlet beside me, flattened out the pages as best I could, and settled down to read what astonished me directly.

TWO: *A MESSAGE IN A BOTTLE*

A. Page One: "A Woman Naked On Her Knees"

"A woman naked on her knees," began the first page underneath the drawing. The words were written in a small and even, unformed yet precise young hand that reminded me of those ancient Arabic scripts whose visual grace at once expanded and confounded their meanings' feelings. "A woman naked on her knees, chained by an iron collar at her neck to the inner bars of an iron cage, arms bound behind her and thighs held wide by leather saddle straps: this is a sight to stop any human eye – especially that of the woman herself, who sees her image in stark reflection when a secret door unexpectedly swings open disclosing, where a library wall of books had been, nothing but a mirror and, beside it in the living flesh, the captor she had recently believed to be her savior.

"That is how I saw myself one evening soon after Master Queen decided it was time to start my training.

"Until a few days earlier I had been, as I believed, his house-guest. He had rescued me while I drifted perhaps close to dying in an aimless dinghy the captain set me in when the ship I'd sailed on hit unlikely rocks and we were wrecked. He had taken me to his home on the quiet shore of his own safe harbor, and had seen to my recuperation. As I became well again and sought to regain myself from the wretched losses I had suffered, which I shall disclose anon, he and a serving woman I later learned he had engaged expressly for my care were the only souls I saw, and the only human beings who knew I was alive. He dressed me in a comforting finery, fed me plentifully, and took me riding in a filigreed carriage pulled by one great white stallion. He even afforded me time to mourn.

"But as my health returned and my griefs receded, my host's attentions waxed as if he meant to woo me. He never said an untoward word, but his stance and bearing became familiar and he no longer waited to enter my rooms after knocking until, one night, he did not knock at all but found me seated by the fire with my sorrows and my memories. I sought to hide my tears from him and so was unprepared to challenge his odd conduct that might, after all, have been an oversight or another form of accident. I could not know his changed behavior was intentional, that he was deliberately breaking down some boundaries with which any lady might protect herself.

"Over the course of the following weeks I found myself submitting more and more to behaviors I would once have thought rude: his words, that I recalled as soft and flowery, were no less beautiful but now also seemed imposing; evening by evening his hand became more intimately acquainted with my neck, back, and shoulders; and gradually his manner toward me came to feel almost commanding if just as kind as before: more like the manner of a man to his most precious pet, than to another human being.

"I did not make much of the changes at the time, perhaps because I was still recovering, perhaps because I was still in mourning, perhaps because I had no experience with men of his flavor and could not accurately gauge what was happening, perhaps for reasons of the heart that I shall tell. And then one morning when the lady he'd engaged came for me, she told me Master Queen had instructed her to pay me special attentions at my bath.

"'Special attentions?' I inquired.

"I was not only to be bathed outside but as it were inside as well. I was to be depilated thoroughly below my eyelashes, which were to be curled. My body was to be massaged and oiled, my lips and cheeks and breasts were to be rouged, all my nails were to be painted, and my hair was to be restyled. There would be further preparations, but my lady in waiting thought that was enough of a preview of the day to come.

"'But what if I object?' I protested.

"The lady just smiled and helped me from my sheets."

B. Pages Two and Three: Juliette

"My name is Juliette," the second page resumed, or, perhaps, began anew, because at first, though it was written in the same tutored yet inexperienced hand, the words seemed to have nothing to do with the page that had preceded it. "I come from France, from 1794, which is known in Paris as Year II – of the Terror. But I am there no longer, because Fate, which I do not claim to understand, has taken me from my life as surely as it has taken my life from me. Where and when I used to live, thousands of people have died in the name of liberty. Those I knew who died were killed because they had the good fortune, since become severe misfortune, to be born noble, or to know someone closely who was himself born noble. I have watched people torn apart alive, I have watched people's beating hearts ripped from their bodies, I have seen men castrated and women raped, I have seen children served up to their parents on spikes. Freedom, such as it may be, does not come cheaply.

"Yet, I am not writing for the benefit of the sea to tell you of these horrors you can read about quite freely in your history books. Instead, I have come to this orange shore in a evening's blue light with these white pages, this black ink, and the empty green bottle I will fill and you will now have emptied again to tell you of a personal tragedy you will never otherwise know about. It is a tragedy that pales compared with the tragedies that are the very definitions of my age, but I came to tell you because it is *my* tragedy, and I *will* have a witness. In particular I will have *you* as a witness, for you and I, as you will see, we are one, as different as we seem, and as different as our lives and times have been. I am writing in the late 18th Century French of the Royal Court and you are reading what I say in early 21st Century American – a language that in many ways hasn't even been invented in my day – because I cannot be present with you in the flesh to answer your inevitable questions, and in this way you will possibly begin to understand me. If what I say sounds strange to you please recongize that if it were anything less than true my letter could not possibly have come to you the way it did.

"In my time I am considered a pretty but not a remarkably pretty young woman, as perhaps you can see from the likeness of myself I have included with this letter, and by your standards I am hardly more than a girl. If you saw me as I write you might think me only twelve or thirteen years of age, although in fact I am nearly seventeen. Not very long ago I was something like a rural princess in a minor province in the south of France. Because I was young and had a good name, and my family was rich enough for me to be considered marriageable, I lived at Court where I sometimes was allowed to attend the Queen. My lover was a young marquis, at first more wealthy in title than in funds and later utterly impoverished by the Revolution. He was supposed to have become count when his father died, pray God they have not both been killed by now.

"In 1791 the Revolutionary government proclaimed that any aristocrat who went into exile committed a crime against the state, and since any aristocrat who was *not* in exile was nearly a *de facto* criminal anyway, my lover and I decided to escape from France, expecting to return home if and when it was safe for us to do so. We planned to travel from Paris to the Normandy coast and there board a ship that was sailing for America, but my marquis had first to settle some painful business that was hampering his free movement and seek to put that set of difficulties behind him. I did not want to go ahead without him; I never wanted to leave him at all. In addition I feared it was impossible to know when or even whether he would return. Nonetheless, with the Revolution all around us and my marquis clearly seeking my own well-being and ours, I agreed to go, praying that the Revolution would end and he recall me to our previous life, which would be best, or, failing that, that he would join me before the ship set sail. I refused entirely to imagine a world or a life apart from him.

"Before we separated my belovèd gave me a star to guide me by. He said it came from the sky when he was a child, and had been red with fire when it fell near his feet. He said he could feel and hear it pass as it burned the wind before his face, struck a flower tree that blossomed two days later, boiled dry the rain-puddle it had fallen into, and then turned ashen in a cloud of steam. He marveled at it for so long it had cooled enough to touch when at last he reached for it. He took up the piece of star and carried it beside his heart for years. He said it had guided him to safety when he needed it, and he wanted me to have a guide in what he believed might be our treacherous times ahead. 'You are never given a wish without the power to make it come true,' he told me. I took the star directly from his palm as he held it out to me. It was phosphorescent and whitish-green, and smooth around its tiny dimples. I could see faces all over its markings. I pressed the star to me and named it Apollo for the sun my marquis was to me.

"For days I travelled alone on roads and through villages that were none too safe for a girl, especially when now and then people sympathetic to the Revolution suspected I might be noble. I feared for my life and felt frighteningly adrift, but I had no choice in my behavior. I thought I was prepared to wait for my marquis as long as necessary, until one night after I had reached the port there were riots, and the captain of the ship we were to sail on came to my rooms to explain he had no choice but to sail immediately, and that I had no choice, if I wanted to live, but to accompany his ship.

"Though he said he would do his best to get word to my marquis, his explanations were incomprehensible to me. I felt horror open in the pit of my stomach along with a new depth of longing to be united with my love that began simultaneously and has to this day never ceased: its intensity has only deepened over time and become a kind of threnody in the sad music of my life. We sailed, he with his ship and I alone, before first light.

"The voyage itself was no more arduous than was to be expected, and nothing attended us worse than ordinary human discomfort. The captain seemed receptive to my plight and treated me tenderly, enjoining me to dine with him and spending a goodly portion of his idler hours in my company, asking about the places I had left and advising me how to proceed in the new land he thought I might call home. He was kind as a grandfather, and to my young ears just as ignorant of the lovelorn heart. Then, in the middle of an ill-omened night, the ship rocked with a tortured symphony of terrible noises, and bucked and fell upon the water. The captain shouted into my room as I stumbled from bed and told me we had struck some rocks. He took me hastily and without provisions to a small boat at the stern of the ship, and set me off on the sea completely alone. I felt rather than saw the ship go down in the dark, and heard cries from men I could not see as my own little boat nearly capsized in the following vortex. After a long while I could hear nothing but the sea, and when dawn broke I could see nothing but the sea. With neither food nor water I do not know how long I drifted. I assumed that I would die. In a day or two I lay down in the bottom of the boat forlorn beyond my ability to imagine, and wept my bitter, grievous loss – not for my young life so much as for my marquis whom I would never see again. I next awoke in a fine feather bed piled high with linens and blankets, and saw the patient face of the man I came to know as Master Queen."

C. Page Four: How I Came to Be There

"When I first set eyes upon him Master Queen was a lean, dark, clean-shaven man with long dark hair on a long firm head, deeply watchful green eyes, a prominent nose, and still lips, lounging rather formally on a sofa in the morning light. He wore wide dark pants and boots, a full-sleeved white blouse open at the throat, and an intricately woven vest of motley silk. He had the air of a man who had been doing nothing with great pleasure for a long while, and who would be perfectly willing to continue doing nothing as long as that was what the moment called for.

"'Do you speak English?' he asked when he saw I was awake.

"'Un peu, Monsieur' I answered slowly, 'very little.'

"'Alors,' he answered with a vigrous nod, 'then I will speak French. Do you know how you came to be here?'

"'Non.'

"He told me how at dawn one morning a few days before, he'd gone to walk the shore of the bay the sea fed where he'd built his house, and seen a little boat riding on soft waves close enough for him to swim to and bring back. In the bottom he'd found a girl he could see was unwell from deprivation and exposure, but very much alive. He'd taken me to his home and with the help of the lady he engaged he'd nursed me till this moment, bringing me food and even holding me in my deleriums. I fell back into my exhausted sleep while he told his tale.

"But on the next day he told it to me again, and in the many days to come I sometimes asked him to tell it over and over. The story became, for me, one of death and resurrection as it took on the power of a myth I could apply beyond myself.

"When I was well enough, seated on his veranda overlooking his calm bay, I told Master Queen my own tale, which he heard with such equanimity I wondered if he believed in my Paris, my escape, my shipwreck, or my marquis. But he listened also with compassion and concern, and was so kind and gracious to me always that I came to trust him fondly. Yet I could not help but frequently regret his kindnesses, for whatever else my life may have been becoming, I did not know my marquis's fate, or how I would ever see his sweet face again. Worse, perhaps, I thought from time to time: we might find each other after years apart, and find each other so drastically changed out of one another's company that we would have but little love compared to our sorrow and grief for the past we'd shared, and for the past of which we'd been deprived."

D. Pages Five and Six: Master Queen

"As Master Queen began to change in his demanor toward me, he also gave me greater acquaintance of his estate. He personally showed me much of the house he'd built, which in summer, he seemed proud to say, was just as cool and dark inside as the day was hot and bright beyond. One particular lengthy carpeted hall turned into a library the likes of which I had never hoped to see again outside Paris. Books lined every wall but one from floor to ceiling, and the other wall was windowed doors that gave onto wide gardens.

"When I exclaimed over his library, Master Queen seemed genuinely pleased. He asked me if I liked the room, and when I said enthusiastically that I did he promised I would see more of it. He showed me the cellar where he kept his wines, drawing rooms where it seemed that sometimes other people must have come, his own bedroom at the top of the house with windows that commanded every direction, the stable where he kept his great white stallion, and the garden full of fruits and roses on a soft, verdant carpet of chamomile, mint, and thyme.

"Yet Master Queen would allow me to be alone no place but my room. He continued firm in his control, but he also continued gentle and considerate beyond reproach of my needs, including my need to come to peace with grief that never fully left me. He sent roses to my bedroom from his garden, brought me pretty frills he liked to see me wear, and saw much further to my comfort than I would ever have dared to ask. In all he was so exceedingly kind it would be fair to say he pampered me. Though I did not yet understand the implications of his behaviors I could see that he had made of me his pet, and that, as he truly seemed to care for me in that capacity, so I had come to truly care for him. Oddly, perhaps, I fell in love with Master Queen, without in any way affecting the very different love I held and hold forever for my marquis.

"I say my falling in love with Master Queen was odd not just because I loved another, as he knew quite well, but also because from the day the serving lady oversaw those special attentions he'd commanded he disclosed to me his bedroom tastes that would not have been out of place in the aristocratic Paris I had left. He introduced me to his pleasures slowly, but there came a night I recognized we had achieved a ritual together, and that while the exercise had begun as something he required, it had become as well something I desired.

"Each night, before I could retire, Master Queen would settle on his sofa with his glass of brandy and bid me stand before him. It did not matter if I was tired, unhappy, or otherwise distraught, whether I stood in love, in pride, in meek surrender, or in boredom or fatigue: it did not matter because he held me with his eyes and will, commanding me as if God Himself had granted that command to him; and quickly or slowly but steadily I grew self-conscious, embarrassed, possessed, and finally shy. I felt myself begin to shrink by increments too small to measure: my head fell slightly forward and to one side as if to shield my face without completely hiding it, my shoulders cleaved toward each other as if to embrace my body, my hips closed in and drew my legs together even so far as to bend one knee, my foot rising to its toes on the furs that made up his thick bedroom rug.

"Then it was, when I had become most vulnerable and almost child-like in demeanor so that even in my heart I was becoming small, then it was he seemed to be most satisfied with *who* I was and started to make me *how* he pleased, commanding the clothing from my body: blouse, skirts, shoes, and every single item of apparel one by one until I stood entirely naked to his eyes. I could not run, could not complain, I could do nothing but obey. Sometimes then he had me turn around and show my back to him, sometimes he had me dance for him, sometimes I touched myself at his direction, sometimes I posed and took positions so subservient and exposed I could not ever have imagined I would stand or sit or lie that way for any man, but he commanded and I obeyed: I *had* to obey: I *could not* do otherwise, as if I were compelled by force of nature. Then, in my confusion, in my shame, and in my never-ending grief, I found my pleasure too: I found I liked my state. One night when he had seen enough of what he wanted and reminded me deeply of my surrender to his words and will, he ordered me to approach the couch whereon he was at rest, and I could tell as far as *I* was concerned he'd *let* me approach him – for in truth I longed to do it.

"As a noble woman I am ashamed to admit it even to this page and to you, who may some day understand and who in any case will not lay eyes upon my writing till my bones have bleached and turned to dust, but there are nights when he commanded my approach and I quite literally threw myself at his feet, crawling, groveling, scrambling naked and sobbing across the floor in my longing and passion to touch his boots, to hold his legs and press them to my breast, to breathe his smell, to feel his heavy hand come gently to my shoulders, to feel him pet my hair, lift me up onto his lap, and hold me in his arms. I gazed into his eyes and touched his skin and felt myself grow wonderfully helpless, eager to do anything to please him, utterly possessed and glad of it. For in this life, this body, I had become his property, just as he intended.

"Then I longed for him to take me to his bosom even knowing what would follow, for all this masquerade was but the prelude to his passion. After he had held and touched me in ways and places even my marquis had never done, he made me say aloud that I am his pet, his slave, his property: from my knees he made me tell this to his face, and that I did. Even though I longed for my marquis I did it: not just because I wanted to, not just because it pleased my Master Queen, oh, no: I did it, sir, because I knew that it was true.

"Was it my Fate? my Destiny? It was the only path that I could tread, though to this day I could never say why. Some nights he made me next recite a list of rights he had in me and then, depending on his mood, he exercised some few of his many prerogatives: he turned me over his knee and spanked me till I wailed and struggled vainly against his stronger arms; he spread me across the sofa back and struck me with a crop as if I were one of his horses, leaving welts and bruises on my back and thighs that sometimes lasted for days; he took me to the trough and there relieved himself upon my person; and there was more, much more. It must sound horrible to your modern ears and eyes, and you may wonder why I did not cry out against his rule or choose to die instead of acquiescing, but coming from the libertinage of Louis XVI's court and then the Terror, nothing human was really foreign to me any more, and as I've said, I'd come to love him in a way. When he took me to his bed and let me nestle softly in his arms and on his chest I found myself not just in love with him but also with what he did to me, and glad for what I was becoming. Even if his pleasures had not been followed by warm baths, soft salves, and the tender ways he used me in the night that made my body sing, I'd have grown to yearn for him to use me as he did, for somehow, held in his command, I was at rest, at peace."

E. Pages Seven and Eight: Letters to the Past and Future
"The greatest difficulty I confronted then was reconciling my deathless love for my marquis with my glad possession by Master Queen. You have doctors of the soul in your tomorrow, as we have different ones in my yesterday: what do they say of this finite passion that is like a Destiny I've dreamed, now playing itself out upon my life? And when they have given their explanations, what do they say of the infinite passion and the way this message came to you? I ask because if you ask them you will find your doctors will not understand any more than mine would have. For understanding in a life like this one must return to the days before Voltaire, when gypsies and wise women knew the secrets of the earth, which even in my day they are starting to forget.

"Let me tell you of two dreams I had, or maybe they were visions. The first came to me in some year long past whose memory escapes me now. It takes place in several times at once: in my day when I am myself and earlier, when I am a poor girl baking bread in Elizabethan England, and later, in a time near yours when young men are hitting balls with sticks and I am one of them, and in very ancient days when the older, white-haired man I am, at peace with his tiller, sets sail his own whole boat in solitude across the blue Aegean, and again in a jungle where the Moors preside and people do not need to write, and again in the Orient where I am a child in the arms of a blue, elephant-headed god, and in other times as well amid peoples and places I can scarcely recognize. In all these times, even as I live, I stand above the clouds somewhere on the arm of my marquis and marvel with him at the wonders of the world. He and I embrace, agreeing to forget all we know in order to learn and teach whatever will serve and save. I take from my heart a crown of black hair and place it on his head; simultaneously I place the same crown on my own head. He opens up his heart with his own bare hands and showers all the world with love. Below us, in all the times on earth, men and women and boys and girls are laughing and crying, making love and fighting wars, giving birth and dying, the sun is rising and setting, and all the images move so fast they become one blur of color and sound that curves over and above us and wraps us in the movements we no longer recognize. Every music on earth plays in my ears at once, and I can distinguish every melody. I feel the touch of every caress and blow, I smell and taste without my senses, I disappear in ecstasy into my memory of my own future.

"The second is more recent. It came to me just a few months ago, as I woke one morning happy in my Master Queen's arms. It is very specific as to time and place, which is in a desert, in a tent at earliest sunrise, so the tent glows orange. I can smell animals nearby and know that I am thirsty. I am lying on my back on a pile of carpets, naked, staked spread out by my wrists and ankles. Abruptly the tent flap is thrown back and I hear a community waking up. My Master Queen enters and secures the flap behind him. All is quiet again. He is dressed in fine silk robes, white and purple, and holds a large, curved knife in his hands he measures against my throat. He steps on my face in an unmistakable gesture. He sets the knife down, opens his robes, and ravishes me repeatedly, forcefully, in every way, in every place that he can reach. Neither of us says a word, although our bodies speak. At last he stands and takes up his knife again, and brings it to my lips. I kiss it and he cuts my bonds. With nothing but gestures of his hand he makes his wishes known. I bow and kiss his feet. I allow him to tie my hands behind me. I allow him to tie a rope around my neck. He leads me naked from the tent. Later I appear dressed only in bracelets, veils, and jewels, seated on a cushion at his feet while he confers with others. When they leave he uses me, not unkindly and with pleasure. I am his catamite, his boy, his girl, or what he wills. He has spared my life and now it belongs to him.

"Those are my visions, my unexpecting friend, *mon semblable, mon frère*: I have come through time to the turn of this foreign century to deliver to you, the man I will be in your day, this partial story of my trials so that when you meet the person my marquis may be in your life you both can read about us, and know that whatever may have happened in our other times and places, whoever we became and loved, wherever the paths we walked may have taken us, in my heart I never betrayed the man he was in *our* lives. I stood by him all the way to today.

"To my dearest love: I send this whole long letter to you over the oceans and through the centuries, beyond space and time, because I know if you are who I have seen *you* to be, and I am the only one *I* could therefore be, that somehow, even if through what people term a miracle, it has to reach you in that other life.

"I have wandered forests, leas, and shores wondering what images of *my* face, what snatches of songs *I* sang you might remember, and that will not leave *your* mind, as *your* face and the songs *you* sang never cease to haunt *my* mind. I wonder what recollected moments cause *your* body to quail in grief as so many of my memories rend *me* over and over again, and tear my life apart.

"Last night I dreamed that you and I were in some mythical, mystical Outdoor World where lavender plants bloomed like bullrushes. We stripped one through our closed hands the way you can strip a real ripe bullrush, and watched as millions of tiny seeds drifted away in the air like so many sparkling stars to seed the world with lavender.

"The thread by which we are connected seems so strong and yet so frail, like a wire spun as fine as spider's silk that reaches its arachnid wisdom from our old Paris to some new America to honor a fealty made in a time out of time which you and I can only live out.

"For years I wrote to you a never-ending letter in my mind about what I see and what it means to me, about what I want to show and see with you; clarifying what I meant, asking you for clarification, posing endless What Ifs, weeping, missing you in the deepest recesses of my heart, pouring out my grief upon the air. You are so much my husband, so much my brother, so much my father and child, that in my wise and innocent blood I do not, cannot, will not feel our bond is wholly severed or erased, and I pray that in the turnings of the world, in hopes of great God's greatest good, I will be allowed to come to you again, and you to me, with joy and peace, relief and grace, instead of this lifetime of loss and grief and worry and want. I love you more than I have ever known I could love, and I know how you love me as well. Maybe that is why I cannot believe this life is done between us. Maybe we will be together forever as we planned, though for now Fate has separated us, and wherever I am, there, somewhere, I am lost. Today the sun's rays, streaming from the sky, look like tears to me, like gold and silver rivers of dismay, as if the very star you gave me pours out his sorrow for us. When it rains it seems as if the heavens weep for us, as if the very gods grieve our little human tragedy. I am not wholly deaf to birds and the songs the powers sing around me, not wholly blind to the beauty of the world: I smell the flowers in the sun and I smell the earth after every rain, I taste sweet fruits and I am not numb by any means, in part because the generosities and love my Master Queen bestows on me bring peace that preserves me, for which I am deeply grateful and which in my measure I am greatly happy to return. Some days I am so glad with him it even seems I am not wholly lost.

"But not even God can help me if I am wholly lost to you.

"With every love on every holy day, I am forever your belovèd,

Juliette du Jour de Fête
"Dated this 14th day of April, 1798"

THREE: *THE MAGIC MIRROR REDUX*

Outside my window the sky was growing blue. I set the pages down beside the bottle on the coverlet, wondering at the narrative I had read, and wondering about the incarnation Juliette described. As I mused I happened to look up and see my face in the mirror where my strange night had begun. The mirror looked no different than it ever had – a large, somewhat ornately framed, reasonably good quality looking glass – but the face I saw reflected back at me had changed: it was mine no longer – or, I should say, it was the face I was familiar with no longer, for mine it surely was: it moved as I moved, and reflected for a moment the same distress I felt, and then, as I began to comprehend, the pretty but not remarkably pretty young woman's face reflected my dawning hope and almost unearthly delight, for in fact it was a face I recognized quite well. I smiled and turned over the pages I had read and took up the drawing with which Juliette had really begun her tale and there I was, the face in the mirror a perfect likeness of the drawing she had sent to me across the centuries. On the coverlet beneath it I saw that the bottle was phosphorescent and whitish-green, and smooth around its tiny dimples. As it shrank I could see faces all over its markings. I whispered "Apollo," and pressed the star to my breast. I knew that my marquis was near again at last.

Like you, my dearest love, I have always led a magic life, but when we were last together and led our magic lives together, hope made it easy for us to misunderstand: a magic life is not necessarily a charmed life, just one in which there is something one must do.

The journey of our lives, together or apart, has never been other than remarkable, my dear, my darling, my eternally belovèd. I have been changed by my journey beyond time and space as I knew I would be, and as I have changed so must you have done. You, too, are someone else now, but like the candle's flame that is different when first it is lit than when it nears its end and is yet the self-same flame, so I know by the drawing before me that you will also be the same. And so I know at last what the star Apollo told me from the first: *You are never given a wish without the power to make it come true.* From one life to another I will always find you: we will always meet again and we will always recognize each other. It cannot be otherwise, for this is the way of fated beings who are partners in process, and have work to do in this and other worlds.

Ponyboy

ONE

"Mr. Benson?" I said; " I don't know any Benson."

"No, sir," Clyde answered over the intercom, "not Benson; Benten, B-E-N-T-E-N. He says he's here to talk to you about horses."

"Oh! Benten! Yes, I can see Benten."

I punched off the intercom and spun my chair around. Today was going to be a high point in a most miraculous year. I stood up and walked to the window, and made sure my shirt was well-tucked, my cuffs shot to the ruby links, my tie knot settled. Twenty-eight floors below San Francisco was spread out before me like a virgin eager to get laid. I could see great mountains of fog retreating back over the Marin Headlands to the Pacific like ethereal white whale ghosts. We'd have clear air everywhere by dinnertime. I took it all as a good omen.

October 29. One year ago I was still a married man, a slave in principle to a gorgeous wife who didn't turn me on in a marriage of convenience I could not afford to leave. I had the old family name her daddy wanted, she had all the money I wanted – and then she had all the money, period. When my picture showed up the in a local gay paper the week before the Folsom Street Fair I was summarily escorted out of the family business: oops, so sorry. It had all been such a joke! Except, of course, the joke was on me. I'd been to the Fair a few years before in shades and cap and vest with my buffed chest and biceps bulging and Richard on my leash wearing the littlest excuse for a codpiece I thought we could get away with. He'd been a big hit at Mark I. Chester's annual photo show, and we even got invited in to Dr. Tech's private bash across the way so people could eyeball Dick up close. I never saw anyone take our picture, but obviously someone did: with Richard bent over a barrel sucking Charlie's Angel while I pumped him with my fist halfway up to the elbow.

Credit where credit is due: the paper didn't run the picture for three years, and when they did the photo was set as part of a nostalgia collage they had the good sense or taste to crop. But anyone who knew me knew it was me, anyone who knew Richard knew he was Gloria's brother, anyone who knew cock-sucking and fist-fucking knew what we were doing, and whoever sent the clipping from the paper to my father, my wife, and my father-in-law knew all of the above.

Shit, you might say, hit the fan. Shit happened. Shit fell on Alabama like stars. I was up shit creek without a paddle. I was in deep shit. In less than three days I was legally disowned and everything but everything was in Gloria's name. I couldn't buy a newspaper without begging for a dime. For two years I suffered in silence, or my best whining imitation of it. I even fucked Glory from time to time. I thought I needed her forgiveness, and a hole's a hole for all of that.

October 30 last year Glory died in an auto accident. Bye-bye.

Sorry. I don't mean to make light of this: family tragedy, personal tragedy, successful youngish woman with still lots to live for, and so forth.

But you have to understand: it changed my life.

A week later, November 6, four days after the funeral, I was sitting in the house on Broadway wondering what I was going to do with my life when the lawyer called and the rest, as they say, is mystery. My story.

What everyone had overlooked was that Glory hadn't changed her will, so I was still the beneficiary and heir unapparent to the last dregs of the Robber Barons' ungodly bank accounts. No trillions, no billions, but many many many millions: enough for me to roll happily in spare change for the rest of my self-indulgent life. And the house, of course: 30 rooms and a lot of history. I sat down in my leather chair in the library off the formal dining room and put my feet on my leather ottoman. I stared out the window down the hill to the marina and the Bay. I rang for Chives – his name is Larry, but I've always called him Chives – and had him pour me some of the better calvados.

The intercom buzzed, and Clyde opened the door for Mr. Benten. I let Clyde close the door, then took two steps in the direction of my guest with my hand stuck out.

"Mr. Benten, a pleasure."

"Mr. Townsend." His voice was quiet, soft, and low as a slow cat's purr. "Call me Preston. Please."

"Edgar. Refreshment, Preston? It's nearly evening."

"Thank you, Edgar." He rapped his leather portfolio twice with his knuckles and smiled as if deferentially. "Yes. One is for 'no,' two is for 'yes.' A cognac?"

I buzzed, two hots and a trot. Clyde came in with the tray, poured, and left. Preston said, "No need for small talk?" I smiled and shook my head. He sat on the couch and opened his portfolio, and spread some photos out. I sat down beside him, picked one up, and felt a rush go through me like the days of wine and poppers. The boy was stunning on his hands and knees, naked, smooth, well-built, and well-hung, wearing a full head harness complete with bits, reins, and bridle, and a big fluffy ponytail just the soft brown color of his hair arching like a fountain out of his ass. The next boy was saddled, with very short stirrups, and the standing man holding him close on reins was wearing shiny lizard cowboy boots with rowels on his spurs. There were saddled boys standing up with hoof-shaped boots, standing boys harnessed in traces pulling sulkies and carts, ponyboys in poses, and ponyboys at ease. They all seemed to be five or ten years younger than I, as Preston was probably that much older.

"When?" I asked Preston.

"Saturday. Come for the afternoon, stay for dinner. You'll enjoy the company."

After Preston left I buzzed for Clyde again. "Close the door," I said when he entered, "and take off your clothes."

"Sir?" he asked.

"Take off your clothes. Don't make me repeat myself."

"Yes, sir."

I never understood why people are obedient, but Clyde did as he was told. Not bad: he could use a gym, but he was young yet. I said, "Get me some ties."

"Ties, sir? Yes, sir."

"And a harness."

"Yes, sir."

Clyde was clearly puzzled, but his naked ass shimmied as he stepped to the closet and brought me a leather harness dotted with cone studs and a handful of Monday-go-to-Meetin' ties. I cinched the harness tight around Clyde's chest, put his back to the side of my desk, strung four of the ties together with bowlines, and ran the thousand-dollar rope I'd made through the O-rings in the back. Then I climbed up on the desk holding the two ends of the rope like reins. "Now: pull," I said. "Lean into the harness and pull. Strain, damn it, let me see your muscles work."

And he did strain, pulling at my huge, landlocked mahogany desk as if it were a lightweight cart on wheels.

Clyde is such a good boy. His shoulders bunched, his rib cage heaved, his back bulged, his thighs and ass cheeks crimped, and he set his jaw so firmly I thought the desk might even move.

I like to see naked men at work. I leapt right down on top of him and threw him to the floor. Before he could say a thing I had my pants open and was fucking him right there without condoms, lube, or anything. I hoped I still was lucky. I came very quickly, and almost immediately felt his sphincters clamp around my dick a half dozen times. Clyde turned his head around to try to see me over his shoulder.

"Edgar!" he whispered.

One is for "no." I rapped his skull once with my knuckle. "Shush," I told him. "Relax. It's only lust."

*T*wo

Saturday I left home earlier than necessary and made a slow drive up into the wine country, consulting the map Preston had given me. I had to get off the Silverado Trail and follow the county road a little less than three miles. A quick right, an obscure left, look for the orange Road Work sign, turn left, and the rest would be apparent.

And it was. Two private guards who were decked out to look like Royal Canadian Mounted Police sat their exquisitely turned out horses – real ones – before a rustic wooden gate. I had the top down on the Quattro, so over my windshield I sang out the word Preston had advised. The Mounties parted like a bright red sea, and the gate swung open like an obedient boy's mouth. I drove in and followed the trail to a tree-shaded parking area full of Boxsters and Benzes and Lexi and one bubble-gum pink Bentley convertible, where more RCMP look-alikes were stationed this side of a huge burgundy velvet curtain. The velvet was artfully suspended between the tops of a couple of telephone poles and draped with old gold ribbon. It had to be thirty feet high and twice as wide, and was perfectly designed to block from sight whatever was on the other side of it. I heard distant music as one attendant took the keys to my car and another passed me through the curtain. On the other side the world was altogether different.

Beneath the shade of a white canvas tent-top big enough for a modest circus, a lawn party was in full swing, composed of well-turned-out men of a certain age dressed in casual silks and linens who would not have been uncomfortable one way or another with my bank account. Sculpted, undressed, and scrupulously shaved rather younger men about my age, wearing bright chrome collars with understated locks, circulated among the guests with trays of food and drink, while a small clutch of strolling musicians played gentle melodies. I took a flute of bubbly off a passing tray and cruised the lawn, taking its measure. I was curious to see a politician I would not have expected to be so bold, and a publicly conspicuous neighbor of mine whose hands on the help appeared to be as forward as his tongue. But a different kind of movement at the lawn's far side caught my eye, so that was where I went, and that was where I found what I had come for.

Beyond the backs of a couple dozen serious connoisseurs the stock was being put through its paces. Lawn chairs were strewn here and there and some were free, but I found a comfortable tree to lean against and watched the show from the shade that it provided.

Among several ponies, each with his own handler, the boy who took my eye completely was the very definition of horsedick, cut by Michelangelo from warm Sienna marble and hanging lower than the five-pound disk of lead weight swinging from balls so swollen they looked like a bulging pairs of chestnuts sheathed in fascia shells. He was got up with silver, blue, and white streamers pinned to his silver bridle, and his arms were locked behind him with his elbows stretched around a chrome bar that matched his collar and pushed his shoulders high and forced his chest forward. He lifted his knees one after the other and brought his feet down with great precision so his fat cock looked like a third leg, while his handler held the owner's end of a ten-foot lead and paced him in a circle where the wide swath of lawn was just beginning to show dark stains of hoofwear. He didn't even glance to the sides though he was wearing no blinders. He really knew how to prance.

The boy had started to perspire, and the weight kept bouncing up and down just above his knees. Even though it had to be causing him some kind of pain every time he took a step his handler made him jump a couple of bars, which he did very gingerly, then stopped him, whispered in his ear, removed the arm bar, and led him away. Everyone else was engaged by a couple other show ponies, but I was so attracted to this boy I wanted to know more about him. I pushed off my tree to follow where his handler led him.

Almost immediately beyond the tent-top they passed a big yellow sign that said No Entry, walked through a gate with automatic locks, then passed a second, similar sign. I slipped my wallet into the gate latch so it couldn't close completely, and when the handler and boy had disappeared I pushed the gate open, retrieved my wallet, and went on after them while the gate closed behind me.

Handler and boy had gone past a structure that looked as if it had once been a small barn, but now seemed like something from a surreal 1960s movie. The wind had torn the roof off long ago, some of the walls had gone with the roof, and what remained was irregular anyway because whole boards and slabs of wood had fallen off, holes had been ripped out here and there, and whatever glass had once stood in the large window frames must have turned to dust before the ponyboy was born. Inside the remaining weather-whitened fragments a dozen men lounged on leather furniture much too fine for the ruins and watched two well-muscled boys Greek wrestle. The handler had taken his ponyboy behind the structure, and I could see at my distance where a split-rail paddock held a dozen other ponyboys more or less like the first who all stood nearly motionless in the shade of a stand of black oaks. I watched from beside a small thicket of madrone.

Inside the corral the handler bent the ponyboy over a sawhorse and pulled out his tail, stuffing it dildo-end down into an obvious bucket of disinfectant. He rubbed the pony from head to hoof with a towel soaked in so much witch hazel I could smell it where I lurked, gave him a pail and let him drink, then chained his hands behind a smaller elbow bar. He lifted the weight on the boy's dark balls, slid it into a narrow slot in the fence in front of the boy, and closed it, then took up the reins of two other boys. He bent first one and then the other over the same sawhorse, and tailed them with ponytails that matched their own hair, then led them out toward the lawn with the same kinds of big weights swaying from their balls.

I waited till the handler had taken the boys away, then moved closer to the fence. The boys saw me, but none of them moved and none of them talked. All their hands were locked behind them and they all wore the same kinds of weights that were pushed through slots to rest on shelves at about thigh level in a way that was designed to relieve the ponies and still secure them. In effect, I had before me a dozen pretty ponyboys, hobbled in the paddock by their balls. None of them *could* move. No one was going anywhere.

I took a bag of chocolates from my jacket and approached the fence, closing in on the ponyboy I'd first seen prance. I admired his companions, and admired him in particular. I opened the bag and nibbled at a little mint.

"You pranced very well on the lawn. Are you hungry?"

It was a little like talking to a real horse. Some of the other boys snickered and one cleared his throat with a kind of luffing warning sound that horses make with their cheeks, but my ponyboy said nothing. Why would a young stud show off his muscle this way? I figured maybe he got off on all the attention, so I gave him some.

"I'd like to see you really run," I said. "I'd like to see you straining at a cart that I was riding in. I'd like to drive you, see your muscles growing taut, see you pulling on the harness, see your veins bulge out, see the sweat run down your back and in between the cheeks of your ass. You have such gorgeous legs, I'd like to see how fast you run. Do you like buggy whips? They feel so elegant in the hand, they sound so vicious in the air, they really sting, they hurt like hell, but the marks they leave are gone in a day. Unless you cut the skin with them. Draw blood. You could really mark a ponyboy with one you know. Do you like to pull a cart?"

I held a chocolate out to him the way you'd hold a piece of sugar toward a horse, but he was having none of it. He didn't come and lip it up the way real horses do. He couldn't turn or move because of the hobble, but his eyes seemed to widen as he leaned away from me and turned his head. I moved closer to the fence and made the chocolate last.

"So I guess you're not supposed to talk with the buyers, is that right? To let us make our minds up on our own? But how can a man know what property he wants unless he has the chance to get to know it. Can I count your teeth at least?"

I finished the chocolate finally, reached out and took his hair in my hand, and tried to turn his face to me. I don't know now if I really wanted to count his teeth or if I was just goofing around with him, but he held his head back with a kind of stubborn equine pride. I shook his head by the hair.

"Don't make me angry, boy. I might just buy you."

"Edgar," I heard Preston's soft voice behind me, "let go of my pony, please."

THREE

I dropped the boy's hair as if I'd been shocked, and turned around. "Preston! Hello! I didn't know he was *your* pony. He's such a handsome lad, and he prances so well – you must be an excellent trainer."

"Thank you," he said in a cool, matter-of-fact tone. He wore jodhpurs and a riding blouse, and slapped at his bootleg with a crop. "I've had experience."

"And you give excellent directions, too. I found the place first try."

"How good," Preston said. The voice I had thought was as warm as a cat's purr just a couple of days ago now sounded feline in a different way: deep in his throat it was almost predatory. "Edgar, how do you come to be back here in the paddock area?"

"Here? I just followed the handler when he brought your boy back from show."

As if on cue the handler appeared from around the Fellini barn, but this time he had no ponyboys in tow. Instead he had a handful of tack, and was accompanied by a couple of Mounties. Preston turned to the handler.

"Gardiner, did you bring Mr. Townsend back here?"

The handler looked at me and back at Preston. "Mr. Townsend? Why, no, sir, I don't bring anyone. That would be against the strictest rules."

Edgar turned back to me.

"I didn't say he *brought* me, Preston. I said I *followed* him."

"Past the No Entry signs? Through the locked gate?"

"Well, yes. I was just so enchanted with the pony that turns out to be yours."

Preston closed his eyes and seemed to meditate on his feet, and time slowed down for me, the moment stretching out so I felt I filled an hour just taking and releasing a single breath. When Preston opened his eyes he was already walking toward the paddock, but when I turned as if to follow I found myself hemmed in by Gardiner and the Mounties. For the first time I felt a wave of apprehension.

Preston went directly to the ponyboy, who was clearly glad to see him: he smiled and bent his head to nuzzle at Preston's touch. Preston spoke a few words to him and actually kissed his pony, then he turned and rejoined us men.

"I think, Edgar, you have misunderstood my invitation."

"Excuse me?"

"I think you expected to enjoy the flesh of other ponyboys."

"Of course I did. What else would I expect here?" Suddenly I felt hollow. "What do you mean, 'other' ponyboys?"

Preston nodded, and I could not have counted to "one" when I felt Gardiner holding my elbows from behind and a Mountie slipped a halter over my head.

"Do not cause trouble, Edgar, and I think you will not be unhappy with the outcome. Or, of course, you can rebel and pay the price."

Gardiner was enormously powerful: if I were to judge by this one encounter he could have wrestled genuine horses and won. Over my protests he held me gently but firmly as the Mounties lifted, twisted, and handled me bodily until they had stripped me naked and set me on the ground among them. To my horror I found myself extremely hard, a fact that Preston did not miss.

"You respond to discipline quite favorably, Edgar. That's a good sign. Get down on your knees. The time has come for a little change."

"Preston!"

"Do not cause trouble, Edgar. I can be very patient, but I am not always." Preston slid his crop across his thigh. I heard bluejays squabble. The first Mountie returned from leaving my folded clothes in a neat pile well outside the circle the four men made. Reluctant and peevish but confused by my combination of growing alarm and growing excitement because by now I was sporting a raging hard-on,

I knelt facing my host, which gave me a chance to notice the delectable bulge in his cavalry twill jodhpurs. Apparently Preston responded quite favorably to discipline as well.

"Good boy," Preston said to me. Good *boy*? "Now: kiss my boot."

"Preston!"

"Kiss my boot, Edgar." He moved so quickly I did not even see the crop slash through space, and the stick whipped the back of my thigh in exactly the spot that allowed the crop to keep on flying and slap hard against my balls. "*Now.*"

With the fresh sting racing around my tingling nerves I nearly fell on my face to obey his command, and as I did I felt rough hands take me from behind. I tried to sit up, but Preston's crop on my other thigh stopped me cold.

"Not a peck, Edgar. Not a little buss. A kiss. You know, with your mouth open, and your tongue wet. Kiss my boots, Edgar. Both of them. Wash them nice and clean."

I tried to comply. Really I did. But those rough hands worked my ass and started to open me with a slick, smooth, relentless pressure. For an instant I felt sharply stretched and I cried out as if I were being torn, then the dildo sank home and I knew that I'd been tailed. One of those same rough hands worked the dildo until I felt that deep-down need for release that has nothing at all to do with cumming, then the other grabbed my balls and stretched them back like salt water taffy, making me ache so I started to buck.

"Kiss my boot, Edgar," Preston said again, and I felt his crop land fast on one cheek and then the other, back and forth even while the dildo pumped my ass and the big hand that squeezed my balls now like silly putty punched them into the deep root of my cock and I tried to say *Yessir* but it sounded to me as if I were drowning in a grilled cheese sandwich when I suddenly realized it was Preston's fine, supple, well-grained, tawny, casual riding boot I was sucking off as if I could get the whole toe of it in between my lips and down my gullet.

Gardiner took my head in his strong hands and pulled me away from Preston's boot. I smelled the thick aroma of deeply soaped tack-leather, very different from the soft, fragrant scent of a well-kept boot. With consummate smoothness he slid a full bridle over my face and cinched it tight and locked it into place. It braced me across the forehead and held my jaw in a soft pocket sewn to straps that ran up the sides of my face and met at the crown of my head. There, one cross-strap ran down in front and split in two around my nose, and became one again at the jaw pocket. The other continued down the back of my neck and locked on a collarpiece that extended from the bottom of the jaw pocket and closed at the back of my neck.

Complete as the bridle was, it was designed to keep my mouth accessible. Now Gardiner forced my mouth apart and pressed a hard, narrow, rubber bit between my teeth. Then he kissed me, right over the bit, and while Preston and the Mounties laughed I finally stopped struggling. I was ready to do whatever Preston said. I felt defeated and I didn't like this feeling, but at the same time I felt thrilled in a way I had never felt before. Naked, on my knees, bridled, a little bit worked over, and helpless at the command of these four big men my cock was so hard it ached, and I *wanted* to kiss Preston's boots, *and* Gardiner's, *and* the Mounties'. I fell forward, but a hard tug on the bridle kept my head suspended.

"Follow," Preston said, and I scrambled to follow the measured movement of his boots as he strolled around the area outside the paddock. He used the reins to keep my head exactly at the height and angle that would make my bearing appear proud, if "proud" is a word I could apply to crawling around in the dirt and praying I would have a chance to grovel for this man's pleasure. He used the slightest pressure to let me know I was to turn to the left or right, and when he wanted me to stop he just tightened his fist on the reins so I felt the thin rubber bit against my cheeks. With every step I felt that dildo rubbing deep in my bowels, filling the cavity, and teaching my asshole to be hungry, as my hips and knees and shoulders and hands moved me along with greater and greater certainty, and the long horsehair tail brushed the backs of my welted thighs all the way past the insides of my knees to tickle my calves.

I had completely lost track of time when Preston brought me up before Gardiner and the Mounties. A pail of water was waiting, and when I tried to direct my head toward it, Preston pulled me up short and took the bit out of my mouth.

"I believe this new pony is thirsty, Gentlemen. Does anyone have something for him to drink? Why, here's something now."

Preston pulled my head up sharply and turned my face to the side at once so my mouth was at just the right height for a very long, slender Mountie cock with beautiful veins that looked like wide blue rivers laid out on a map of heaven. The lines and ridges and marks on its head were the intricate byways God had set up to make the sinner's journey entertaining. I wanted to travel each little one-way street so slowly I could come to a full stop at every twist and turn, but the Mountie with the open fly interrupted my reverie. He took my hair in one hand and his cock in the other, and jerked my mouth open and jammed himself straight past my gag reflex and out, and in and out, and he never even stopped to find out if I could handle meat that long, and by the time I could cough for the first time he was cumming so far down my throat I never even tasted him till he pulled out gradually, like a hungry snake reluctantly leaving the warmth of its sun-spotted burrow, wiping the head of his dick on my tongue as he passed.

I was gasping more than the Mountie, but I was getting the hang of it: if this was going to be the future I started to see how I could have some unexpected fun, and I was ready for Mountie Number Two. He was thick as a plug, but I clamped him in my lips like a hose in an O-ring and sucked up a vacuum that must have yanked his balls straight into his body and shot them out into my mouth, which is how he came, One-Two. *His* mouth fell open but mine stayed shut, and I did not meet his eyes as I smiled to myself. I expected Gardiner next, but Preston put me in front of the bucket and I drank what ponies are supposed to drink.

While I drank I smelled something hot, as if a little piece of air was burning, and when I was through one of the Mounties threw a little piece of meat to the ground in front of me. Was I supposed to eat it? Preston stabbed it with a tiny iron, and it crackled and sizzled and smoked. He pulled the iron away and there was an arrow branded into the meat.

"I like the way you work, Edgar. That is a pleasant surprise. If you continue to please me this meat might be you someday. If you continue. But today we have a different task. Stand up."

Beyond the paddock was a hedge. As Preston led me toward it I could see the hedge was made entirely of holly maybe two feet thick and dense with hard, curled leaves that were so pointed that the hedge was effectively made of thorns. From closer up the hedge seemed curved, and in a few more steps I saw that its curve hid a gap maybe twice the width of a real, large horse. Preston led me inside the hedge, and then I could see it was completely circular, containing a grassy area maybe half the size of a soccer field, with a second gap about the same size set directly across from the first.

Preston removed the reins from the bridle on my face. "You will wear the bridle and you will wear the tail," he said, "but otherwise you will be free to run. If you can escape the enclosure through either opening before I capture you I will bring you the ponyboy you seemed to admire so much, and put you out to stud with him for the weekend. If I capture you, however, you will join my stable and maybe pull a race cart I will let him drive."

Gardiner appeared in the gap behind us, leading an English-saddled roan that had to be eighteen hands.

"I'll give you a little head-start," Preston said, "but I have never yet lost this contest. Enjoy yourself. Run."

I made the same mistake I suppose anyone would make just then: I ran. But instead of maneuvering for position at close range and plunging through the gap we'd just come through, where I might have really had a chance, I ran for the far gap, supposing sort of automatically that with the little head start I might outrun him. Outrun a horse. A big horse.

The dildo stretched my asshole and wallowed in my rectum and almost brought me to my knees all by itself. The bridle cramped my face and restricted my breathing. My bare feet were exquisitely sensitive to the nuances of little divots and pebbles and gopher holes, and the searing points of dry grasses and nettle seeds nearly threw me to the ground repeatedly. My unsupported balls bounced more heavily than I would have imagined, and hurt surprisingly. Maybe this wasn't going to be quite as much fun as I'd thought a little while ago. And only then did I realize I was a naked man with a bridle on my head and a horsetail dildo up my ass, running beneath the sky as if my life depended on it across an open, empty field. I turned my head to look behind me and saw Preston sitting in the saddle, leaning forward with his arms folded against the horse's neck, laughing. Now *he* was the one having fun. Fuck him. Preston reined his horse and started it in to walk, and then to trot, and then to canter. I turned for the far gap and bolted as fast as I could.

Preston never meant me harm, I know: this was just a game for him, and I was learning to play. But I have never been so terrified in my entire life as when I heard the rapid beat of horse hooves pounding on the ground behind me, closer with every set of steps. My eyes were blurred with sweat the first time he swept past me and sliced the skin of my ass with some kind of whip. I'm sure I screamed, but I kept on running. He described a wide arc in front of me, swept around behind me again, and I felt the terror again as I heard him coming up on me at a dead run when the whip cut my ass again. The breath was rasping in my throat and I'd forgotten all my pain, keeping my eyes on the gap that now seemed miles away. I heard Preston shouting from behind, "Run! Run! Run!" and then a lasso settled over me and pinned my arms to my sides and the horse just stopped, jerking me to the ground.

Preston was on me as if I were a steer, tying my wrists behind me, tying my ankles together, and trussing me up in record seconds. I was panting hoarsely, trying to catch some breath, and Preston's shirt wasn't even ruffled. That made me mad.

"If you were me I bet you'd fuck me now, wouldn't you?" he whispered in my ear. At first I didn't have the strength to reply, but he took my balls in one of his hands. "Shall I geld you, Edgar?" And then I found my voice.

"Please, Preston, no. Please no."

"Well then, what shall I do with you?"

Suddenly I had caught my breath. I was exhausted more from the adrenaline that had been coursing through me than from the run itself, and I knew that I would ache by morning. But I realized that Preston was lying almost completely on top of me, holding my balls in his hand, and looking into my eyes.

Lying beneath him naked and bound, bridled and tailed, I got coy and almost smiled. I made music with my voice as if I were an olde-time sweater queen batting my eyelashes at a butch. "Will you please brand me, Preston?"

Hah! I thought. He wasn't expecting *that*.

But he didn't miss a beat. "In time, perhaps, but you haven't earned that honor yet, Edgar. This is just the first day of your training. Perhaps I'll keep you or perhaps you'll fetch a pretty price when I get through with you, but you're an orphan for the moment. You're in my keeping but you don't belong to anyone just now, and you have a great deal yet to learn. And by the way, to you my name is Mr. Benten. But of course, ponies don't talk and you are not allowed to speak again. Do you understand me?"

I wanted to spit in his face and I wanted to kiss him, I wanted to rip myself out of my bonds and destroy him and I wanted him to beat my rebellion out of me with his whip, I wanted him to make love to me and I wanted him to crush my balls in his warm, soft, exceptionally certain hand. It was difficult, hog-tied as I was, but this was going to be even more fun than I'd thought. I lifted my legs together and let them drop on the ground: one, two: yes.

Fire Island 1974:
A Bedtime Story

[That names have not been changed does not imply the people are real. – JW]

ONE: JAMES

Look: tinted pink in dawn's early light, the failing moon is falling like the last mnemonic remnant of a brain, long since torn from its grey stem and twisting imperceptibly toward the near horizon in a brief, irregular ellipsis. Yet, we are still awake. That is your doing. I wanted to lull myself to sleep recalling a story of erotic indulgence that was true, as if any erotic story were not, however flagrant or pedestrian. But stories are stored, as they are conceived, in recall and other imaginative data, so their truths must lie in those most miscible grounds where what was so and what was not become the equal property of anyone who makes a claim on history.

Remember *Rashomon**? Seven different people recalled a single murder in a grove in seven different ways, and all were telling the truth. I will tell you the truth in these last moments of the night, and maybe we will sleep at last. It is up to you to find the other witnesses – unless, of course, you want me to be them too.

---

* Rashomon, *the famous movie (1950) directed by Akira Kurosawa, and starring Toshiro Mifune, among other great Japanese actors, was based on two stories by Ryunosuke Akutagawa (1892 - 1927), "Rashomon," and "In a Grove." In*

The story I will tell takes place on Fire Island, New York, in July of 1974. My aunt, let us say, a Mame-like figure given to flamboyancies of all the senses, owns a home there one village block from the water in a family community, a couple of miles up-beach from the red-hot center where, those few short-sleeved years past Stonewall, pink angora sweaters and dry martinis still survive at night, and rumors persist amidst longneck beers by day.

In her ordinarily theatrical drive to clarify something, anything, for the good of those she loves, my aunt has become fast if temporary friends with Joe, a radical stage director, and has invited him to weekend at her weekend house. Her brain-surgeon husband, a good-natured fellow who is comfortably indulgent of her bohemias, is absent – and, shortly, absent so is she: back to Queens to care for her children, too young to have begun to have children of their own. The stage director has brought along a friend and colleague and sometime boyfriend named Harry, who is himself a minor playwright with a wife and daughter lost back in Los Angeles to the age of ebullient sexual experimentation.

I – once a mediocre amateur actor, and so on plausible terms with them both – had met the director years before in his Soho loft, where he plied me with not enough drinks and then, quite rightly, dismissed me as too jejune. Now we meet again, and, friendly at least to his hostess's nephew, he shows me his round and mustachioed friend who is never in the breath of a thousand infanticides the kind of man I would spread my legs for, but:

But Harry is sweet. Without a beat we make the sort of meaningful contact people usually flirt to achieve, and though I pretend that nothing is changed, I know from that moment the die is cast. His cock is in my mouth already, my still-tight asshole is reaching around his girth, I am lying beneath him while he labors to come, and if he is really so heterosexual as to please his wife, then he makes of me a happy girl.

This is as much a vision as any I have ever had: it has no pictures, no beliefs, no words, and no melody, but I can dance to its distant beat. If in some far-off world I do already know what's going to happen, back here I smile and go to help make dinner.

---

the former story, set in the ruins of what once had been Kyoto's great Rashomon gate, a servant recently fired by an unnamed samurai debates whether to become a thief or to starve honorably. It is in the latter that the seven testimonies to a single murder conflict so as to make truth itself unknowable.

Later that night I eat a little yellowed windowpane of acid and decide to go for a walk. I can't help the acid – it's a configuration of my generation as surely as gin was of Fitzgerald's. Does it make the evening resonant, or would the night have shimmered over the ocean anyway, its ranked clouds scudding like cotton soldiers in the fully moon-lit sky? It looks to me like the Erté cover of a 1920s *Vogue*. I walk on sand packed hard by lapping wavelets, and stroll in foam lit Coke-bottle green by the milky stars. Each time I pass another group of houses up beyond the beach I pass another little village. In between are spaces large enough for twice as many villages more, where reeds stand still in a breezeless air. By the time I realize I'm growing tired I have not yet reached my destination, the bright extravagance of Cherry Hill.

Do I dare go on? My feet, accustomed to city pavement, are beginning to give out in the sand. Home for the night is many towns away. I turn and start back. Little waves as curved as clams and mussels riffle on the water and sizzle in the sand like cooking cockles. The moon, it seems, has moved no farther, nor have the ranked clouds stirred since I set out. It is not the bones and muscles in my feet that now decline to carry me, but the tendons that give up, weak as Achilles': my feet are flopping like hooked fish, like hanged men on the gibbet when the floor has flown away, like the stranger-limbs they are that have been severed from my body except for some integument. They will not hold me, yet I must get home: I have a mission that makes no sense.

Dropping to the sand I crawl – what else? Hands and arms, shoulders and chest, knees and thighs, I call upon them all to carry me over the foot-sized dunes I sometimes fall face-forward into. Once I think I find nirvana. Looking at the static sky that has not changed the whole time I've been out, I think I must be happy. By the time I recognize the beach that fronts my aunt's house's village, all my limbs are quivering when I use them and twitching when I don't. I'm crawling now with my nose too close for comfort to the creosote-soaked wood, the boardwalk that serves as footpath here, and think I ought to sob with gratitude when I find the entrance to the square compound where my bed is waiting and I'll have to crawl no more. The rooms of the house are built around a central open space sheltering more boardwalk and a Fire Island pine. Insects chirp and rasp and chirr and I can hear the ocean's slop-slop-slop even here. Of mammals there is not a sound or scent or sight I can discern.

Falling on my face at every other lunge I pass the sliding glass that is my room and crawl directly to the very next one. The door is open to the night, a mattress splayed like a spilt milk across the unpolished, carpetless floor. As I approach, the sheet is quietly thrown back like an opening mouth, and without any words I take his tight balls into my own open mouth and roll them softly, menacingly, on my tongue. I slide up his cock like some priapic devotee and ride it with my throat. I hear him hiss, and when he comes the inside of my mouth feels the way it does when I eat quail egg sushi and crush the yolk against my palate: everything inside is swimming in a warm, thick, liquid, and perfectly frictionless *smooth*. There is no such thing as HIV on Fire Island in 1974, a cure for the clap is just a shot away. I drink his every shudder till he's shining and starting to grow hard again. He pulls me up along his bearishly haired body and we kiss at last. We have never said a word to one another.

_T_ WO: _HARRY_

From Los Angeles to New York is a six-hour flight; from Hollywood to Fire Island is a journey of a thousand miles. When I first stepped off the plane at Kennedy I saw armed guards keeping visitors, greeters, and well-wishers at bay. We have grown accustomed to maltreatment and the infringements of our humanity in these original, heady, end-of-the-empire decades, and some of the early coarseness has been smoothed over by triumphant oligarchs, but in the summer of 1974, for the first time in America, you could not walk a friend to an airport gate nor meet one at a landing flight, and when I got off the plane I had to scan a clutch of anxious, eager, irritated people waiting at the end of the corridor like a fist full of fingers at the end of an angry arm just to find Joe's familiar face.

Joe was literally leaning on a cop. Nearly swallowed in an ancient grey raincoat that hung down to the tops of his threadbare hi-tops, he balanced perilously on his cane as if the blue-suited elbow were a necessity. He seemed to have aged forty years in the three weeks since I'd seen him, and when he hailed me his voice quavered like a very old man's before he broke down in a fit of rasping coughs.

I hurried to the barricade and put my arm around the body I expected would feel frail. I was so surprised to feel his yogic muscles ripple at my touch that I remembered I'd forgotten he had taken body language seriously and trained himself to speak what his voice sometimes could not.

"Haerrry, Haerrry, Haerrry my boy, how glad I am to see you," he cracked and whistled as if through dentures he had never worn. "Take me home and let me get you out of this heat."

I tried to take him from the cop who saw that we were separated by the makeshift wall and simply moved it for me as if I were not a terrorist. Nodding in a sort of proletarian-brother kind of gratitude I slipped out of the arrival gate's enclosure and embraced what looked like an infirm, dying man. "Joe," I said. "Joe, it's gonna be all right." I looked into the cop's wholly unsuspecting eyes. "Thank you, officer. Do you have a wheelchair?"

The cop looked startled but Joe took over. "No, no, Haerrry, don't make me ride in one of those damn things today. Let me walk again. Let me remember I'm a man."

I looked down on his shrunken form. "Sure, Joe. Sure. You just take my arm, and then we'll walk." I winked at the cop as if conspiratorially, though what our conspiracy might have been would take a Senate subcommittee to decide.

We tottered down the corridor, never breaking Joe's shuffling stride until we'd turned two corners and were headed for the baggage claim. Then Joe was my height again, fully formed, laughing and turning pirouettes with the grey coat rising up around his hips like a Hassid's skirts – or no, like a dirty canvas tutu.

"'Thank you, officer,' he sang, 'Do you have a wheelchair?' He-ha-ha-ha-ho-ho-heee. 'Thank you, officer,' he twirled around the last redcap who skeedaddled outta there, 'Do you have a wheelchair?' Harry you were priceless, *priceless*, PRICELESS! You *have* to consider a career on stage!"

"Schmuck! How could you know I'd understand what you were doing? Schmuck! We could both be in jail by now!"

"He-he-ha-ha-ho-ho-heee."

✦✦

When we docked at Fire Island late that July afternoon the air was thick and still as custard. The sea was as calm as Bing Crosby on Quaaludes. The sky was like Dale Evans waiting for Roy Rogers to go to bed. We found a Red Flyer wagon to load my lonesome bag in, and as we trundled off down the boardwalk hand in hand I felt as if I were in some out-take of a rough cut of *The Lady Eve*, heretofore lost on the cutting room floor.

Joe had shed the geezer drag and was scrumptiously tanned in white Ann-Margaret hot pants. I remembered why we'd become lovers, and forgot why we had stopped. The deal, he said as we strolled in step, was a weekend of fun 'n' sun, no muss no fuss, and a few days in Soho before I went back home to Miriam. Gulls wheeled and kids at a distance shouted. The sea was in the air everywhere and I put my arm around my friend. But at the house there was another man, a man I wasn't counting on, and Joe could tell right away I wasn't going to sleep with *him*.

He came to me in the middle of the night smelling sweaty with beach and sea and boardwalk. I'd lain awake stroking myself and licking the precum off my fingers while the moon made my room grow bright and brighter then darker and dark, listening to the crickets' whirr; when they stopped I knew the time had come. I'd been hard for hours on and off and I was very ready. He *crawled* to me that first night, honey, literally crawled across the doorsill of my room, and when I let the covers fall away he sucked me off in thirty seconds. When I was hard again I pulled him up to kiss him, pushed him over on his belly, spit on my hand and spread his asshole with my fingers, then I came twice more while I fucked him till my dick gave out.

THREE: JOE

"I'll never forgive Harry for leaving me," Joe said. Something by Lizst was playing too loudly for background but not loudly enough for him to listen to.

"He didn't leave you," Liza countered mincing shallots on the maple cutting board. She paused to listen to a climbing arpeggio of triplets that resolved like a waterfall. "He went home to his wife."

"I rest my case," Joe said. Moodily, he watched the oblong shallots shatter into tiny flecks beneath Liza's knife, so sharp and quick it left no juice behind. If he imagined himself very far above the table he could see them all collecting like a crowd of hunky dandruff at a hair bar. He wondered what each would order: *'Brylcream: just a little dab'll do me, Joe.' 'Wildroot Cream Oil, Charlie.'* Liza slid her wide blade underneath them all at once and flipped them into a pan where they started to sizzle instantly. *'That's what Head 'n' Shoulders will do, Gentlemen: cut us down like a knife. It must be stopped at all costs.'*

Liza started slicing morels. "Joe, he always goes back to Miriam. He always *will* go back to Miriam. He fools around, but he's a deeply married man."

"He didn't look so married when I took him to the St. Mark's Baths."

"He fools around."

"And he's not going to look so married sleeping with your nephew, either."

"They both fool around. Maybe they're made for each other."

"I'll never forgive him."

Humming an intricate counterpoint Lizst left out she tossed the mushrooms into the oil and stirred them with the shallots, adding herbs and spices from the bountiful rack beside her like an ancient mandarin calculating the age of the world on an abacus. "Did you set the camera up?"

"Oh yeah," he answered tracing runes to the music with his finger in the sparse dunes of fresh ground pepper her mill had left behind. "Yeah, the camera's in and loaded with film, I double-checked the infrared sight, the sound is perfectly muffled, and the knothole's so big you can turn the lens to any place in the room they could possibly reach. There'll be a motorboat named *Judy* waiting at the slip from midnight on to take the film to Cherry Hill. The guy will work all night and bring you prints for breakfast." He saw that they might just spell *'Joe,'* but wondered what the signs he'd made could really mean.

"Excellent," she said. "Thank you." She drizzled brandy into the pan and a minute later a little cream, turned off the heat, and poured and spooned the mixture onto plates of fresh-popped toast points. As she left the pan in the sink and the plates on the table she pulled from the refrigerator two small bowls of endive, watercress, jicama, and mango loosely chopped together under a sesame oil and balsamic vinaigrette, and a bottle of unlabeled white wine. As he always did, he got the bread: a cibatta this time that needed some shoulder to slice. He sat down and she put her arms around him from behind, dropping her hot mouth to his neck and sliding her hands along his naked chest. She gripped his nipples between her thumbs and forefingers, and pinched and chewed for a long minute until he said,

"The ice cubes are getting cold." Then she stood up with a sigh and sat down to eat.

"Well, Liza, I'm gay, you know. I can't help it, I just don't respond to women. You wouldn't respond so well yourself if I were a woman coming on to you."

She raised her eyebrows at him.

"Well then to a sheep. You wouldn't turn on to a sheep nuzzling at your teats now, would you?"

Her expression didn't change.

"Well for Christ's sake then, fuck what you want to fuck but leave me alone with my boys."

The music ended with a brave sort of flourish. Liza took a bite of the soaking toast and smiled. "I love lunch," she said.

✦✦

There were actually three cameras in all, each with its own roll of thirty-six exposures. She enjoyed watching Harry play with himself, but only started to take pictures when he lifted the sheet as James crawled toward him from the door across the floor. She took pictures of Harry's balls and cock both in and out of James's mouth and of his cock both in and out of James's ass. She took pictures of James's cock and balls growing fat and heavy while Harry fucked him. She took pictures of Harry's face engorged with James's genitals. She took pictures of the two men sleeping naked in each other's arms. By that time she was intolerably wet, so she went to Joe's room with a strap-on dildo in one hand and a jar of Vaseline in the other. Joe was sound asleep but he woke right up when she grabbed his balls. She was hunkered down so her face was level with his. "Now listen here, my friend, I know you're gay but that can't be helped. I am your hostess, your friend, your confidant, and your pimp, and I am a lady in need. Either you fuck me or I fuck you. Which will it be?"

FOUR: TOMÀS

He knew she'd come home because the front door was ajar. He shut it and locked it, picked up his mail from the round marble table under the Tiffany chandelier, and took the letters and bills and journals into the kitchen where she'd also left a lot of food on the table. He held the pile of envelopes in his left hand and peered at the repast over his horn-rim glasses, which he secured on the bridge of his nose with the index finger of his right hand. A basket of bread, of course; a plate of cheeses, of course; a bowl of fruit, of course; a green salad, of course. Some casserole: he bent forward and lifted the lid of the orange pan, sniffing gingerly: cassoulet. The chafing dish held pieces of grilled rabbit swaddled in rosemary. He lifted the cover off a small plate to find rows of braised endive with leeks and red peppers. His glasses started to slide off his face and he dropped the plate's cover onto the endive trying to catch them. Oily juice started to leak out onto the table where he could see the cover had cracked the plate. He put down his mail and took off his tie, sopped up the liquid with it as best he could, then used it to make a sort of dam around the base of the plate.

At the sink he filled the bottom of a kettle with water, then he put the kettle on the stove and turned one burner on. He took a cup from the cupboard and a teabag from a canister nearby, dropped the teabag into the cup, and waited for the kettle to whistle. Out the window over the sink evening was starting to shut Queens down. A single bird sat on the topmost branch of Liza's lady apple tree facing west, as if watching the impending sunset. "Tee-wee-wee-wee-wee," it said.

Tee-wee-wee-wee-wee also said the kettle. He turned off the burner and poured water into his cup. He carried the cup to the table and put it down while he wrenched a poorly cut slice of bread from the basket. He put the bread in his jacket pocket and picked up the mail in his left hand and the tea in his right, then went back past the marble table and up one flight of stairs to his room. He put the tea cup down on his dresser and threw the bag into his wastebasket. He put his mail next to the tea cup and the slice of bread next to the pile of mail. He took off his suit coat and hung it in the closet, then took tea, bread, and mail to a soft chair in the bay window where he sat down.

He sipped the tea and set the cup and bread on the floor beside him. He looked through the envelopes without changing his expression, and flipped them one after another unopened into the wastebasket. There were a great many envelopes, most of them white, some manila, a few in odd colors like green or red. Now and then he slid an envelope underneath the ones that remained in his hand, and when he came to the topmost envelope of those he'd saved he opened it and perused the letter before throwing it away. He kept a small pile of bills and magazines out from their envelopes on the floor and finally held only one last envelope all by itself. He hefted it to judge the weight, held it up to the fading light at the window though he could see nothing through it, smelled it, held it up to his ear. He sipped his tea again and finally opened the envelope and spilled onto his lap 108 5" x 7" glossy photographs of two naked men having sex. He vaguely registered that he vaguely recognized his nephew. He sorted through the pictures, now quickly and now idly, until he had divided them into a large pile and a small pile. He scooped the large pile back into the envelope and pushed the small one over beside his slice of bread, and he looked through the pictures until it was too dark to see anything clearly.

He stood up and tossed all the pictures on the bed. He picked up the pile of bills and magazines and set it on the dresser. He undressed slowly, hanging up his suit pants with the jacket, lining up his shoes on the closet rack, dropping his shirt and socks and underpants into the hamper in the bathroom. After he turned on a dim lamp over the toilet he set his glasses beside the sink and drew a hot bath without beads or oils or any other additions, then settled into it wordlessly and quite comfortably. When the water became too cool he got out and dried himself, draped a robe over his shoulders, put on his glasses, took the envelope with the large pile of pictures in his left hand and the small pile of loose pictures in his right, and went back downstairs. He left the envelope on the marble table in the foyer and continued on into the kitchen. He looked at the table full of food and ate a piece of rabbit. He spread the pile of pictures out before him on the table and, with a small smile, masturbated into the cassoulet. The doorbell rang and someone started pounding on the door itself.

FIVE: LIZA

He breathed a little sigh of exasperation and went to open the door. The small and very angry blonde woman standing on his porch didn't even seem to notice that his robe was open and that his penis, recently released, was oozing one thin, fine, translucent liquid string depending to his knees and swaying in the draft.

"I want my husband back!" she shouted up toward his face.

He pushed his sliding glasses up the bridge of his nose. "Why on Earth?"

"Why? *Why*? WHY?" She did not seem to have an answer.

"Why – why on Earth are you telling *me*?"

"Where is my husband?"

He thought about the man who'd died in surgery that afternoon, but the hospital should have handled that. Besides, the man had not been married.

The woman shouldered past him into the foyer, brushing his robe onto the floor. He tried to catch the robe but his glasses began to fall and he had to use both hands to catch them instead. By the time he put them on his face again the woman was well into the house. He followed her in some consternation and when he caught up with her she was already standing stock still at the kitchen table. Slowly she turned toward him. Her face had gone quite firm. She was holding a photograph. She spoke quietly and very deliberately.

"Where. Is. My. Husband."

"James?"

"Harry. HARRY. WHERE IS MY HUSBAND?"

From the doorway where she was leaning with one hand on the jamb Liza asked, "Perhaps I can be of some help?"

The woman whirled on her. "Who are you? Where is my husband?"

"With regard to the first question, since you're standing in *my* kitchen where you weren't invited, I might better ask who are *you*? And with regard to the second, since you're standing here with *my* husband, who is naked as a skunk and has clearly just had an orgasm, I might also better ask you some questions."

The woman seemed to actually notice the man for the first time. She looked him in the face, then looked him up and down and found that he was, in fact, naked. And, like Liza, she could also see that he had recently come. She held out the photograph and Liza could tell by her crumpling face that the woman had just begun to recognize what could be seen to be her own predicament. "But Harry," she started to cry. "I want my husband."

"You must be Miriam," Liza offered, coming down from the wall and walking toward the woman who nodded as if afraid to trust her voice. "Did you come all the way from Los Angeles?" The woman nodded some more. "Then you must be hungry," Liza said patting the woman's cheek with maternal certainty as she reached for a plate and spoon. "No one with a tongue can eat the nasty crap they feed their captives on a plane. Come on, sit down and have some supper; then we'll talk."

Obediently, Miriam sat down before the plate Liza had set before her and started to eat.

"Do you like it?" Liza prompted. Miriam nodded as if that was all she could remember to do, and then she found her voice. "Good," she said, "what is it?"

Liza smiled, happy that her food was at work. "Cassoulet."

IX: JAMES

Even with models in place it takes a long time to shoot a roll of film if you know only approximately what you want in your pictures and you don't have the luxury of a motor-drive. I hear the first distinctive *sssnk* of a shutter about the time Harry lifts up his sheet, and by the time I take his balls into my mouth I could if I had to point to one of three knotholes the camera has to be hidden behind. Perhaps it's the acid, but tonight I seem to be able to do two things at once, and, reticent as I usually am, putting on a show seems like an entertaining other choice. Making love with Harry I reach down deep into my repertoire and pull out all the stage tricks I remember about highlight lighting, use of shadows, and position for effect. I make sure to show the juicy parts except every now and then when I feel like being a tease or I want to make the camera drop a few frames. It simply doesn't occur to me for days to wonder how anyone could have planned for me to be here when I didn't know myself that I was coming till I'd arrived. Maybe Harry was expecting someone else who never came. When I get around to thinking about tonight it makes me nervous about the pictures' future, but by then it's really too late to worry.

Later, when Harry has fallen asleep and the camera is gone, I find that I'm hungry for more night air. I still can't walk and I'm only taking it on faith that I will ever be able to walk again, so I crawl naked into the Fire Island night on my sandburned knees and then I crawl all the way to the beach. Exhausted and exhilarated with my night full of efforts I sit against a tree that has become driftwood, and marvel as the brilliant pearl of a moon I saw earlier first melts to a yellow puddle on the flat black sea and then almost immediately becomes an equally flat dull copper shining wanly across the Island from somewhere west of Brooklyn. In this briefly two-dimensional night the sky holds not a single cloud, nor does it show a single star.

Who am I now, I wonder, *and what have I made up? How could I describe tonight's history, and who would believe me?* I hear a shuffling in the sand, and someone very softly calls my name. Does that mean I'm not alone? Is there someone else who could tell my tale? I answer the mystery voice – "Hello?" – and Harry walks into the rancid moonlight dappled like a camouflaged soldier.

"You aren't wearing any clothes," are the first words he ever says to me.

I look down at my body and it's true. I look back at him.

"You going to stay up awhile?"

"Yes," I say, breaking my own silence with him. "Awhile."

"You'll get cold. Or busted. I'm going back to bed. Take this," and he peels off his sweatshirt and hands it to me. Then he takes off his pants and hands them over too. Now Harry is bare as the day he was born, plus a lot of body hair. I kiss his cock which for me is just at face height. "Good night, sweetheart." He bends down to kiss me and I kiss him back, and then I'm alone again. I put Harry's clothes on the sand beside me. The air is soft and warm and moist and feels like an extension of my skin so that if I don't move my muscles I can imagine my body's disappeared. In the mind that remains I say aloud that I could die at peace right here, right now; then, far away at what must be the end of the island, I see the lights of a dune buggy start to come my way. This is how Frank O'Hara died, I muse, run over drunk on a Fire Island beach. I am not so ready to meet my unmaker as I thought I was. I scrabble out of its presumptive path and instantly its lights go dark.

Now: the moon has set. Pull down the blinds, my love, and let's go to sleep.

Ritual Cycle

for L

ONE: *APRIL FOOL*

The days are growing longer once again.
Hour by hour the very minutes seem
To stretch like fingers and arms on the hands of a clock,
Like flowers reaching petals toward the sun,
Like me reaching toward you from my knees.
Yet, though daylight lingers in the pink
And pearl blue high western clouds,
All sky and air turn night
Just as they do on December 21st. Light
Is not a metaphor, nor is night.
Everything begins and ends again.

Two: Occult Blood

My tea leaves say your patience will be rewarded.
The lines in my palm say my life is in your hands.
Even the stars line up in my skies to spell
Your name. I have become the grail I sought
For you. I have become the road itself to you.

Three: The Fisher Bride

Like a long-line trawler you set your hook for me.
I swim right up to you: I *want* to be caught.
The trouble is, I can't live on land and you
Have sworn to throw nothing back. What more is there to say?
I take the bait. The sea surrounds you, eats your little craft.

Four: Sunset at Glass Beach

In the rattle of the surf I *heard* the bony voices of my ancestors: this
Mother and that, all the fathers, grandparents, you,
You, and always you, all the way back down the phylla,
All the way back to your goddess. Surf sounded like wind in the treetops yesterday,
That danced as the holy serpents dance in the cave of your sacred vulva
Filling me as you fill me when I lie on the beach at night with my hands beneath you,
Lift you to my mouth like a great bowl of sky,
And drink the stars of the milky way
Through your bright, open, terribly full moon.

FIVE: MANGOES

For your kiss my breasts are mangoes.
Sweet juice runs from between your teeth,
covers my chest, the sheets,
the bed, the floor, the street.
It's a good thing I'm not a sea of turtles.
You'd turn each one on its back
and this is not a game
for you.

SIX: YOUR SIMPLE KISS

We drove from summer to 1953
over peninsulas of pines, and came at last
to a river running beside the road like a ghost.
"Home," you said, and took me from the car.
The house went on as far as I could see
but you remarked on nothing. Cosmos stole
the light, while your simple kiss took me over
and over, as if I were sleeping with God. Night
fell, the river faded, the house disappeared.
Did we notice? Did we care? Did we?

SEVEN: WHITE ROSES

These white roses spread their petals
Like a pet boy's thighs before his Mistress's desire.
Nothing in the wide ocean of this flower
Could have been predicted in the raindrop of its bud,
Yet, when you gaze down upon your property
The whole world grows hot and damp,
Fields of flowers reign on earth and I
Rise and bloom expressly for your eyes.

Straight Boy

Back in the bad old days, when rubber was what your Corvette laid in its five-second skid from zero to sixty, I used to get my kicks at the Eiffel Baths in San Francisco. Things were so loose for a while in that town that the place even ran suggestive ads in the big city dailies, and now and again some Bette Midler impersonator made a local splash singing a run of "boy" songs: Water Boy, Drummer Boy, Danny Boy, and the like. Since I kept up with the music scene, the bath house concerts and the bath house itself became part of my Sunday Supplement consciousness.

The Eye-full, as it was known on the street, was also famous for its raunchy help – attendants were rumored to be routinely found with their ankles behind their ears amidst the sheets they were supposed to be changing – and because it was reputed to be the only fuck-bath house in history that admitted women. As a consequence, a number of straight guys came there looking to hit on the females they figured would be swinging from the chandeliers. Also as a consequence, since very few straight women actually ever did show up, house policy provided perfect cover for a straight boy to learn that the smell and feel and taste of cock could make him pant and sweat and squirm just like any other faggot.

That straight boy – that was me. Among my regular buddies I was just another regular buddy: I worked my nine-to-five, kicked back on weekends, and went through women like a hot tongue went through soft ice cream.

But what none of my good buddies ever guessed was that some nights, around the time the bars shut down, I got a peculiar tightness in my nuts that tingled like electricity. It felt different from wanting to fuck my number-one girl and different from wanting to fuck some other girl, and it was more than just wanting to get my rocks off or I could have hobbled home to Mrs. Hand and her five daughters. It was urgent and overwhelming, like the sudden need to pee little kids have that makes them dance and clutch their crotches and come away with wet hands.

On those nights I'd pretend I didn't feel a thing and start to head for home. But then, curious, hopeful, frightened, and so excited my hands were sweaty and my mouth was dry, I'd find myself motoring over south of Market Street as if I hadn't done the driving. Soon I passed through those disco doorways where fifty or a hundred or two hundred men groped down dark warrens with thin trick towels tucked around their waists or draped like leis around their necks.

By that time my head was hot with anxiety and a fear bred of sheer dumb ignorance. Never quite knowing or admitting to myself what I was doing there, I descended the wide redwood stairs and let my eyeballs do the walking, scoping out the game room, the t.v. lounge, the snack bar, the indoor hot tub. I went to my little cell and stripped, and then, with my own towel split up my thigh like a fan-dancer's banner, my heart gushing in my throat like some fountain of youth, and my head prickling as if I had brain fever, I checked the outdoor tub, the sauna and the fantasy dungeon. After a shower and some heat to calm myself down, I stopped pretending I'd come looking for quim. That's when I really relaxed.

Up the halls and down the halls, pacing myself around the stations of the maze, I loved the ritual of cruising: that flicker of the eye, that twist of a finger, that tiny movement of the towel that said Yes. Lingering kisses with strangers in the shower. Butts for touching and butts for looking only. Coy jokes and promises to get together later, if something better didn't work out.

The first time I passed Kelly I got so confused I fled back to my private cot in the dark red light. If he had been a woman, I told myself, I'd have known just what to do. But the way he shot his skinny hip out to block off half the aisle, the way he had his hair crew cut, the arrogant way his face set up with its wide lips and its arching nose like a condor's beak, even I could tell that he was not just going to be a man, he was going to be a man in charge, and I didn't understand exactly why my legs began to tremble and my heart to pound all over again.

When I passed Kelly the second time he had a boy with a Nautilus body pinned against the wall outside a group room. The boy's two wrists were gripped above his head in Kelly's one enormous hand, while with his other hand he gently traced the outline of the boy's face: jaw to chin, lips, forehead all at once, then the eyes. I had time to watch him lift his knee precisely underneath the boy's big balls and slowly press them up between his thighs. The balls spread apart and straddled Kelly's knee. He jigged his leg once and both balls fell to the left. His dick made his towel billow like a tent. He caught the boy's whole sack between his knee and the boy's own thick thigh. The boy's eyes opened wider and wider while Kelly looked straight back and deep, as if he were looking through the irises of that boy's eyes and into the meat and memory of his brain.

Kelly's hamstring stood out taut against the flesh of his back leg, the toes of his floorbound foot dug down for traction, his bent knee pushed up harder against the root of the boy's hot cock, and his hand still soft as a lover's breath lay calm upon the twisted face as the boy gasped and groaned and shot so hard his own mouth and Kelly's both got wet.

Gradually, Kelly let the boy's hands go. His head fell onto Kelly's shoulder, and Kelly put his arms around the boy and held him close. Finally he kissed the boy and wiped his face. He turned around and looked directly at me. Then he walked away.

I saw Kelly the third time when I'd already decided this was not my night. I was headed for my closet, planning to dress and go home, when I almost stepped on Kelly's foot. He held out one arm as if to stop me and his fingers grazed my belly. I was hard before my foot hit the floor.

"I saw you watching me," he said.

"What?"

"Third time's the charm."

Kelly was as tall as I am, a good six feet or more, but very wiry where I used to be thought of as a hunk. He pushed me backwards gently. My towel fell off my hips and a curtain parted behind me. I kept walking backwards, propelled by his three fingers resting just below my navel. My cock was dripping sticky webs that trailed from his forearm where I kept bumping him.

"What happens in here?" I asked, abrupt anxiety making me stupid as a virgin.

Kelly didn't buy my innocence for a moment. He pinched his lips together and said, "I fuck you in here, just like you've been wanting me to do all night."

I stammered as if I were protesting, but my cock was so hard it hurt all the way up to my heart, my balls were screaming tight, and for the first time in my life I felt neither straight nor bi: right then I was a gay man, and Kelly's dick was all I wanted in the world.

The backs of my legs bumped against a mattress and Kelly's fingers pushed me down upon it. I lay back and opened up my legs and arms. He opened his towel and tossed it on the bed, showing a long, thick, hard dick glistening at its single eye. He settled down on top of me with his cock against my cock, and my joint and asshole twitched as if I were going to come.

"Uh-uh," he said, squeezing the tip of my cock with a thumb and finger. "Don't you dare."

I swallowed and took a couple of deep breaths, holding back until I calmed down some.

"Better," he said, nodding. "I want you hard when I fuck you."

He kissed me, and slid up my body till his cock was at my mouth. For the first time I understood cock-hunger, and reached for him with my tongue and lips and my whole head, but he wouldn't let me touch. He didn't even tease. He just waited, holding himself above me on his hands and knees, watching me intently as I pleaded to his face. Then, when I was just about to beg, he pushed his cock deep into my mouth and let me suck him while his balls in their soft skin hung beneath my chin down toward my neck.

He slid out of my face when I started to gag.

"Breathe," he said.

I sucked in air, then his cock was down my throat again. Out. "Breathe." In. Out. "Breathe." In.

"Turn over."

"No, please. Fuck me from the front. I want to see you."

One corner of his mouth ticked up a fraction of an inch. Kelly was smiling. He knelt between my legs and I hiked myself up, holding the backs of my thighs in my hands. He spit in his palm and lubed my ass, then brought his cock up against me.

"You a straight boy?" he asked. "You're so tight you must be really scared. Hmm?"

I nodded.

"Too bad," he said, and pushed his way in.

I felt as if my whole body were being torn apart. The pain was like a burn that seared me from my asshole to my gut. My face must have passed through a lot of emotions because Kelly finally laughed out loud. He braced himself on the backs of my thighs, and then as he pumped me full of himself I felt my asshole open up, my stomach open up, my heart and face and head open up. I felt complete and full. I threw back my arms and head and howled.

◆-◆

In the bad old days relationships didn't blossom out of chance encounters at the baths. Fuck-buddies might meet up there from time to time, and regulars had familiar faces. Friends might even come and go together, but the whole idea was to have happy, dirty, mindless, guiltless, anonymous sex in surroundings that were more sensuous and comfortable than glory holes, back alleys, or the parks.

After Kelly wiped his cock I figured we were over. The gay stud had had his straight boy, and the straight boy had had his limits and his asshole stretched for good. So I was surprised when he wiped me down as well, and said, "Why don't you come over to brunch tomorrow?"

I was even more surprised when I heard myself reply, "Where? What time?"

Kelly told me his name then, and gave me an address in the heart of the Castro, a couple of blocks from what was in those days the Elephant Walk. "Show up at one or two," he said. "No one will be up till then anyway." Then he picked up his towel and walked back out through the curtains.

It must have taken me a quarter of an hour to get myself mobile. I had been most righteously swived, and my body was relaxed to the point of indolence. More important, my mind had been thoroughly fucked as well. In my lethargy I pictured Kelly's cock in front of me, and felt my own cock swell. I wondered what made me think that I was straight.

Another man peered into the room and eyed my hard-on as I lay supine upon the wet, chilly sheet. I gave him a faint smile and shook my head, he shrugged and went away. I got up on shakey legs and headed for the shower. There, as I cleaned up, I looked at the other men who joked with one another, or displayed themselves self-consciously, or hurried through their ritual ablutions. I could see no difference between us, nor could they.

Someone began to soap my back.

"That feels good," I told him over my slippery shoulder, "but I'm through for the night."

He paused for a moment, then put the soap in my hand. "You do me, then. I'm just beginning."

And so I soaped his back and leaned around to soap his chest, playing with his nipples till they stood out hard. I soaped down his arms to where his hands rested quietly below his hips. I soaped his hips and his ass, working my hands between his thighs to soap one of his legs all the way down to his foot, then I soaped the other leg all the way up to his crotch. I soaped his cock and balls until his cock was stiff, and after I helped him get rinsed off I knelt on the public shower floor and sucked him till his breathing started to heat up.

I stood up and gave him a quick kiss. "That's to get your evening off to a good start," I said, and I went back to my little cubicle and dressed and walked out into the dawn.

Just for curiosity's sake I drove to the address Kelly had given me and parked across the street with my car's engine idling and the city birds chirruping all around. I had no idea why I was there, miles across town from my own apartment at five o'clock on a Saturday morning. I was vaguely troubled by what I had done at the Eiffel, and confused by what I was feeling now that I was outside in the tired, slanting, early light.

The door to Kelly's place opened and a beautiful young man dressed all in white stepped onto the sidewalk closing the door discreetly behind him. He stretched like a cat, looked up and down the block, looked at me sitting in my car, and turned to walk away toward Castro Street.

Somehow he was the sign that I'd been waiting for. I was still worried about what I had done, but I was no longer confused about what I was feeling. I wanted to see Kelly again. I wanted to feel him lying in my arms, and I wanted to feel his dick up my ass. Now I knew that I would come to brunch, and see what other lessons Kelly had to teach me. My cock got hard as if I hadn't come all night, and

I felt my nuts start tingling all over again. I put my car in gear and turned myself toward home. I was grinning as if I'd drunk too much caffeine. I didn't know if I could wait till one. I opened a couple of buttons on my jeans and wrapped two fingers around my pulsing cock, glad my current number-one girl had taught me to wear no underpants.

Every Picture Tells a Story

It started with a picture in a magazine. Two women were on a beach. The younger one, with long, straight chestnut hair and a black leather jacket so thin it looked like tissue, was, oh, maybe 20. The older one, with longer, straighter, shining black hair and an even softer black leather jacket open to show her black lace camisole was probably 20, and maybe half an inch taller than the younger one. Their skins looked translucent as the inside of a wet clam shell, as if you could see through layer after layer to something shimmering with pinks and blues and browns but you could never reach it. Behind them the water was so blue it looked like, oh, I don't know, the sky, the sea, your eyes if they were blue, no: yes: the water was so blue it looked like the sea in tourist brochure photographs of Greece, and the beach was that same postcardy white sand that stretched to the jagged cliffs all craggy and edgy and shadowed dark, and you could tell the sun was in the sky because everything was all so light, but the sun was not in the picture, just the women.

Just the women. The older one had her arm around the younger one's shoulder and looked straight out into the camera with her mouth pursed and her lips very relaxed and full like she could care, looked straight into your eyes when you were looking at the picture as if, *What are you looking at, bitch?* while the younger one with both her elbows bent and tucked to make herself look small and both her soft hands on the older woman's chest stared almost pouting at the painted tip of her own single finger where it traced the scalloped lace of the older woman's camisole, watching her own finger move so slowly even she was not aware of it moving toward the other's aureole just almost barely visible behind the scallop, below the low-cut line of lace, and you knew if you watched the picture long enough you would see it, see her nipple, see the younger one's finger reach it and touch it the way you would see the colors in their skins if you could wait that long and still you knew that no one could.

I wanted to be in that magazine with you. I wanted to be on that beach with you. I wanted to fold up into you, fragile as a bird, to trace your camisole with the tiniest tip of my one finger, touching you so softly it was like skating on a hair but you could feel me, and I could feel your arm and the look on your face protecting me against intruders' eyes, against the sun, against the night to come while I felt your warm skin heat my finger in the breeze, and I knew already that I wanted to touch you without stopping, to fall down in the sand with you right there, and I looked up from the magazine and found my face was wet and my pants were wet and I went to bed alone again and cried and cried and came and cried and cried, but it was the crying I fell asleep from.

I and Thou

Her son had been killed by... someone who didn't exist.... Abruptly, a great sob tore through her body, and she wept uncontrollably. That passed. She laughed, giving the thing on the floor an almost jeering glance. "Well, kid, it's only one throat, huh?" And then she went out of the room and the hotel, and out into the City of Angels. —Jim Thompson, The Grifters

arlos rolled down the grassy incline, turning over and over in the sweet hot sun, smelling the chlorophyll crushed in his passing, laughing in remembered, imagined free-fall, and came to rest with his head spinning and dizzy in a pile of leaves, half in, half out of a great oak's shade. Jane was on him before the leaves stopped rustling, locking his head in the crook of her elbow, kissing his face, prying his mouth open with her tongue, forcing his not unwilling thighs apart with her knee, taking hold of his bare balls with her free hand, gently sliding one well-lubed finger into his ass and reveling as she felt him gasp, felt his sphincters loosen, felt his belly soften, felt his jaws relax, felt him take her into him everywhere. His arms went around her neck, his legs went around her hips, she released his balls to get two, then three fingers inside him, pushed up on his balls with her knee a few times, and started to fuck them with her vulva while she pumped him with her hand. He was crying to her rhythms already, crying real tears, whimpering beside her ear, pressing his face against

I and Thou   [123]

her face, shaking from convulsions in his belly, almost there, almost out of control, almost out of his mind, she fucked his mouth, she fucked his balls, she fucked his ass and then he roared and shouted and rocked and she felt his body clutch at her and release her, clutch and release, clutch and release and then his contractions started to subside and he was open wide, soft as a sleeping kitten. She gently pinned his wrists to the ground, settled her clit on his cock, and started the ride that would take her off. Later she would let him come in the more conventional mode, shooting and wet, but for now she had him where she wanted him and he was moving his hips in time to hers, a piece of living meat happily at her service. "Fuck me, baby," he whispered in her ear. "Come on now: come in me."

She woke when she heard the boot break a twig beside her face. She could see it right there, close enough to kiss, and felt the presence of someone else above her, straddling her where she lay on top of Carlos. Someone's bare ass sat on her bare ass and she felt her hair grabbed from behind, tightly, right at the back of her skull. Her head was pulled up just far enough for her to see a long, curved, glinting knife held out for her eyes' benefit, then the hand pushed her face down again. The sudden weight had wakened Carlos. His eyes and mouth shot open almost at the same time, and the boot stepped quickly on his hand. His eyes went up above the boot to where the knife would be, and then came back to hers. She said nothing and did not move. He was frightened, she knew, but there was nothing either of them could do. She felt a meaty, greasy hand spread the cheeks of her ass, slide forward, and spread her vulva lips. She was still swollen from riding Carlos, and the hand's rough touch would still find her wet. Legs moved against her thighs and dragged along her hips. She hoped she would not get pregnant or diseased, and then the dick came into her hard, fast, and all at once. He came almost immediately. She could feel his penis pulsing and his spunk spurting inside her. If she had the knife she would happily cut his balls off and make him eat them while she watched. Carlos was immobile.

This man climbed off her. The other man who had held the blade moved behind her, out of sight. She heard his belt and zipper, and felt him squat on top of her. Two hands spread her cheeks and shoved fingers one two three rudely up her. She tried to relax but the man was too fast pulling out his fingers and then too large and she bit her lip to keep from crying out as he pushed himself up her ass so she felt stretched violently but not yet torn, then he stopped and didn't move, buried in her to his belly. She felt him twitch but he didn't come. Instead he took her hair in one hand and wrapped his other hand around her face like a muzzle, then slowly began to move her, move in her, move with her, make her move. "Now you're my little pony, girlie," he whispered in her ear. "Your ass is my saddle and I really like to ride. I want to hear you whinny for me. Whinny." She was silent. He jerked her head up by her hair so hard her whole torso rose off Carlos, and stated to slap her throat, slap her face, slap her breasts, slap her anywhere his free hand could reach, slightly at first but then quickly harder and harder till he was pummeling her and she felt real danger for the first time. "Whinny, bitch. Whinny a *lot*."

So she whinnied as well as she could in her position and the man laughed loudly in a great good humor while he rocked on top of her and his penis went even farther into her and out to the tip of its head, then in again and out, in and out. He pulled her up on all fours and slapped her flanks, slapped her ass and made her rock some more while he straddled her and did not come, going in and out, in and out. He tore the sleeve off his own shirt and wrapped it tightly around her mouth and tied it very securely, throwing her head around by the cloth as if it were a bridle. He pushed her down on top of Carlos again and pulled her hands behind her and tied them with rope from somewhere, too tightly she could tell. He pulled himself out of her, not kindly, and hauled her to her feet, holding the ropes that bound her hands. "This one's coming home with me," he said, and started to drag her away backwards. "What about the guy?" asked the man who was now holding the knife. "Kill him," the man who held her said, and just kept going. He was so strong, and moving so fast, it was all she could do to keep herself upright. Twigs and stones cut her feet and she stumbled and fell and stumbled and never saw or heard a sound from Carlos ever again.

She had fallen over and over. Sometimes he bent down and set her upright, sometimes he picked her up altogether and almost hurled her forward, sometimes he just kept dragging and she had to scramble up somehow or be ripped apart by the tree roots and fallen branches on the forest floor. She was cut and scratched and welted and when she tried to scream through he gag he hit her once, so hard her mouth was still bleeding on the cloth and down her throat. He had never bothered to put on his pants, he just carried them in the hand that wasn't holding on to her. They came to a slow, shallow riverbed full of stones, with a pathetic trickle of a creek staining the center crevice a thin, watery yellow-brown. At one point the stones gave way to a jut of dirty sand shaded by a little stand of jagged trees. He stopped, threw down his pants, and looked at her. "We're going to finish what we started," he said, but I want you to understand something first. Remember when I slapped you?" She still hated him when she nodded very slightly and suddenly his fist smashed into her belly. Everything went black, and she felt white streaks behind her eyes she couldn't see. Her gut was roiling and she wondered vaguely if she was hemorrhaging, if she was going to die.

She found she was lying on her back. She opened her eyes. He was still standing near his pants. He had knocked her at least ten feet with the punch. She felt deathly ill. He came and stood over her. "I've slapped you and I've hit you and I'll do it again if I have to. Shut up and behave and I won't have to. Got it?" She nodded. "Turn over." She struggled but she turned. He cut the rope or untied it and freed her hands. He tied the rope around her neck, loose enough so she could breathe but tight enough that he could stop her. He held the other end of the rope. "Run in place." She started to move without even thinking, stepping as well as she could, but she hurt and she was dizzy and she was very very scared. "Faster," he said and switched her ass with a thin green twig he must have taken from a nearby tree. "Faster." She tried to high-step and he laughed, swiping at her buttocks with the switch and drawing blood she knew, she could see, slapping at her breasts with his hands and they were aching, then he pulled on the rope and said "Stop."

She was panting and sweating and crying and her legs were trembling so badly she thought she was going to fall. She hurt all over and was trying not to pass out. "Get on your hands and knees." And she did. She did whatever he said. She was going to do whatever he said. She hoped she would feel differently someday, but now she felt broken and she knew she felt broken. He made her crawl around in circles on the rope he used as a tether while he switched and kicked her ass and thighs, he yanked her to him and cut the shirt sleeve from her mouth and made her lick the dust and sand and rotted leaf parts from his boots and from the soles of his boots, he sat down heavily on her face made her kiss his ass deeply and with her tongue, she could feel him try to shit but he only farted. He did not make her suck his cock. "You know why?" he asked. She shook her head. "Because you'd still bite it." He laughed at her, and then he threw her onto her back on the sand. The sand abraded her raw skin, and grains that stuck to her lips slipped into her vulva and scratched her inside. He knelt down between her legs and tugged the rope left and right and cut off her air just to let her know how precarious was her purchase on anything. He hiked her thighs up over his shoulders and then he smiled broadly and almost nicely because he was having such a lot of fun, jammed her with his fist, and swiftly sank himself into her, fucking her faster and harder than she knew a man could move. After some long relentless time she felt she had nothing left at all any more and did not even care that she was alive. She wept without restraint and knew that that was when he came, but that didn't matter either.

She was with them long enough to lose track of the progression of days in some sort of rustic cabin. Sometimes the first one, who might have killed Carlos, stuck himself into her, but mostly he didn't seem to want to bother. Often he was gone anyway. The second one used her frequently, to fuck or just to bat around. He liked to slap at her, shove her, kick her, beat her so she bruised, scourge her with branches where the stripes began to scar. He liked to watch her fall or fold into a helpless, hopeless bundle shaking at his feet and do whatever might have been demeaning in another life: crawl and beg him not to hurt her, grovel for a meal or drink of water, choose between his thick belt across her thighs or a fresh thin willow switch across her breasts. He made her piss and shit in a hole she had to dig outside while he watched, he made her drink his own piss by the glassful and eat his shit off plates for the amusement of the other man. He tied her up and stuck her under his bed at night and after a while he came home with a black steel cage built to contain a large strong dog and locked her in it to sleep and any other time he wanted to shut her out of the way. Sometimes he took her behind the cabin to what looked like an old horse trough full of cold water and put her in it and scrubbed her with a brush and soap, but each time he got distracted and ended up squeezing her breasts and ass and fucking her on the ground. One day he took her to the trough and let her bathe herself while he sat on a tree stump and told her what to wash and how. He gave her a small plastic razor and told her to shave her legs and her underarms. He gave her a brush and told her to take better care of her hair. He took her to his bed and tied a rope around her neck as he had done the first day, and held it so that he could break her neck with a finger, then he fucked her mouth for the first of many times. She never had any clothing.

One day the first man came in in a great hurry, and the two men conferred and then sat at the table. A couple of times they looked at her, huddled up against a wall. He snapped his fingers and she scuttled to his chair. He showed her again the long curved knife that he set out of her reach on the table, then pushed her face to the floor, stood up, and rested one foot on the back of her neck. She heard him remove his pants and felt him sit on her ass again. He spread her cheeks again and roughly pushed himself inside her again. He clutched her hair in one fist and bounced her head around a couple of times. "Move," he said, and she began to buck her hips. "Don't stop moving till I tell you to." She bucked and felt him thrusting in her ass. "We have to be going now," he said. "But only us, not you." She wondered if he would set her free but she saw him reach to the table top. "Keep moving," he said, moving faster himself. "Don't stop moving till I tell you to."

The world is a voluptuous place, full of attributes exciting to our human appetites. After years in the desert we hunger to see green, after hours of silence we hear music amid the motes in the air, after days of bread and water we thirst for even salt. We are made to take in data through our senses: they are made to be appeased. And where we are angels we long to see the face of God.

My Life As a Wife

Non ministrari sed ministrare (Not to be served, but to serve) — *Wellesley College Motto*

ONE: *THE COURTSHIP*

When my mother used to speak of being chained to her kitchen back in the days of six kids, three dogs, one cat, and two husbands, we all knew it was just a metaphor: her way of complaining without complaining about the meatloaf tedium her formerly champagne-and-oysters life had become. So after my neighbor Renée graduated from Wellesley and told me that she wanted me to be her wife and planned to keep me chained to her kitchen, I assumed it was a kind of family in-joke. After all, she knew my family lore just as I knew about her father's collection of pornography and her mother's fancy lingerie. As kids we'd gone trick-or-treating together, sung Christmas carols together, and even played doctor together when we were the right age, with Renée always the doctor. So I laughed when she said it, she laughed, and only days later I realized I had heard in her laughter a different note than the merry mirth I meant for her to hear in mine, and by that time I'd already accepted her invitation to visit the country house she had finally inherited from a wealthy aunt. Later still I would even remember the tone of her laughter as sinister, but I think that was just a trick of memory. Anyway, by that time I'd already become so reconciled to exactly the life she had planned for me that I wouldn't have left it even if I could. But on that lovely, fateful day in early May when I first heard her say it, I heard her laughter only as sincere and almost playful, so if I had any apprehensions I stanched them and drove far out of town the following Saturday.

I always admired Renée when we were growing up, and for awhile in primary school I used to follow her around like a sappy puppy. Maybe she thought I was kind of a pest, but maybe not: I was smart, I paid attention to her, I could carry on a real conversation, and I liked to help her do things, so in retrospect I think maybe she encouraged me. As a teen and young adult I came to look up to her moral strength and integrity, but when we were kids I just looked up at her: she was tall, yes, but she was also extraordinary to look at in other ways, and that was enough to inspire awe in me. Even as a little girl she was already large-boned, rangy, and vitally athletic, and she grew up to be the kind of woman to whom someone must certainly apply the word *handsome* every day. She had a thick mane of tawny hair and long, broad teeth she worked in her jaws as if she were constantly hungry.

By high school her lips had grown as meaty and pale as macaroons, and although she rarely wore make-up she did take to biting them deliberately until they blushed the color of fresh cream clouded with raspberries. Her wide, peat-colored eyes were so remarkably hooded they made her seem mysterious and even dangerous back then. They had also started to shade slightly yellow when she turned them up at night so they caught the moonlight, as I noticed the one time I dated her near the end of our junior year. But she wasn't turning her face up to kiss me that time: she was just watching a nightbird cross the sky.

By that time I was in awe of other things beside her looks. She liked to dance, for example, and I was in awe of the way she always wanted to lead, stalking me up as she stalked all her partners, hip to hip. She walked the same way she danced, with a lilting, hypnotic, predatory rhythm, as if she were the boss and knew it and expected *you* to know it, and I walked beside her as I danced beside her, happy to follow her lead because I liked the way she smiled when I obeyed. I didn't really put two and two together back then, or I wouldn't have been surprised when she turned out to be the first really ardent feminist in our class. In a school that worshipped football players and pom-pom cheerleaders Renée canvassed for women politicians, ran almost successfully for class president, and tried to get the quarterback to run for homecoming queen.

Attractive and extremely modern as she was, though, Renée could not have been more certain in her rectitude or more sure of herself and her opinions if she had been an old-fashioned biddy with a netted, grey-streaked bun wearing high-necked dresses and tightly buttoned high-top boots. It was as true when she was grown up as it had been when she was a child: however honeyed the tone of her speech might be, she always said what she meant and meant what she said, and the ringbolts she'd had countersunk into the stone and structural beams all over the country house were not, by the time I saw them, designed to be removed. As it turned out, the ones I noticed first emerged from the black slate moldings around the kitchen's highly varnished floor like steady, silvery eyes: one near the sink, one near the stove, and one, fitted out that day with a length of fairly heavy chain, right near the breakfast table overlooking the garden where she sat and sipped her coffee as she said to me, "Take off your clothes, my dear. I've just quit your job for you."

"Excuse me?" I croaked incredulously, although even as I spoke my heart skipped and my palms grew damp because I knew that I had heard her right.

"Take off your clothes and come over here. Your new life has just begun."

I have never known anyone who could actually disobey Renée face-to-face, and, as I said, I, for one, had never wanted to: I liked the way she smiled when she was pleased, and I liked especially to be the one who brought that insidious smile to her face. Maybe I was already in love with her, maybe that came later, maybe it doesn't matter. She had the same effect on other men. Salesmen begged to find her bargains, m'aitre d's in crowded restaurants found her intimate tables at the last minute on Saturday night. She was never uncomfortable speaking directly, and she expected results. The attitude with which she lived her life entertained her friends as much as it confused her teachers in school and angered adults then and later who thought they were supposed to tell her what to do, especially because once she'd stated her desires she didn't want to argue. She tantalized me, however, and since she'd stated her desire to have me naked now, I was not about to disobey her, anxious as I was. Her eyes shone like burnished brass while I hurried to heap what I'd been wearing onto the kitchen counter beside the sink: sweater and pants and briefs, good-bye. The socks I left in the shoes on the floor. I never saw any of them again.

When she crooked her finger at me twice I knew Renée was having fun because she never liked to repeat herself for someone else's benefit. Pleased that I could be the source of even that small pleasure for her I stepped smartly up beside the table as she rummaged through a canvas bag beside her coffee cup and removed a wide, shiny, silver-colored metal ring. I was close enough for her to touch me, and she did: she grabbed my balls – not gently – in one large, smooth, red-nailed hand and smiled up at me. Her eyes turned yellow as if I were the moon, and my mouth went dry.

"Put your hands behind your head until I tell you to move them," she said, and I, of course, obeyed. One-handed she fiddled with the ring until it popped open. She put the ring around my scrotum above my balls and closed it with a click so it fit like a too-snug cuff. She lifted the chain up from the floor and fit that to the cuff and closed it with another click. She stood and strolled insouciantly to the sink dragging the chain behind her, dragging me by the balls as well. She clicked the other end of the chain to the ringbolt there, then sat back down and took up her coffee again. "I've been waiting twenty years for this, and I'm going to like it as much as I thought I would," she said. "You can move your hands now. Walk around the room."

I did a quick perusal of her handiwork and found that everything she'd put in place was locked. I took a backward step and stammered.

"Cute," she said approvingly, "but not enough. I want to see you drag the chain now, *not* with your hands. Move farther. Get me some cream for my coffee. It's in the 'fridge."

The walk was only a half-dozen steps each way, but I guessed the ring itself weighed close to a pound and the couple feet of chain I dragged were probably four or five times as heavy even before the links reached the floor, and I had to pull another fifteen feet of it. The chain trailed behind me from between my legs like a link metal tail. It pulled on my balls as she'd obviously wanted it to do, so each time I took a step my thighs got in the way. Finally I bowed my legs to walk, and the weight of the chain pulled my balls back behind me as well as down my thighs. I was just beginning to register the way this ached, starting inside my balls and rising into my lower abdomen, then spreading out across the underside of my belly like the heat from an interminable elastic that never stops contracting. "Yes," she said, "now *that's* right."

I found the cream in a little covered green and white pitcher that said *cream* in floral script, and after I took it out I closed the refrigerator door very deliberately, trying for my own sake not to make any sudden moves. I wondered briefly what I looked like to her as I stood chained and bare-assed in her kitchen, and when I turned around with the cream in my hand I saw from her lascivious, mischievous face that she was enjoying herself immensely.

I carried the cream back just as carefully as I'd closed the refrigerator door, the chain weight tugging on my balls at every step, and when I stood before her she said, "Now: when you present things to me, kneel and bow your head just slightly, keep your back straight, and hold the pitcher or whatever it is out and up above your head with both hands, like an offering. Think of me as your Queen if you need to, and think of yourself as my slave. Or think of me as the head of this household, and think of yourself as my very old-fashioned wife, which is more or less what you are going to be. If you forget, remember how many locks are holding you that you don't know how to open, and how far we are from anyone who could hear you if you called."

In conventional terms Queen and slave were probably closer to the truth, but *wife* is the word she wanted and *wife* is what I turned out to be, and in that spirit I did just what she had said. First I thought about this house in the country where I'd attended teenage parties six and seven and eight years ago, and recalled that the closest other house before the turnoff onto what she called "My Road" was at least twenty minutes north driving flat-out with nothing in the way. I thought of what I knew about Renée and how partial she was to getting her way, and I thought it likely we were very much alone. Then I remembered how the ring and chain had looked and felt: not only couldn't I open them, I couldn't even see where they were locked: they were totally smooth, hard metal to my touch without so much as a seam I could discern. And then I got really scared and I thought of supplicating her: please, Renée, let me out of these things! Please! I'm not a slave, I'm not a wife, I'm just a guy getting started in my life! *Please!* I want to go home!

In that spirit I knelt before her and proffered the pitcher, but instead of taking it from me she took the lid off and made me tip the pitcher into her cup. In a moment she tilted my hands back into position, covered the pitcher, and said, "I'm finished. You may take this back to the 'fridge. But – " when I started to move she pulled up on the chain so suddenly and hard I squealed and fell over, clutching at myself and trying not to spill the cream. I looked up into her deep, hungry eyes from the floor where I was trying not to wince and got a terrible, terrifying chill that matched the abrupt coldness in her voice as she resumed – "but, first, don't you ever, *ever* move away from me until I have dismissed you. Second, you are to crawl both there and back. I plan to see you crawl a *lot*, everyplace, on your hands and knees, with your face to the floor. I want to see your balls in chains, dragged down between your thighs, behind your ass, I want to see you learn that you're *possessed*, a piece of *property*: that you're *my* property. So, third, when you have put the cream away and you turn around and *beg* to come back to me just as you are, naked and crawling and locked in my chains, I want to see in your supplicating face that you have started to know this is really going to be your life: that I am all you have any more and all you are ever going to have from now on, so you had better start to love it because I have no intention of *ever* setting you free." She prodded me to my hands and knees with the pointed tip of her shoe, then slapped my flank with an open hand, not playfully. "Now," she said: "go."

T WO: *THE PROPOSAL*

The life Renée promised was *not* the one I wanted. Yes, she liked to be served; yes, she had known since we were young that I was glad to serve her; and yes, she had harbored a vision of the future she wanted since even before highschool, and now that we were grown up she had decided she was going to make her dream come true.

But her dream was not *my* dream. When I say that I liked to serve her I mean I used to like to hold her coat for her, or open the door for her, or carry her books: I never wanted to disappear into the well of anyone else's world. But disappear is exactly what I did, because over the next few days and weeks and months I came to learn that what she told me as I lay grimacing at her feet was exactly true. She had taken me prisoner, in a way, and inasmuch as I could learn to collaborate in my captivity and serve her the way *she* wanted, I could find a strangely peaceful happiness. If I could not, she promised in no uncertain terms, she would make the rest of my life one long, unending misery.

From that first day I was never free to come and go again. Even when she believed, with good reason, that I had capitulated utterly and was no more or less than what she wanted me to be, I was always physically bound to her or to her house somehow, held captive by one unforgiving force or another. The chains were just the first, dramatic, and very clear example. So was the way she told the truth. Using the phone I was never allowed to even see except when she was using it, she really had quit my job for me in the very hour I was driving to her house. As she explained, she had told my boss she worked for a branch of the government she could not disclose, said that I was needed for a special assignment, and said that she was sorry I could not give notice myself or give more of it, but that I was already en route and they should not expect my return. In a voice no one would recognize she had left a similar message for my sister, who was all of my big family I had left by now. Then Renée let me approve the person she'd chosen to close up my apartment and in that way made me complicit in my own imprisonment, because while I pondered the correctness of her choice, I didn't even think to tell her No.

With more of the metal bands she liked, Renée manacled my wrists behind my back and shackled my ankles together; she chained my ankles to my balls with a short chain so I could only shuffle along with slow and careful steps, and then she hauled me around by the first heavy, long chain, using it like a leash while she acquainted me with the kitchen and pantry and made sure I knew where she kept the pots and plates and food. When she was through with that room she took me off the kitchen ringbolt and led me through her house at a pace I could barely keep, panting and stumbling for my own self-preservation. When I tried to run a little, with the quick small steps that were all my hampered state would allow, the chain pulled and swayed and beat on my cuffed balls till I began to feel ill. When Renée saw I'd realized she was moving fast to make the chain swing like that on purpose she laughed out loud, but she didn't stop. She showed me where to find the laundry and cleaning supplies, and where she kept her linens.

"You know why I'm showing you these things, don't you?" she asked as she closed the linen closet. I had an idea but I hesitated, and the pause apparently did not please her because she slapped me across the face with an open hand. I was so surprised I just stared at her dumbly and never even knew if the slap had hurt. "You!" she said, "pay attention! Why am I showing you these things?"

"Because…" I said. "Because…." I knew the answer: I just couldn't bring myself to say it yet.

"Yes? Because? Because what?"

"Because… I'm supposed to use them. Because… I'm supposed to be… your wife."

"Yes!" she beamed, "that's right! Good for you." She stroked my cheek where a minute before she'd slapped me. She even petted me for the first time, and I became greatly confused because bound and hurting and in her power as I was, I felt thankful for her display of affection. I had started to see it as her *right* to command me and slap me, as it was her right to pet me, because she had taken the right to object away from me. Blushing, I found that in some ways I was actually *glad* the rights were hers.

She must have liked my reaction because she petted me some more, caressing my face and head. But naked as I was, and with my arms trussed up behind me, I couldn't hide how much her attentions were also getting to me in another way. She saw that movement and looked down and grinned, "You like it when I pet you?" And then without letting go of the chain she moved her free hand from my face to pet my penis, instantly making me even more aroused. After a minute she turned and started to walk away again. Leashed by her chain as I was, I had no choice but to follow; but now I was also aroused and it was not only the chains that held me: in addition to her other rights she had suddenly become the woman who controlled my arousal, and like any man in thrall to that power I *wanted* to stay near her.

Renée led me into the living room whose floor I was to come to know as well as I knew the chains. In the center, a wide semi-circle of fawn-colored leather couches showed off an intricate beige Chinese rug that covered a huge square of the inlaid hardwood, right up to the granite flagstone hearth of the broad stone fireplace. Low, curved glass tables with deftly rounded corners and edges, thick enough to seem a pale sea green, were spaced before the couches so that anyone who was seated could reach one easily, and anyone who wanted to sit on the couches could pass between them. Off to the far side of the fireplace setting a half-dozen conversation chairs and small, round marble tables were casually spaced near a wet bar. On the close side, ebony end tables countered by four deep wing chairs flanked another couch, covered, like the chairs, in burgundy leather as dark as grapes. The couch and chairs were all set to face a great leaded picture window whose stained etchings and bevels showed the Goddess Diana watching over the young Endymion barely covered with a provocative robe as he sleeps in a field with his flock of sheep in the background. Dressed in a short tunic and sandals, Diana holds her long bow in one hand; a quiver of arrows shows at her back. In her other hand she holds the leashes of a brace of collared animals straining slightly on all fours out from their Mistress toward Endymion; but clearly contained and obedient as they are, these animals are naked men, not dogs.

Renée sat down in one of the chairs and used the chain to pull me to my knees in front of her, then she took my sore, weighted balls in one hand and picked up my penis again in the other.

"Hands behind your head," she said. "Move."

"Move, Renée?"

"Move your hips for me. Back and forth. Pretend you're fucking me. Wouldn't you like to fuck me? Haven't you *always* wanted to fuck me? Move your hips."

She was stroking me already as if to give me a clear idea of what she wanted, and I have to say I moved, yes I did. Her hand was firm and soft and warm and she knew exactly how and where to use it to bring me closer and closer to release, and no matter how embarrassed I was already, and no matter how embarrassed I thought I was going to become, I got harder and harder and I started to think *O Jesus! I'm going to come* when suddenly she said, "Stop," and let go of me and settled back in her chair and – smirked. She did: with a smile she almost refused to show, she was silently laughing at my baffled discomfort. There I was: naked and on my knees at the feet of this woman who literally had me by the balls, shackled ankles locked to those aching balls with chains that only she could open, she was in the midst of jerking me off and then bang! she left me hanging. My cock was twitching but I wasn't quite there yet, and there was nothing I could do to keep her touching me, and with my arms locked behind my back there was no way I could touch myself.

I groaned and pleaded and panted for a minute or two and just when I was starting to recover and take deep breaths she leaned forward again and took me in her hand again and said "Move" again and move I did – until she said "Stop" again, and so it went, back and forth for an hour or more with her stroking me hard and making me move until I was crying out and pumping my hips at her, flailing my head around and pleading with her, *begging* her to let me come, and each time she'd stop and maybe let go or maybe keep holding me, sometimes pinching the head of my penis, sometimes bouncing my balls around on the chain and watching me try to figure out how to get her to let me come, and when I tried to lean up against her like some heat-crazed dog she kicked me not too lightly with that pointed shoe, and then she kicked the chain between my balls and ankles to make it shake and jerk on me – but all this must have been part of her plan. Coming was *my* idea: in all that time *she* never even *thought* she was going to let me come. My knees were sore and my hips were sore, my shoulders were sore, my balls were extremely sore, and even my toes were sore from pushing against the carpet, my jaws hurt from clenching my teeth, and I was light-headed from all the stimulation as if I'd taken sixteen kinds of drugs and stayed up all night, and I would really, literally, absolutely have done anything, anything, *any*thing she told me to do in hopes that she would finally, at last, *please* let me come and that is when she said, "That's enough for now. We have other things to do."

I almost fell over when she let me go. I could not believe she would leave me in the state she'd taken me to, but I greatly underestimated Renée.

"Now this," she said as she took my balls and cock in her hand again and shook them till the chains went rattling merrily up and down my thighs, "this is mine and you do not get to touch it. In fact, if you ever do touch it without my permission – *ever* – I will become extremely cross and I will punish you more severely than you can imagine. But because I would prefer not to punish you I will provide some help to protect you against that unpleasant possibility. Stand up."

With some difficulty I stood. She took off the chain that held my balls to my ankles and took off the band that, with the weight of the chain, had squeezed my balls down to a tiny, tight, exquisitely sensitive package in their thin sac, and for one foolish, innocent moment I breathed in hope, thinking she had had her fun and this game was all over. But then she opened a drawer in the closest ebony table and pulled out a pliable silvery metal band, narrow with softly rounded edges. She wrapped it around my waist like a belt so it fit just above my hip bones as closely as if it had been measured just for me. From the center of the belt's back a second pliable metal band hung down with a smooth, gently curved metal gulley welded snugly to the bottom of an upright shield that was maybe just the height and width of a woman's hand laid flat. The gulley was open at the bottom rather than the top, like a cover rather than a bowl, and she pushed my partly-softened penis up into it as she wrapped the second belt under me, between my legs and up. Then, when she raised the end of the second belt to the front of the first, the shield pressed against my pubis and forced my metal-covered penis down, separating my balls from each other and forcing them apart, presenting them out to either side of the penis cover as painfully tight as drumheads and with no place to move at all. Renée tugged and patted and adjusted the belts until she was satisfied, locked the second belt to the first just above my pubic bone using one of those seamless metal locks, and flicked my tender balls with one abrupt finger making me wince. She locked a leash-length chain to the base of the shield and then she smiled one of those radiant smiles I loved.

"In fact," she said, "this is mine and you *can't* touch it." As I looked at her handiwork I could see how right she was. Except for my very vulnerable balls, now pressed out to the sides where she could reach them readily, I was entirely packed away. The second belt had a wide, smooth spread in the back of it, and the trough was narrowly open at its end so I could use the toilet. Renée had locked me in a chastity belt.

THREE: *THE ACCEPTANCE*

Maybe the real definition of a nightmare is living someone else's fantasy, and maybe the real definition of a dream is coming happily to terms with the fantasy you're in. Certainly the dream I was in belonged to Renée, and although my first reaction to my dawning awareness that I was really, truly, genuinely enslaved by my childhood neighbor and playmate was a kind of hopeless horror, I found that I was fascinated at the same time. No one in the world knew where I was except Renée, no one could hear me if I complained or yelled or cried or even died except Renée, and no one could affect my life in any way except Renée, who could affect it completely, any way she pleased. The chains were real, the locks were real, the chastity belt was real, and Renée's delight in my helpless vulnerability was so palpably real that she flushed on and off like a woman in heat. It was obvious that whether I liked my present circumstances or not was irrelevant: she did, and that was all that mattered.

Renée studied the changes in my face as I moved through each of these realizations, and when I saw that the shield she'd locked on me was etched with a single, ornate floral *R*. When at last I looked up from my bondage and met her eyes I was even further along in resigning myself to my most unusual fate. Renée neither smiled nor primped nor made any gesture I could interpret, but only stood quietly in front of me. She was wearing low stacked heels that peeked out from beneath a simple pastel floral summer dress, and a triple rope of pearls at her throat. Her unpretentious clothing made my nakedness more plain, and the casual way she held the loose end of the chain both showed the ease and grace with which she held her power over me, and emphasized the status she'd reduced me to. In just these few hours I was already far past crawling to her from the refrigerator. There was nothing for me to do but show I understood, and so, slowly, without taking my eyes from hers, I lowered myself to my knees again; then slowly, reverently, I bowed and kissed her feet, one at a time, and remained bowed before her with my face on the floor, waiting for her command.

Her command was as eloquent as her eyes. She said not a word, but after a long minute she turned on her heel and began to walk away. Without thinking, I followed her feet as I followed the leash, scampering on all fours as quickly as I could. "It's a long time since you were here last," she said as if I were a cordially invited guest. "Let me show you the grounds again." She pushed the door open and I followed her outside.

The changes I noticed most around the grounds were the new horse-head hitching posts she'd placed strategically so that when she chained me to their iron rings, as she has done over and over in the months and years since then, I could still reach to pick fruit from the small, well-ordered orchard, or tend the herbs and vegetables in the victory garden off the kitchen, or hold her towel or bring her lemonade when she swam or lounged beside the tree-shaded pool. In and around the house there were several structures she said she'd designed to use with, for, or on me, as she chose or needed to. Some of those were purely functional devices like the ringbolts and hitching posts, intended for frequent use and easy access. Others — such as the hammock-like suspensions, the waist-high padded benches, the rack of tack and miniature English saddles in the barn above the gaily painted two-seater sulky – she assured me I would learn about in time. Several items, she soberly explained, were strictly for punishment. Pointing toward a flight of stairs that led down to some sort of basement off the kitchen she said she hoped I would never have to learn what she kept in *there*.

The rest of that day and in the weeks to come Renée trained me to my new duties as her version of a wife. I learned to clean her house and wash her clothes and linens either by hand or by machine, depending on the item and material. I learned to make and serve her coffee the way she preferred. I made and served her meals and cleaned up afterwards, then bowed my face to eat from her plate that she set on the floor at her feet. I learned to wash her hands and feet, and then I learned to bathe, lotion, and massage her whole body, although, contained as I was in the chastity belt that prevented me from even getting hard, I often shivered when I set my hands on her. I learned to wait on my hands and knees and face outside the bathroom when she was using it, and to clean her, if she wished, with my lips and tongue: I learned to worship even this about her. While she stood over me I used old papers for my own indoor toilet, and outdoors I dug and filled and covered a hole with lime while she watched my discomfort and embarrassment.

And every night when she was ready for me to go to sleep she led me to a closet in the hallway near her bedroom and lay me down on a ticking-covered pallet. She chained my wrists and ankles to more ringbolts so I could not use them to reach myself. Kindly, she stroked and petted my face, and sometimes, grinning with a nearly sadistic delight, she massage and slapped at my tender balls until I cried out and screamed and begged for her to stop. Finally, she tested the lock on the chastity belt and left me, closing the door behind her. Each morning, when she was ready, she took me from the closet to the yard where I washed in a small horse trough, where she herself kept my body clean of the little hair it grew.

In this way I soon lost track of the number of days that had passed since I had vanished into Renée's life. In its outline one day was very much like the last, though in its particulars each was unique: what I picked from the garden; how I cooked; when I attended her; whether she played with me as she sometimes did by tossing the panties she'd been wearing for me to fetch and retrieve on all fours; how when I brought them to her in my mouth she would pet and praise me; how I came to know the intimate smell and taste of her until I found the very notion of the game exciting and wanted to play again; how I cringed with shame and still felt longing at the same time just to know she watched me writhe when I pushed my face into that creamy, musky lace, and knew I did not want to let it go when I delivered it to her waiting fingers; how she looked when she walked out to the car she had directed me to sign over to her and then had had repainted the opalescent silver of a cartoon moon; how she went away, leaving me alone.

Renée went away every few days for some hours. Sometimes she brought back items for the house or kitchen, sometimes she did not. Always when she went away she locked me down beyond any possible purpose but her lust, taking more precautions against my implausible escape than any team of locksmiths or horses could have freed me from in a week, it seemed, with multiple locks at every binding and hobble chains that kept my movements rigidly confined. After awhile I came to fear her ventures out, not so much because of the discomfort they subjected me to or my fear of what would become of me if for some reason she never returned, but because she had become my keeper, my owner, my mistress, my husband, my human, my something, my everything: she was the key to my life by now. Without her permission I could not feed or drink, I could not relieve myself, I could not even sleep except in a pile on the floor wherever her chains might reach. I had no one to talk to and no one to hear unless she commanded or conversed with me. It was she who played the only music I heard, or read to me or had me read to her the only words I knew of someone else's, or walked me in the gardens and orchard, or brought me any breath of life at all from beyond the silence of her walls.

For her to leave became a torture to me worse than when she chained me to a bench so tightly I could not even roll my hips and then slowly, delicately, daintily, tapped with a pair of lightweight plastic chopsticks in monotonous, relentless rhythm on my nipples, on my inner thighs, or on my chastity belt-tightened balls for such long minutes that my whole existence became a single, centered rack of agony where I lost myself in shrieking, weeping, pleading. Afterwards, sometimes, she removed the chastity belt to stroke me and pet me and make me move and bring me close again, but never, never, never to allow me the blessèd release I used to take so easily for granted. Once, early in my stay, I fell asleep on the floor beside her favorite chair when she was gone, and was ripped from slumber by an explosive wet dream in which I only kissed her fingers. When she came home and found the crusted evidence on the chastity belt she bodily threw me over her knee and spanked me with a hairbrush so long and horribly that I bled, and the bruises didn't heal for a couple of weeks; then she shackled me to the bare floor of an outhouse-sized shed off the back porch for long enough that I drained the two-gallon jug of water poised with a nipple tube beside my face, and fouled myself repeatedly. My tears and cries availed me nothing: for all I knew she had left the property entirely. Maybe two days later, maybe three, she watched me silently as I cleaned the room by hand, and took me to the horse trough to bathe. But bad as the silence was, the worst punishment by far was her disgusted look of displeasure when she first discovered my transgression. I taught myself to wake before I ever spilled again.

And still, if I had ever needed them, the bindings had long since ceased to be necessary to hold me. I was hopelessly locked down by more than chains, and if I cannot say with certainty that I had completely fallen in love with Renée quite yet, I can surely say that by that time I would have been hard pressed to leave my captivity. Prisoner, slave, chattel, or wife, the depth to which I had come to belong to Renée no longer could be measured, and all I could imagine was that she had meant for this to happen, just as it had done.

Sometime soon thereafter Renée began to use me for her sexual gratification. It started with a game of panty-fetch that, while once I had really played only for her entertainment, by now I also played for the odd erotic intimacy it brought me into with her. On the day in question she had removed the panties in my full view, which she had never done before. Although the chastity belt that doubled my ache surely prevented her from seeing the full nature of my interest, Renée understood that I had never been immune to her. Perhaps she had not intended me to be immune to this game she had devised herself. In any case, she took the panties from my mouth when I returned them to her for the third or fourth time, then sat in her chair and held them tight against my face and made me breathe through them repeatedly. If I had not been aroused before I certainly would have become so then, so when she lifted up her skirts and parted her firm thighs and commanded my mouth to her I wanted almost nothing but to obey.

Her pleasures went on and on, from the shimmering pulses in her swollen clitoris down the slopes of her soft, full outer lips to the rolling folds of her inner lips, the corrugated recesses of her vaginal walls, and the slow, rich pulsing wells that made her roll her hips and press her wet flesh flush against my face until I was glistening with her from chest to scalp. Long before she'd finished she'd come off the leather chair and pushed me onto the carpet on my back and straddled my face and ridden me as if I were some bareback racing horse. I'd heard that women had capacity to make men shamed and jealous, but I'd never known I could please someone in a way that would satisfy me so greatly. She began in the afternoon and it was dark before she finished, languorous to be certain, but also energized and clearly ... happy. Happy in a way I had not seen Renée happy in all the years I'd known her. Something in her was wonderfully fulfilled, either by the simple physical pleasure she took or by taking it this way or by taking it with me, from me. And so, although I could never predict when in the morning, afternoon, or night she would command it, some such form of sexual service became an almost daily ritual for me. Though it never included my release, I saw from the very first time that she conferred an honor on me when she permitted me to honor her like this, and each time I was overcome with gratitude.

One day when the light was getting short and brilliant as I knew it did in fall, I woke on my pallet unusually sore. I had scrubbed the house the entire day before, and then Renée whom I maybe loved had douched me and shaved me without the chastity belt. She had taken me to the orchard and cut a long, fine, narrow willow branch, then bent me over the side of a padded stool and methodically switched a stinging ladder of tight red stripes up my hot thighs and ass. She had worked my balls over till they were swollen to twice the swollen size they usually were by then, stroked and petted me and made me move for her until I fell and then made me do it again, and when she replaced the chastity belt that felt whole inches smaller than it had before, she fit a lubricated rubber plug into the hole at its rear and pushed it firmly into me before locking the belt in place. After that she used my mouth and face, and locked me up for sleep. Waking, I felt the need for every kind of release, yet I could do nothing but lie in my bonds and moon over my absent jailer.

When Renée finally came to take me to the yard I begged her openly for pity, for release of any kind, and for the very first time she granted me a boon: she agreed to take the plug out until evening, when she was to have visitors. I worked especially hard to show her my appreciation as I devoted the entire day to preparations. I set the table in the dining room for seven, with all the best she had to offer in linens, crystal, china, and silver, and I set about preparing the dinner menu I found in the kitchen in her studied floral hand. Toward the end of the afternoon she took me to my papers, washed me, replaced the plug, and sent me back to work. In the early evening's light I laid and lit the fire, and as I was polishing the last glass on the wet bar in the living room I heard a car, then two, drive up as if they arrived together; shortly after that the doorbell rang.

I removed myself to the kitchen, as Renée had said I was to do, walking carefully with the long chain limiting my immediate movements more than it limited my range in and out of the house's main rooms. I heard the front door open and close amid the music of women's voices greeting women they were glad to see, and after awhile I smelled sage burning and then delicate and pungent incenses. I heard a series of lilting chants in women's voices, and a voice that was not Renée's but spoke with similar authority. Later I heard other voices, one and many at a time, Renée's among them, and I heard more women's singing. But I understood that what was going on in the living room was not for me, and that if I were to serve Renée as well as I could it was important for me to know – and to show I knew – my place.

I had been lost for an hour or more garnishing dishes and making other final adjustments when Renée rang for me. I did not fully grasp my situation until I stepped into the living room prepared to kneel and bow as she liked me to do. Six women in addition to Renée were sitting or standing in the burgundy wing, all, like Renée, dressed splendidly in long white robes with jewels at their throats and on their hands and in their hair that glistened where they tossed the light from dozens of white tapers. A couple of the women were still talking between themselves, but all were watching my entrance. Clearly chained to the house most intimately, plugged, welted, and wearing nothing but the chastity belt that pushed my swollen balls out painfully before my thighs, I had never felt more thoroughly exposed and humiliated in my life. I fell rather than sank to my knees, and bowed to Renée with my astonished, reddening face in the rug.

FOUR: THE WEDDING

"Come," I heard Renée command, and embarrassed, ashamed, even frightened in my consternation, I made myself move forward, hand and knee, hand and knee, dragging the chain behind me until I arrived at her bare feet. I kissed each one and then stayed there, lips pressed down upon her bones because I didn't know what else to do.

"This is going to be my wife," I heard her say.

"I like the chastity belt," one woman said, and another said, "The chain's a nice touch. Do you still need it?"

"I don't think I ever did," Renée answered, walking away from my face, "but I like what it says and I can't imagine him running off and leaving those behind."

To the accompaniment of light laughter she gripped my hair in her hand the way a cat grips a kitten's scruff in its teeth and walked me from woman to woman, indicating with a slight thrust of her fingers as we came to each guest that I was to bow and kiss her feet as well, and so I did, though not as lingeringly as I did Renée's. I did not think about myself or what I was doing until the last of the women, who was seated on the couch, placed the foot I was not kissing on my head, indicating that I might not move. "Why do you bow and kiss our feet, boy?"

I had not spoken to anyone but Renée for months and months, I had not been briefed about how to answer questions the women might ask or how to address them, and Renée did not prompt me now. I had to make myself up as well as I could dare.

"Renée commanded me," I said, and added because it felt right to me then, "my Lady."

"And why do you suppose Renée commanded you?"

How was I to know? For a moment I think I panicked, wholly miserable, and then I realized I just did not want to fail Renée. The rest was suddenly very simple. What I knew of Renée was all I could rely on, so I made up an answer I thought she would like.

"You are a woman," I replied, "and I am a man. You are my natural superior, and I am your natural servant. I am Renée's … wife, and I hope to honor her by honoring her guests. My Lady."

The woman moved her foot from my head and I scuttled close to Renée. I leaned against her and held onto her legs as if I might in some way hide from the woman who had questioned me. I was abruptly aware of the red marks Renée's switch had left on me, as if they still hurt and as if they mattered. Then I was very aware of the plug. And the belt. And my nakedness. And my physical position on the floor.

"That's a very pretty speech," the woman said. "I like a male to know his place."

I heard assent from among the women, but buried in the loose folds of Renée's skirts my face was burning. She took me by the hair again and led me to the woman whose feet I had first kissed, standing close to the Diana window. "Repeat what you said to my other friend," she said. Again I bowed from my hands and knees.

"You are a woman and I am a man," I said to her shoes. "You are my natural superior, I am your natural servant, my Lady."

I got no further when Renée pulled me by the hair again, leading me around the room again, and when I had proclaimed my subordination to every woman there she took a seat beside the fire and took my head in her lap and caressed me as I had longed for her to do all day. I could not help myself, and trembled as if in fright, but it was not fright: it was my pleasure at her slightest touch. At last she told me to kneel up, brushed my face, and smiled that smile at me: *at me.* How could my heart be glad when I had just abased myself before a roomful of strangers? But I had done so at her command, and so it was: my heart was glad. I smiled up at her, and if I had not been in love before I certainly did fall in love forever with Renée at that moment.

I had forgotten that whom the gods would ruin they first raise high.

Laughing and talking among themselves the other women formed a loose group that was more an oval than a circle, all of them facing into it and the woman who had questioned me first standing closest to the Diana window at what appeared to be the oval's head. The other women seemed to wait for her or follow her lead, and when they had become so quiet that the only sound was the evening wind outside it was she who broke the human silence.

"We have a purpose here tonight that requires our serious attention," she said. "Our sister Renée proposes to take this male to wife, and has asked us six to witness, approve or disapprove, and celebrate the outcome of our mutual decision, whatever it may be.

"Most of the work for this ceremony has already been performed, so we can keep this last part brief. Each of us has sought in solo ritual and its subsequent meditation the protection and advice of the goddess spirits closest to her heart. Together we have met and asked protection and advice from the goddess spirits who guard the four portals, the heavens and the earth, the worlds outside us and within us. We have purified the space and purified the moment, and each of us has given her reply.

"Now the time for the final ritual has come."

At that Renée rose from her chair and, gripping me by the hair as she had done when she led me around before the women, walked into the center of the circle where she pushed my face down and let go of my hair. Slowly she turned in place, as I could see by watching her feet, facing each woman one by one. Then she came to rest facing the woman I had come to think of as the Priestess.

"This could be the moment for a long narration," she said, "describing my history, which you all know, or telling about the choice that seems to have been made for me long ago. I could tell you tales about this male, or why it is he and not another. But apart from what you already know I think that those are data for the personal conversations we will have in time, I with you who are my sisters. At this time, here in this circle, it is enough to say that I have made my choice, to thank you for your considerations, and to learn what all of that might mean."

Renée bent down and with a motion I could not discern, or with a key I had not seen her take from anyplace, she unlocked the chain from the chastity belt and let it fall to the floor between my feet. "Up," she said, and I knelt up for her. She unlocked the chastity belt itself and gently let it pull away as the room's air cooled my crumpled genitals. As it always did, my awareness of this little freedom rushed on me like blood. I shuddered and wanted to weep with loud relief, but she pushed me forward at the shoulder and I bowed again while she pulled the plug out of me and folded it away in a bag nearby.

"Stand." I stood, a bit uncertainly. Turning me this way and that she looked me up and down, into my eyes, at my face, at my body, at the stripes she'd left across my ass and the backs of my thighs, at my poor penis and balls hanging out before me. Then she turned and walked away from me, out of the circle and into the foyer. Immediately I felt frightened, but I watched her instead of the other women, and I held my tongue and kept my place. I heard her open the big front door and felt a bite of autumn evening wind. The flames on all the candles flared and danced, and she returned to stand in front of me.

"Get out," she said. "Go away just as you are, naked and free. Take the car – the key is in the ignition, there is money on the seat, and there's a suitcase full of clothes in the trunk. Make your way, live any life you choose, and never let me hear from you again."

I felt a vast hole tear open the pit of my stomach, I broke into a cold sweat, and my legs began to shake. Then she resumed, "Or else go close the door on all of that forever, and come back on the floor, as abject on your hands and knees as you know how to be. Crawl to the inside of this circle and pass every woman's feet until you fall before me prostrate with your empty palms up, showing me and all these women that you freely choose the life I've shown to you: subject to my will, obedient to my command, to serve me on your honor, mine to have and hold and use as I wish as long as you may live. And then if I do not walk away from you, you may beg me to take you as my wife."

Could there have been a choice for me? Maybe, once, before the day I'd come to visit her. But now what she asked was nothing, because there was nothing I'd have stopped at to remain where I had come to belong. I did not even question why. I simply turned from her and walked to the door, closed it firmly, and turned the bolt to lock it. I wanted to take no chance that anyone could misunderstand. Then, there on the literal threshold of her home, I knelt and bowed across whatever the distance between us might still mean, and proud as I was to be who I was and where I was, doing what I was doing, I crawled as abjectly I could, glad in my heart to pass back across the stone floor of the foyer, onto the carpet and into the circle of women, around past each one till I came to rest hands up on my belly at her feet.

A moment passed and then another, but she did not go away. Finally I stretched my fingers out and touched her toes, and pulled my face up far enough to speak. "Please, Renée, I come to you as you commanded me to do, naked and free, to ask you to let me love, honor, and obey you, to be the wife you want to have and hold and use as you wish as long as I live. Please, Renée, I beg you to take me as your wife."

After another long moment I felt her hand in my hair and she raised me up. A woman from the circle handed her the chastity belt, which she locked once again where it belonged. She made me use my mouth to place the chain end in her hand and I was taken aback by how very heavy it was to my unaccustomed jaws and head. When she locked it to the bottom of the belt I never knew if the groan that escaped me was at the burden of its weight, or at my joy that all the questions were at an end. For the first time ever she wrapped a collar around my neck, and as if it were a ring, the woman I thought of as the Priestess said, "I now pronounce you woman and wife: you may do whatever you wish to with the bride." There was the general laughter of release and Renée said, "Serve the food and serve my guests. I will do exactly what I want with you when I am good and ready." Amid more laughter I crawled from the room.

In the foyer I stood and started to make my way back to the kitchen. In the hall I passed the guest mirror I rarely saw because I came to the front hall so infrequently, but now I stopped before it and looked at myself, naked, belted, and chained as I have described. My hair was awry, my face was streaked with tears and sweat, the switch stripes were still quite red across my thighs, but I was no longer hot, nor blushing with fear, embarrassment, or shame. I felt secure, proud to be exactly where I belonged. I saw my balls protruding from beneath the belt's shield and almost touched them but caught myself in time. Now I was a wife indeed. I went on to the kitchen.

FIVE: THE HONEYMOON

Was dinner uneventful, or merely anticlimactic? Or did I miss whatever was important because my head was in the night-time clouds? I know I brought hors d'oeuvres and then refreshed the women's drinks. I know the women came to table and in order, with wines, I served them chestnut soup made silken with tofu; fresh fettuccine tossed lightly with shiitakes and truffle shavings; tiny perch from Renée's own pond bathed quickly in hot shallot oil; a roast with jeweled baby peas and carrots; arugula salad almost as naked as I was;

chocolates and tarte tatin with coffee and teas; cheeses and brandies and ports.

I know I left the kitchen to clean in the morning because Renée wanted to feed me before her guests: to show them how I crouched between her feet for her, haunches in the air and face in her leavings, for no reason but that she desired it. She played a round of panty-fetch with me for the women's amusement, and kept me after for her footrest while the evening talk wound down. Someplace in the midst of things she took me to use the papers and announced her agenda so deliberately beforehand I knew she intended to shame or test me in her speech, and, when two of the women followed us out to the porch professing curiosity, I knew she intended to shame or test me in my performance as well. Like some conquering potentate she used the occasion of her wedding to compel repeated demonstrations of my absolute surrender to her absolute authority, and I think therefore I must have missed much of what transpired because my emotions were confused, caught in the straits between the Scylla of my embarrassment and chagrin, and the Charibdis of my unspeakably proud happiness.

Is it strange to read that I felt proud and happy? We are raised in this society to believe that we want freedom, yet everywhere people are, as they have always been, eagerly yet unhappily enslaved, and they do not even know it: they are slaves to their bosses and slaves to their jobs, slaves to their families and slaves to their possessions, slaves to their passions and slaves to their desires, slaves to their notions of decorum and propriety, slaves to their religions, slaves to their politics, and slaves to all the other unexamined prejudices they call ideas but that make their every thought and word and move and deed as predictable and manipulable as they are baldly programmed.

But I was no longer ignorant: I knew the nature and context of the life I chose. Free of all that history, I had both knowledge and fortune on my side. Renée had showed me exactly what my life could be, and when she offered me the door I knew exactly why I declined to go. I closed the door to keep our precious moments safe. I bolted the door to keep the sorry world at bay. I no longer had the stomach or heart to live the lie of freedom that was not free. In begging her to let me be her wife, I begged Renée for freedom in her chains; and as Renée has *always* loved me, even when I was just a child in awe, she granted this life to me.

We are also raised in our society to believe that it is and ought to be a man's world, but what have men given us but war and ravages, domination of the small by the brute force of the large, a planet despoiled and dying with every bite we eat or breath we take or mile we travel, murderous religions of despair derived from politics of greed, art that's rarely more than commerce, and commerce that's the root of those religions? As a class we men have not done well in our chosen careers as leaders, and as a class we are too desperate to see what grim horrors we have really done, or what abysmal charlatans in some fantastical heaven's name we've willingly become. Not only did Renée give me my freedom, she let me lay this foolish burden down. And so I did pass through the straits unharmed, and left chagrin, embarrassment, and shame behind. I was proud she'd chosen me, and happy to have this unexpected life with her.

In time the guests departed, and as the two groups took their leave Renée walked the women to the door, leading me on a braided leather leash she clipped to the collar as if I were some favored Borzoi or a hound-man from the Diana window, and I followed more than willingly. When the last woman had walked off down the path among the scents of jasmine and star magnolia and echoes of honeysuckle from the day, the night had grown still and almost wintry cold. Departing headlights curled and disappeared and left us, one standing, one kneeling, and both shivering in the dark beneath very bright stars that were less like little jewels stuck in the spirit of kitsch on a teenaged giant's black velvet ceiling than they were like the light of the biblical heaven shining down through uncountable holes in the cosmic colander turned upside down to spill night over us like comfort. I pressed my cheek against Renée's thigh while a little figment of a moon sidled through the orchard on its side, ruffled at its curve like the lacy edge of Renée's inner lips. When I looked up at her, Renée was already looking down at me.

"So, wife, I've made an honest boy out of you at last."

"I'm sorry if I was slow, Renée. I didn't even know I was lost till you found me." In the time it takes a falling star to vanish I was overcome so much by love and gratitude I had fallen on my face for her. My arms were wrapped around her ankles, my hands were clutching up her calves, my lips were on her chilly feet which I kissed and sought to warm with my grateful breath. My body hummed in what was now a familiar wave of spasms, and when it settled down Renée pushed at me with one toe.

"Up," she said with a gentle smile. "You did very well tonight, and I have something yet to do with you."

I knelt but she shook her head, and when I stood as she indicated I should do, she did the most remarkable thing she had ever done to me till then: she put one arm around me, bent, and with her other arm caught my legs up and out from under me. I threw my arms around her in a simple fear response and found that I was lying in her arms. I sank back into her and she stepped forward, carrying me across the threshold. Inside she kissed me as I lay against her chest, and I melted happily into her. Only after she took her mouth from mine and I opened my eyes to hers did she set me down on hands and knees to close the door. Then, leashed again, I followed her to the sill of the main floor bathroom, where she tethered me to one of those ubiquitous ringbolts. "I think you're probably tired," she said softly. "You may lie down till I come out." I sighed appreciatively to the closing door and all but fell into a pile.

Renée must have been in the bathroom for a longer time than usual, and I must have drowsed or dozed because a sudden light from the open door and her rending cry of angry dismay startled me from somewhere.

"*You do not have permission!*" she shouted down at me, "*You may not betray me on a night like this!*"

I was still befuddled, dazed and remembering myself and where I was as if I had been dreaming something when I realized simultaneously and scrambled to my knees and pulled my hand away I had insinuated fingers underneath the belt somehow and somehow had been touching, however slightly I could reach, my penis as I had been prohibited from doing.

Immediately I knew the depth of my treason. Immediately I knew the trouble I had found.

"No!" I cried worthlessly, falling back face down upon her feet. "No please! I was asleep, I didn't mean to, I didn't know!"

She pulled away from me as if my lips were dirt, grabbed the leash from the ringbolt and marched herself off as if in a fury with me stumbling on my knees and toes and hands behind her, all the way crying tears of despair that I had betrayed her and betrayed myself. I felt so destitute that my little shames before her guests seemed contemptible now, and petty. I had lost control of myself and thereby become a traitor to us both.

Renée led me through the house and out the kitchen door, down the stairs to the isolated room she once had warned me about. She kicked at the hewn-wood door that was braced by iron bars and shoved it open with her fist. She took away the leash and threw me to the floor by my hair, hissed at me, then flipped a switch that lit the room in harsh, white, cold, bright light. There were no windows I could see, and the door was heavy as a wall. I did not know what had kept it closed before, but now Renée braced it shut from the inside with a plank as thick as a castle rafter. Against the stone walls of the room I saw the frame of a medieval torture rack, updated to stand on end and stripped of the wheel that made it infamous, so it could stretch and expose a victim but never rip him into quarters. Renée pulled me up and strapped me to the rack at my chest, wrists, ankles, thighs, and upper arms. From an iron hoop suspended from the ceiling that had once been a pillar candelabra, she selected from among a dozen or more one whip with many tails and a second with just one, and vigorously started to beat my back. At first I winced, and in a very short time I pled; soon I started to yell, then to shriek and curse, and then to cry, and all the while I was begging for her mercy.

She must have liked to hear me beg because she told me to beg some more and just kept scourging me with the flogging whip, grunting with fierce effort as she brought it down left and right across my shoulders and my back and cut me in between bouts with the snake. I begged and begged though my rasping throat, I made myself hoarse with begging to please her, and when I was so broken and hysterical I couldn't even do that I just hung limp against the rack with tears and snot all over my face, gasping and barely even bothering to breathe.

At last she laid the whips aside. She was panting and sweating herself when she unwrapped the straps and turned me around. She took my muddy face in one hand and for a moment I thought she meant to caress me, then she slapped me with her other hand with such force my head would have snapped had she not been holding me.

She opened the door and turned off the lights and started to drag me away by the leash. With what little will I had remaining I struggled to follow the woman I loved back up the stairs, through the house, to the closet that was my bed. She threw me in and didn't even bother with the chains but just slammed and locked the door behind me. I heard noises, but I couldn't be certain what they were.

I have never experienced a worse night ever in my life: sore in body but not nearly so sore as I was in heart; despondent beyond my ability to cry; cold, bereft, and left alone with my recognition that what I had done might have cost me everything I loved, everything I had become, and everything I had earned so dearly. I moaned, I'm sure, and whimpered or sobbed. I must have slept because my mouth felt foul and my eyes felt gritty when I recognized the short, wan stripe of light that marked the floor at the closet door and meant that dawn had passed and morning had come to Renée's house. I waited and waited and waited, and my great reward was to hear Renée's footsteps as she approached the closet, and then to hear the sound of her key in the lock. When the door swung open I was already bowed with my face where her feet would appear, and I could most certainly cry again.

IX: THE MARRIAGE

"I do not wish to hurt you ever, in this kind of way at least," Renée said to me when she had placed her coffee cup back in its saucer on my outstretched palm. She was dressed in an icy lace, all brilliant white with a faint blue under tinge, and it seemed to soothe the air that felt hot around my beaten body. "I get no pleasure from it: quite the contrary, it's hard work. I wasn't even angry, just surprised. I'd thought you learned your lesson months ago, when you had that dream without permission. But last night you became forgetful again, and even if it was a minor lapse, and even if it did occur in a moment of exhausted sleep, you must understand that there is never, *ever* any excuse for you to disobey me. Ever. Even if I don't want to punish you it is sometimes my job to do so, and I take my job as seriously as I take my marriage. Keeping you in line is one of the ways I take care of my wife, and I am perfectly willing and able to bring you to your senses when I must. But what happened last night was only the first level of punishment that could befall you now that I have taken you in ceremony. I would prefer never to show you the second, but I will not have you be unruly. Do you understand me?"

"Yes, Renée," I answered in a whisper even I could barely hear.

"The explain to me what you understand."

"You are right, of course. I know that as your wife I must obey you without lapses. I know that is what pleases you, and pleasing you is what I want to do. Pleasing you is *all* I want to do. I regret I caused you pain through my disobedience, and I am ready to accept whatever further punishment you choose."

Earlier that morning Renée had taken me out of the closet without anger, violence, or even a trace of evident rancor, but rather in the soft way sorrow can make some people gentle. Wordlessly, she had led me to the trough, removed the collar and chastity belt, douched me deeply, and bathed me carefully, shaving my small growths of hair as she went and cleaning my wounds without exacerbating them. After she dried me off she put the collar around my neck again, and instead of the chastity belt she locked on my balls the same metal cuff she had locked on me the day I first came to her. Then she wrapped a different belt around my waist that was made of leather and sported metal circles like the ringbolts she had all around the property, and closed a matching set of narrow cuffs around my wrists. She led me to the kitchen, which was full of last night's unwashed memories, and listened to Gregorian chants while I cleared some space and prepared the breakfast she commanded me to serve in this unusual posture.

"I know you are sorry, and I know you want to obey me. Otherwise I would never have called you to me in the first place. I've known who you are for years, even while you were busy trying to figure out what was wrong in your male world."

"But now I am your wife."

Renée's smile emerged from deep behind her facial mask the way a slow sun comes out from behind long clouds, and then she did the second most remarkable thing she had ever done to me till then. As I knelt before her with her coffee cup on one hand and her muffin plate on the other, naked and collared and cut and bruised and weary from the beating she had given me and from my grief and from the lack of sleep my torment had demanded, she leaned forward and kissed me like a bride again. She took my mouth with her mouth, opening my lips with her lips and entering me with her tongue, rolling my own tongue around with hers, and nipping at my lips with her teeth. I clutched at her with my mouth and somehow I did not drop the plates although I trembled and started to cry again, and when I opened my eyes she was looking directly into them.

"You *are* my wife, you know."

"I know, Renée."

"And you wouldn't be here if I didn't love you."

"I know that too, Renée. Thank you."

"Or if you didn't love me."

"I do, with my heart, my life, my soul. I have loved you since at least the day I saw you as a child, although I only came to understand that here, locked in chains to your home and your life. As I begged of you last night, so I beg again, to love you always, to honor and obey you."

"It is the only way for me."

"And so it is the only way for me as well."

She took a piece of muffin from the plate and held it to my mouth, and then another. I fed and nuzzled her fingers till she had me suck them free of crumbs.

"Put those down," she said, indicating the plates and cup, so I set them on the table. "Come," she said, and so I crawled behind her.

Renée led me to the living room and back to the wing with the Diana window. A towel mat was folded on the carpet in front of her favorite chair, but it didn't make me wonder till she had me kneel before her on it. She had me lift my wrists up to my waist and locked the cuffs to belt rings at the back of my hips so I could not use them; she kissed me again; and then she did another remarkable thing, that would have been the most remarkable thing she had ever done to me till then if she had not kissed me twice in the past twelve hours. She poured some lotion in her hands, then took my balls in one hand and my penis in the other. "Remember this?" she said, and when I nodded she said "Move."

There was only one thing for me to do. I started to sway forward and back with my knees and hips, moving my sex in her lotioned hand as I grew hard the way men are supposed to do for women.

"Move more," she said. "Move faster. More. Faster. More. Faster."

"Oh, please, Renée, I won't be able to stop, I can't ...."

"Then you may come," she said, and I looked up at her as my mouth fell open, I shouted and cried out and I fell against her, my body erupted in her hands, I fell on the floor, I rolled around, I pressed myself into her sweet, wet palm, and I came and I came as I felt a world of pain released in me deep down and out, and still I came or thought I did because even as my hips were moving as she wanted them to do, out of my control, even then I was struggling up to reach her, kneeling with my face in her lap, sobbing with relief and thanking her and thanking her and oh! I knew she had let me come as if she had deflowered me as a virgin on the far end of our wedding night, and the towel she had placed for me to come on was her evidence like bloodied sheets, and the release that she permitted me she also took from me as yet another seal on my compact as her wife because I knew without her telling me that it was her pleasure and not mine that mattered, and that as long as I lived I would only ever come when she, not I, decreed.

She let me down to the floor again where I fell for a timeless time into a dreamless slumber. I woke to feel a different towel, damp and soft and warm, sponging off my thighs and genitals and belly, and I lay still, watching while she took the cuffs and then the belt away. With a gesture she let me know she wanted me to kneel.

"Do you know why you were allowed to come?" she asked.

"It must have pleased you to permit me."

She stroked my cheek. "Despite your lapse last night you are generally very apt." She replaced the chastity belt and then she did an even *more* remarkable thing, the very most remarkable thing she had *ever* done to me till then. Keeping me on my hands and knees she took hold of the collar at my neck with her hand and led me by it out from the living room and across the hall into her bedroom and to the foot of her bed where suddenly directly in front of me I was facing a heavy black steel cage with its gate standing open like a menacing invitation. It was long enough for a man to lie down in but only high enough to kneel in, not to stand. The green corduroy cushion on the bottom of the cage and the white water-filled bowl braced to the bars in its far corner both bore my name in contrasting colors and in the same floral script I'd seen on her menus, on the chastity belt, and first on her cream pitcher many months ago. She let me stare, though there was no need to understand exactly who and what the cage was for.

"Do you like it?" she asked.

Like it? I was completely taken aback. How do you say you like your jail? My mouth and throat were dry and I could hardly speak. "I.... I.... It's very ... pretty," I replied.

"Good. I want to keep my wife close to me, so I want you out of that closet and in my bedroom, as long as you behave. It's your new room. Get in."

Crawling like a docile animal into a cage another person owns is not the same as entering a room or even being shut up in a closet. The meaning bars impose is different than the meanings of a wall or door, and the fact that you are imprisoned is only part of it. From a cage you can see out from your prison, so you can see how small your jailer makes your space in the space of the bigger world. There is no place to be where you cannot be seen, and so, in a way, even when you are alone you are always watched, and when she is physically present you can even see that you are watched, as well as when, how, from where, with what attitude, and by whom. You can see your jailer close the gate and turn the keys that close the locks, all while looking into your helpless eyes. It altogether changes the nature of confinement, to be caged, and when, as in Renée's bedroom, mirrors are extensive parts of the décor, you even become your own witness to your own imprisonment, seeing as if through another's eyes that, nevertheless, are still your own, exactly how you appear to the woman you love when, because it is her preference, you are always naked and always collared and always wearing a chastity belt while crawling about on your hands and knees in a space that is barely big enough to turn around in and is surrounded everywhere by solid iron bars where you have agreed out of love and a passion to serve her that you will live for as long as she desires.

I knelt up so I could hold those bars and stared out at Renée who was lounging on her bed. Within the chastity belt I could feel I was aroused by the look in her eyes, and even, now, by the feel of the belt. Yet, I knew that made no difference. I longed to feel her hand on me, I longed to touch her skin with my fingers, I longed to smell her close to me, I longed to kiss her, I yearned for her so far away across the room and I must have looked as plaintive as I felt because I saw that she was smiling more and more happily. Never letting my eyes leave hers, slowly I sank down on the cushion as my hands slid down to the lowest of the three cross-bars. I gripped that bar and just as slowly lay down, using my folded arm for a pillow, and stared and stared and stared at Renée, who looked back at me saying nothing. The sun moved slowly across the sky and shadows moved slowly across her room and just as slowly they moved across mine. This was indeed the life that she had planned for me, and I was indeed the special kind of wife she said she had always wanted.

I Bow

I bow
The Master bows
I bow
The Master bows
Have I attained
Enlightenment?
The night sky
Shines with stars.

O Christ, I thought, she's at it again.

I left the poem on the refrigerator, stuck there with an ancient, rusted magnet of Divine in *Pink Flamingoes*, and hiked down to the boathouse to find Lurline. She'd been losing her mind for four or five years now, and episodically her rambles led her through some thickets of Zen practice. Last time she raked the entire quarter-mile of driveway to a fare-thee-well, so that nary a rock nor grain of sand was out of place for all that length till Roto-Rooter came and sent dust flying everywhere. I thought she'd be despondent but she sat by her rake and smiled radiantly while the guy with the snake plumbed the bowels of the house, and when his truck was gone she stayed cross-legged on the lawn all night.

The boathouse was maybe half a mile away, down across a bunch of lawn and through a stand of beech and maple, flanked by weeping willows full of tiny translucent worms that hung by thin wet threads of gluey saliva till you entered their domain. Then in the tent of the willow branches they stuck to your clothes and hair and skin as if you

---

were going to be lunch for some very, very, very large spider. I forgot about the worms in my plunge to find Lurline and became entangled with a feeling of disgust that made me want to retch. This of course was my own damn fault for failing to keep tabs on her, but I had the property to care for, and the help to manage, a job to hold, and a girlfriend whose grown-up kids would like to see me drown. The least she could do is keep tabs on herself.

Beyond the curtain of worms the ancient boathouse looked more like a boatwreck, sagging down into the water's lap, showing its rotting planks through peeling paint that must have once been white simply because all boathouses were white in this part of the world. What of the window glass remained, jagged where deliberate rocks or inadvertent canoe bows had broken through, was greasy black with cobwebs, or speckled with some yellow-green lichen that assumed vaguely entomological forms and glowed in the dark, or spray-painted with faded adolescent notions of pornography such as spurting sticks and the sort of gash slashes drawn only by people who tell but do not know.

And there in the sand with her feet in the water sat my skinny, wrinkled, spinster sister, naked but for the grey rope of hair that hung like a wrung wet mop exactly down her entire spine to her coccyx.

"Jesus Christ, Lurline, it's March: you'll catch cold like that."

"March starch cold mold."

"Well, have you seen God yet, then?"

"Larch parch gouache menarche. Bold fold gold hold polled rolled sold tolled voled wold."

"Gouache?"

She pointed to a very high, wholly silent jet slicing across the morning sky with the precision of a computer-guided laser scalpel. It left a contrail line that devolved into a series of puffs that degenerated very softly into a long fat squiggle and then began to fuzz out at the edges growing indistinct and merging slowly with the early cirrus still clotting the upper airway, just the way a patient hopes his surgical incision will disappear into skin, just the way we lose our desires for sex, just the way we lose our minds and, if we're lucky, our lives. Here on earth nothing breathed, it seemed, until a pointed bird shot like an arrowhead from one worm-infested tree to another and got caught in a curtain of threads. For a handful of seconds it thrashed around like the fly invited into the spider's den, and then broke free. It headed off to somewhere else, and when I looked back at Lurline she was pointing a finger straight at my heart.

"I've been meditating for forty years and you want to make an aphorism of me."

"Oh my dear, I don't want to make anything of you. I just want you to stop wandering off in your skinny when the difference between the temperature and your age could vote all by itself. It's no fun for you when you're sick, and it's sure as shit no fun for me. Come on back to the house and put on some clothes and I'll make you a cup of tea."

"A pot. I want a whole pot."

"A pot then. Yes, a pot."

"Darjeeling."

"Darjeeling. Yes. Anything. Just get up and let's go."

"You don't care about me and my tea, you just want me to do what you say. You're trying to bribe me."

"Yes, Lurline, I'm trying to bribe you. I'm also offering to make you some tea and trying to keep you from getting sick. Bashō wouldn't have sat in the water naked at this time of year."

"How do you know what Bashō would or wouldn't have done? Have you been holding out on me?" But she was standing up, which was the first important part. I wished I'd thought to bring a towel or a blanket or something. Whatever once was cloth in the boathouse was too diseased or infested or molded or falling apart to even consider, and I wasn't wearing a jacket either. She turned toward the house and me and I was struck all over again at how amazingly naked her grey bush made her look. I'm of an age myself where I know from first-hand experience that we all get a little thin down there when we get quite that grey, and yet Lurline had a mop-colored mop as thick as the hair on her head and it made all the rest of her look as fragile as a dried-up washed-out stick that's been tumbled on the seashore for a hundred years. I opened up my arms and she came into them like a timid little girl. I chafed her back and arms in order to restore some circulation, then walked her around the worm trees, across the scrofulous, neglected lawn, and up the seven haggard wooden steps to the door of the old Great House.

"And lemon. I want lemon with my tea."

I opened the door for us. Some days it hardly seemed worth it to just keep going on.

Moon

oonlight woke me, silent, pale, passing through the window like water that is not there, passing across the glass like a ghost ship passing across the moon, passing like these last minutes of the night, last nights of the year, last years of my life, passing without a cloud.

Behind me, also lying on his side, my sleeping lover wraps his arms around me, pulls himself up close to spoon. I feel his knees beneath my knees, his thighs beneath my thighs, as if I'm sitting on his lap lying down, his broadly sculpted athlete's arms around my graceful poet's chest.

I feel his penis stiffen, wide and muscular, like a third thigh at my back, and then his breathing deepens, the way the moon gets darker when I cannot keep my eyes from closing into sleep. He is awake. I watch the moon in its slow trajectory across the pane. His strong hand falls across my hip, his long fingers reach down softly, softly close around my balls as if he's protecting a bag of bubbles. He splays them, dandles them like spun sugar candies in their bag that's soft like eyelids, lifts his fingers to match the delicate length of my own penis hardly thicker than his thumb. His second hand moves beneath me, spreads my cheeks, and makes me moist as if he kissed me open with his tongue, wider and wider for that part of him that now, in gentle increments, replaces his fingers, his hand, and enters me with a mind of its own, thick as an animal itself. I feel him moving farther into me like moonlight entering the room, like nothing that is everything. He fills me the way the moonlight fills the room until I can see each piece of furniture, each article of clothing, every sepal and petal on every one of the dozen white roses he left for me to say I love you, just the way he fills me till I feel tears overflowing, running down my cheeks into the pillow case. I am so glad of this bright moon.

I feel him everywhere. There is no room left anyplace in me. When he begins to move my hips on him his forearms lift me by themselves, raising me toward the moon and pulling me back until I'm lying on his lap again, pierced utterly, pierced through, pressed so deep his very lap is in me. He lifts me toward the moon again and when he pulls me back to him I feel he is the moon come up and out of me to light the room, the sky, the night. He lifts and pulls and lifts and pulls until the night passes into dawn, the moon becomes a pale witness slyly leaving sleeping dogs to lie, and I would fall asleep again to the gentle rhythm of his love when in a small frenzy he shakes the whole of me on his excited moment and the fading moon just shatters into stars.

Red Nails In the Sunset

It is all unconscious, he knows, unintended, yet it sometimes seems to be deliberate: the way she hides any bit of information, no matter how irrelevant or innocuous: speaking of individuals in the plural so no person's sex or gender can be discerned; lunching with "a friend" as if there is mystery afoot although if he inquires it turns out to be always the same friend; going "shopping" but never saying where or for what.

She does not mean to be secretive, or so he thinks: she is just hidden. Maybe it's a female function, like keeping nearly all her arousal and release within herself, so very unlike him and other men who stain their underwear, their pants, their worlds with even unfulfilled excitement – it's enough to make a preacher howl.

She comes home late again, according to his lights, some hours after he'd said that he'd arrive. Out the living room window the sun is just about to dip into the last layer of horizon-bound clouds, and light is already spreading up and down and out in Deco rays and shafts. Of course she'd be befuddled, even miffed, and rightly, if he should mention this, since she'd not said a word about her own arrival time and he'd neglected to ask, as he always did, assuming she'd be home about the same time he was if she didn't tell him otherwise. He believes that he will never learn to ask, any more than it will ever occur to her to volunteer. He knows this discrepancy does not bode well for them, but he also knows it will take awhile for one of them to wear down – probably himself. She swings the door open and doesn't even see him, sitting in the living room in his cozy easy chair, his

---

stockinged feet up on the dog that wags its tail and strains to bark and run and greet her but knows better than to move just now, a dark hardback book without a jacket and stained with a jumble of rings where drinks have been set down on it shut over his long slender fingers. He peers at her in the foyer over the dwindling ice cubes in his lowball glass. She puts a couple of parcels on the floor and fingers her key from the loose, once-jimmied lock, puts it in her purse, shuts the door, shuts the purse, picks up the bags and boxes, and is on her way.

"Good evening, Love," he says softly, so as not to startle her.

"Oh!" she says deliberately, like a matron auditioning for the ingénue part in a B-movie that will never be made. She turns her head toward him at exactly the same pace that she opens her small mouth into a single, lonely, perfect vowel. He sees her red lips pucker, how the dark skin crinkles and purses, moist beneath the bright red lipstick she likes to wear. He thinks of her other dark skin, crinkled and pursed, moist and puckered, and sets his book down underneath his glass so the condensation will not stain rings on the dark mahogany piano. He moves his feet and the dog, released, bounds forward, prancing and yipping around the woman who feeds and walks her. He comes forward and relieves her of her packages, all but the one she clutches to her bosom. He sees how the pale box presses the black silk jacket back into the red silk blouse, back into the red lace lingerie, back into the warm flesh he knows is yielding when she lets him touch it with his thankful fingers, his smooth, inquisitive palm. He thinks of the dark skin there, crinkled, pursed, and puckered but not moist unless she lets him touch it with his lips, his tongue. All of a sudden he wants to cry: to give up hope, and with it all the tension in his body, not just the tension of the stressors in his life the doctor warned about, but even the tension that holds his body up, the tension that holds the parcels in his hand, that holds his hand in its peculiar shape, that holds his arm up, that holds his head up on his neck. He wants to cry and fall down in a puddle, melting like the wicked witch of the west, like a sno-cone, like a fancy candle, like a cube of butter worshipping the sun. He is the east, and Juliet is the sun.

The sun has disappeared in the living room window. It throws its light upward from beneath the horizon leaving golden clouds magenta mauve and rose backlit with orange and fiery red. He falls down on his knees. He lets himself go and slides to the floor, her parcels splayed around him like the legs of a spine-shot fawn. His knees don't hold him either, and he slides the rest of the way. He feels his fingers twitch as if they want to reach for her but do not have the strength and only brush lightly over the tops of her black suede pumps as he completes his fall in space and lies prostrate just where her next step would have been.

"Oh!" she says, turning her head downward at exactly the same pace that he falls.

The dog looks up at her, snuffles around his face, looks up at her again, balances from paw to paw in unmistakable uncertainty.

Is he all right? Can he get up? Does it matter? What would happen if he stayed right here? What would happen if he had to stay right here? Her foot is merely inches from his mouth and so he kisses it, a delicate brushing of his lips across the bones that show above the vamp, and then another kiss neither delicate nor slow but firm and lingering. He lets his tongue out, licks the weave of nylon, wishes for her skin. Her foot smells distantly of the lavender she wears all over, he can also smell the very expensive suede. He lets his tongue get underneath her arch and she says, "Oh!" and grasps the stairway balustrade, lowers herself discreetly, without looking, into the hallway chair.

He has never noticed before how inefficient their housekeeper is. Dustballs have gathered against the floorboard molding like families of cowering mice knit together with doghair shirts. Spider families no doubt extinct have ceased to feed on carcasses of flies and moths that fell with Carthage. The dog is lying in the doorway that is the path to kitchen and kibble, the doorway she would walk through next, if she were walking. The dog is resting her head on her paws but her brows are knit like long-lost relatives that met only recently, and her eyes switch back and forth like windshield washers keeping her vision clear from the master on the floor to the mistress in the chair and back again and back again.

Why not? What's to stop him? He removes one shoe and sets it carefully aside. He kisses all the stockinged toes at once. He removes the other shoe and does the same with it and with the toes on the other foot. He considers his position; then, since nothing seems to happen unless he makes it so, he takes the sole of one foot in each hand and wraps the foot in his long fingers from the longitudinal arch to the instep. Has he ever noticed how very much smaller she is than he? The whole of her frame is a scaled-down model of what he has always thought was human. He sees her as a different sort of animal and wonders if his bulk offends her, or if she simply sees him as she'd see a horse, an ox: a fairly domesticated larger animal, clumsy but not intentionally dangerous, best handled circumspectly, fit for heavier labors than she likes to undertake.

Still, everything waits. He sets her far foot down again and raises both his hands along her closer foot and leg, exploring the curves of ankle and metatarsal, heel and Achilles' tendon, pinch of shank, swelling calf, and shin. In front the knee is rounded at the cap, in the back not even nylon can disguise the skittishness of skin as tentative as scrotum, labia, eyelid. Now he has reached her thigh, and as the volume of her leg expands he feels the sticking rubberized lace that announces to his fingertips the top of her dark stocking. There is skin beyond, warm, beckoning if you asked him, and he could ride his fingers forward he expects, up the skin to the next lacy station – but.

The dog emits a single whine, not even a whimper, then, sighing, settles more completely on the floor, eyes largely closed as if nothing is happening but still you never can tell. He pulls down slowly with his eight fingers, two thumbs poised for tasks that are not certain yet, and the top of the stocking rolls down into a round rubber band, a circular cuff descending that thickens as he lets his fingers do a little spider dance extruding smooth bare skin where once there was only nylon.

The stocking is low enough now to grow loose on the conical cylinder of her thigh, and he grips it with thumbs and fingers to pull it more swiftly down. Below her knee there is no longer any secret, and he takes it to her foot when he unexpectedly – hits a snag? No: he feels her fingers on his head, stops, looks up at her. Her eyes are wide: this is not the greeting she expected, if she expected any greeting at all. But her lips are moist and her bosom moves. It is pleasure he descries and, "Use your mouth," she says.

Use your mouth, she says. Use your mouth, she says. This is not the greeting he expected, if he expected any greeting at all. He lowers his face from hers again and brings his lips down to her toes. No. He bends his neck so his lips can get a grip on the roll of nylon above her heel, at her Achilles' tendon. He tugs it down behind her heel, over the back of her foot, and then the rest is easy, he pulls forward from the back and feels it slide right off. He leans back so he can look up at her and sees she has extended her hand. He nods forward and deposits the ball of stocking in her open palm. It is the most natural movement to settle back, and as his body falls face forward toward the floor again to encounter and encompass with his lips, his tongue, his entire mouth the foot he has made naked. "Oh!" she says, and her arch flexes, her toes extend and spread, he licks where there is room between them for his tongue and "Oh!" she says, her foot gives a little kick against his soft palate, his head turns up and down and around at exactly the same pace that her toes twitch.

The western sky has gone all pearl grey blue and lilac except one scalloped high fringe of pink. He slants his eyes in her direction so he can look up at her and sees she has extended her hand, a small red object in it. He lets her foot go free from his mouth, surprised when she wipes it thoroughly dry in his hair, front and top and bottom and back. He looks more closely at the thing she holds out to him and sees it is not red but contains red: nail polish. He looks into her eyes and she nods forward and deposits the little bottle in his open palm. He closes his hand around it, such a small hard thing, and thinks back to what he knows. He shakes the bottle, listening for the telltale rattle to thicken up and stop, unscrews the cap and pulls it with its densely coated brush. He takes her foot from his head with his free hand, supporting without clutching her warm sole in his long fingers so her toes extend up on his pulsing wrist. He bends forward in the gloaming and with great precision paints a broad red swath along the center of her great toe from just above the cuticle all the way to the nail's smooth edge. Two more careful strokes, one on either side of the first, and he holds the foot out so he can see his handiwork. He puts the brush away without screwing on the bottle cap, blows cautiously across her foot until he thinks the coat is tacky, takes up the brush again, squinting to see her next toe, trying to gauge his line. The dog's right hind leg twitches in her sleep and she mews, it sounds to him, plaintively, chasing rabbits. The pink is gone, the grey is gone, blue gone, lilac gone. Darkness finally settles in.

Civilization and Its Discontents: My Justine, Part One

Medication
Don't do me no good,
Meditation don't
Like it should,
Masturbation
Probably would,
If you weren't looking over my shoulder....
– *Mark Malkas*, Living with the Worm

I've been gazing at the underwear models in the latest catalogue from Victoria's Secret, trying to see beneath the satin and lace where subtle shadows trace their nipples, and inside the soft elastic bands where their professional bikini trims stop and their narrow pubic patches start. Since I was eleven or twelve I've liked to look at human ads for women's underwear, and these frilly garter belts lapping Victoria's slick-teddied honeys are much more what I ever had in mind than the massively corsetted bras and boxerette shorts that were plugged in the Sunday supplements of my 1950s adolescence.

It's not just that I enjoy pictures of women *dishabille*: I like pictures of men, too, and naked pictures, and scantily clad undressers live and in the flesh. For years I had a flirtatious correspondence with a woman who lived in a foreign country and with whom I had once had a hot affair. I teasingly urged her to send me a photo of herself in the buff and at long last she did, suggesting I reciprocate. How I came to have that wang-a-dangle beefcake shot I sent her is a story for another time, but when she returned to California we ended up in bed again, and again, and again, taking minimal time out for only the plain necessities. In the midst of this second of our honeymoon affairs I slipped out to the lingerie shop one afternoon and bought her a white lace g-string with a butt-strap that kissed her arsehole when she bent over, and that is how I happen to be on the Victoria's Secret mailing list. My very own silk briefs were likewise a present from her from there, but while my gift was a deliberate suggestion, hers was just a lark: Justine is straighter than I am in every way, and if she receives the catalogue at all I doubt she explores it with my kind of relish.

A few days ago she and I were leaning on the plush rail in the rotunda at Davies Symphony Hall, waiting to hear Yo-Yo Ma play the Schumann cello concerto. Justine sipped a scotch-and-water and I nibbled cognac. "One guy cross-dressed and walked around town for a day," I said, explaining the optional assignments in a workshop I was taking in Human Sexuality. "Another hired a dominatrix to whip him for a half-hour: that sort of thing. But I really don't see any projects for me this time." I sighed and stared out the window where I saw myself reflected against the oncoming concert-goers. "Once upon a time I would have leapt at the chance, but by now I've pretty much done the things I wanted, I'm not especially curious about yet another hunt, and anyway – " I sort of looked sidewise at her to avoid letting her see me looking at her looking at me – "this is such a good sexual relationship that within its boundaries I feel I am free to do anything." She smiled and offered a little sigh of agreement. "The only thing I could think of was that I could try monogamy."

"*Try* monogamy?" She was quick, and there was a little fire in her voice. "Aren't you *being* monogamous?"

"Well yes, but I meant, you know, as a project, for a month, for the workshop."

"Don't you dare," she shuddered. "Don't you dare make a project of it. The first thing that will happen is you'll decide that monogamy is an obligation, then you'll think you have to deny the obligation and you'll go out and fuck someone else."

The problem with a really good lover is that she is liable to know something about who you are, and since I was enjoying the present regime I did not sign up for a special project. But the idea that I could have undertaken yet another new unfettered eroticism stirred my blood and led me to fantasies based on what had come before: of pillows and dildoes and mirrors and creams, of whips and ropes and clamps and rings, of theatres and elevators and airplanes and parks, of men and women in groups and at random, of high-minded celibacy and tender affection and even the vicious morass of moral guilt. And I thought of the struggles that freedom entails, and the desperation with which we must sometimes announce ourselves when in the throes of self-discovery.

It was Oscar Wilde, more than a century ago, who called homosexuality the love that dared not speak its name, and it was some blighted editor at *Time* magazine about eighty-five years later who rechristened it the love that could not keep its mouth shut. It seems that in my lifetime many of my fellows and I, and not just the homosexuals among us, have felt the *Time* magazine sort of need to expose the sexual parts of our natures: coming out, as it were, for reasons I can only hope are fundamentally honest. While I celebrate the individual and collective freedoms we have gained from stepping forward to be more fully who we are, and the intimacies we have enhanced with everyone else in the world by doing so; and while I applaud some of the political and social reforms that have resulted directly or indirectly from our exhibitions, such as consenting adult statutes and the various steps toward domestic partner recognition: still, I have often felt a social and intellectual – as well as a personal and emotional – embarrassment at my own seeming need to proclaim in public what I feel are acts essentially as private as prayers. In other words, I distrust the making of manifestoes in the cause of liberating personal expression, for despite my willingness to see myself as a metaphor to be transcended, I am a very private person and think, as the song says, it ain't nobody's bidniss but my own.

When Justine observed that in *trying* monogamy I would feel myself *obliged* to be monogamous, she was poking around the crux of one of the great issues of sexual politics: exactly how is it that we *should* behave? Who do we think we are that we should behave that way? And who do we think we are that we have the right to tell anyone else what they can, must, or ought to do with their bodies, minds, souls, or lives?

As I thought about what Justine said I realized how much I am bothered when other people believe they have answers and all I can see is questions. I stand in a kind of queasy awe before those who are ready and willing to assert and even enforce the universal importance of their individual beliefs. Perhaps because I am male; perhaps because I've been beating my meat since about the time I started looking at Sunday Supplement underwear; perhaps because I've happily tried a variety of sexualities since soon thereafter: in any case I grow frightened and angry when someone tells me I should only do it his or her special way, whether that person wants me to eat only Spaghetti-Os and cola, or only lobster and champagne.

As far as I can tell people express themselves sexually – homo, hetero, bi, pan, auto, a, or ab – in different ways at different times along the same continuum. We have a capacity to slide back and forth on this scale the way we have the capacity to eat different kinds of foods: Mexican today, Chinese tomorrow, French, Greek, English, Eritrean, and Thai. Some cuisines may not be to our liking, but any single cuisine is as limiting as it is limited: that's one value of experimentation; why variety is the spice of life. And despite the wagging tongues of sexual fascists on the right and left, I never know when the vagaries of my own mind and dynamic circumstances may make my own joint twitch.

One wonderful thing about Yo-Yo Ma is that he does not tell us how someone is supposed to play the cello, or even how the rest of us are supposed to listen to it; he does not have to fuck around, because what he does with that big instrument between his legs makes Schumann's erotic music move us beyond ourselves without ever demanding that we give ourselves up – as sex can also do.

Twenty years ago – before I knew about Victoria's Secret but after I'd ceased getting off on department store white sales – turning pages in the *New Yorker*, I came upon a henna-haired beauty on her knees, wearing just three tiny yellow triangles; and though her face was turned away from me and shaded by the curves of her *pas de Basque* arm, she stopped the breath in my addled throat. Did she touch the lust in my heart? Yes; and she looked exactly like my former wife. I carried the picture in my notebook for months, and wrote a romantic story about a man who dreams of such a woman repeatedly, until she takes over his waking life and steals his sleep.

The Unconscionable Treachery of Fate: My Justine, Part Two

If sex were all, then every trembling hand
Could make us squeak, like dolls, the wished-for words.
But note the unconscionable treachery of fate,
That makes us weep, laugh, grunt and groan, and shout
Doleful heroics, pinching gestures forth
From madness to delight, without regard
To that first, foremost law.
– Wallace Stevens, Le Monocle de Mon Oncle

ONE: DIERDRE'S WEDDING

The logs in the fireplace split and spit; a tendril from an ivy vine grew in between two rafters; cameras snapped like shots before the merciless organ; and everywhere were candles and white flowers. Between my pleasant social face and the face I'd chosen to submerge, a pressure built of sudden, unexpected tears I *would* not show because this was her day, her celebration, and I did not want to steal the least bit of her lightning, and because I felt my estate that afternoon – I had argued with Justine again, who was not with me because of it, and who was leaving me again not even, it turned out, for the last time – had fallen too low for me to want to let it become visible.

Dierdre's family did not know what to make of me, there, then, in that holy, hopeful place. I sat in the very last pew among forgotten friends I might be thought to have known on my own, hoping to go unnoticed with my back against the wall; but sorrow ambushed me when the dozen faces I had neither seen nor thought about for years, unprepared for mine, went puzzled and confused; and when long-lost old acquaintances asked, "What of you?" I could not even lie: I just replied, "Hard day."

They thought they knew what I was talking about, and I let them believe it for my ease's sake. But I was not sorry to see her marry, to see nostalgia, trepidation, joy, and anticipation mingle in her impy grin, or see her put her arms around another man and kiss him before God. She and I had parted clean, with love and admiration and a certainty that we were not quite right for one another: we had let each other go, and I was glad for her although I knew that even the friendship we'd maintained would settle now, slowly, out of reach. I felt a little like a father, not a former lover; or neither like a father nor a lover but like someone with no rights at all in the matter, no right to even be there, no right to be blue, and it was this sense of isolation in the midst of the solemn, hysterical happiness that was mother to my pain. I was suddenly seeing my love as if it were a ship adrift, without even an anchor to cast into another's heart, and I was feeling sorry for myself.

Two: In the Steamroom

In the steamroom at the gym the other day, where men and women generally wear bathing suits, one woman sat down barely arm's reach from my face with only a towel wrapped around her; and when she stood up enough of it fell away that her buoyant young buttocks winked at me once. She gathered her dignity around her like a cloak and saw me try to look away in time, then flounced out through the fog as if she'd sniffed an aristocratic nose. I would not recognize her – nor, I imagine, would she recognize me – if tomorrow we were lifting the very same weight. But her ass remains in my mind's lascivious eye, and I would guess that when I am an old man it will return to me one night, creaseless and pink and pumped as a basketball, inviting me to fantasy.

In that fantasy she will know that you don't wear a towel into that kind of steam room if you don't want to be noticed; she will let it fall with grace, without believing she is obliged to pretend it was all an accident, and I won't pretend, too: I will look at her body from top to toe, from front to back, from alpha to omega, and she will enjoy the pleasure I take in seeing the word made flesh. She will look at me as well, when I slip off my steaming trunks, and then... and then... and then....

Reality is full of sweat and razor nicks, pimples, and the slatherings of Crisco. But in the joys of sex our bodies' chemistries grant us enough selective blindness that we may see perfection in a wart. In sex we see our lovers as if through a vaselined lens; we live in a literal fantasy world, where pain and cold and hunger disappear as data from the brain. Like male mantises we lose our heads for a moment's embrace with our own ideal, but unlike the eager insect that must die of it, we fall prey not to our mates, but to ourselves. We live! and so may be embarrassed when the flush has fled to find, however perfectly we regard it, that we have worshipped a wart indeed.

*T*HREE: *THE FOOD OF LOVE*

I fled the reception with an honest alibi but felt frantic by the time I got out the door. I had not wanted to be at the wedding alone, and now I saw that, apart from her company, I had wanted Justine to provide camouflage. Mated, I'd have been more celebratory company for the kith and kin of my dearly belovèd ex; alone, I was a vague disturbance. Mated, I'd have been another new beginning; alone, I was an old ending, standing too close for comfort. Besides, if she had been there everyone I knew would have had to ask about her, and I could have said something wonderful and proud.

I drove to her home and took her out for drinks and dinner and a concert. At first the air was icy, though her distant wrath was hot. We talked and explained ourselves and maybe we took the turn that will truly save us or bring us down at last. Neither of us was satisfied, but we are friends and could hold hands and show we cared about each other by the time the music started.

The first piece was a requiem, atonal and dissonant in a tradition that was rebellious generations ago. I moved into another state of consciousness almost with the opening bars, that took me from my body to the women in the concert chorus. I went from one to another to another, seeing how each was beautiful: the fat and the lean, the young and the old, white, yellow, black, and brown, passionate and rational, tall and short, I felt as if each woman showed me what was perfect in her. I saw myself go arch-satyric, thrusting and thumping from alto to soprano. Sex was the art and the aesthetic. Where we debauched our faces shone with glee and perspiration, and when the music ended I returned to watch the composer, a gaunt, unsmiling man, accept the audience's polite accolades.

After intermission Vladimir Ashkenazy played Brahms' hyper-romantic first piano concerto. Violins and celloes, bassoons and piccolos, orchestra and soloist rolled around together in the music. Ashkenazy's fingers leapt like light white spiders in the ivory web, and caught black notes like insects. Later we went back to Justine's house and worshipped each other's bodies. She told me again she needed my commitment; stuck as a pincushion, I could not move.

FOUR: SCHLEPPING WOOD AND BURYING WATER

Sex is not all, but it can be a model for all: a spiritual or alchemical road on which the insights, intuitions, or perceptions of imagination may transform reality and bring us proudly to our knees. This road's intensity invites us to surrender, face to face with God in each other, face to face with God in ourselves: the same God who, once known, can never be entirely forgotten.

For a long time at least we in the west pretended that we were not animals; therefore, we thought we had to love someone or even marry before we had a right to fuck. But that belief may have been part of a bygone era of idol worship: a part of the Cartesian revolution that split mind from body from spirit for three-hundred years.

Recently, it seems, we have grown more religious. We have begun to recognize that not just a trembling hand, but *anything* can make us squeak the wished-for words, if we wish for it to do so, and there stands God: for there is no squeak without surrender, and surrender is what creates Divinity. The body turns out to be neither a dirty burden to be abjured, nor a motel to be kept pure for the transient holy spirit, but flesh *as* spirit incarnate, that offers us the opportunity to discover where love of self and love of others and love of God are one and the same experience.

FIVE: THE FIRST, FOREMOST LAW, GIVE OR TAKE A COUPLE

a. Saying Uncle

Long after midnight the night of our second date, I parked with Dierdre at the Marina to watch the spring moon set and listen to sailboats' lines chime against their metal masts. We kissed, we cuddled, I opened up her clothes, and as I found her wet and evidently willing I wondered how many men she'd done this with before me. It wasn't that I wanted her to be a virgin, but that I wanted her to be all mine, which is not the same thing at all; and I could nearly hear the voice of my long-ago psychiatrist telling me, with reference to another woman years before, that if she did it with me she had done it with others too.

Jealousy does not rear its head in this tale, but I almost did not push my luck that night for fear of finding there was no question in Dierdre's mind. Almost. And for a while thereafter we fell to any vacant couch or bed or floor as new young lovers will. But some months later, after we began to live together, our sex life dwindled to the occasional missionary fuck and, for me at least, a lot of masturbation. I'd had a ribald and promiscuous youth and hungered for the eager pubic kiss. I'd thought I could let it go easily, but abandoning wanton sex is like relinquishing cigarettes: it demands an earnest commitment that, as later with Justine, I could or would not muster.

I very much desired not to sleep with someone else for fear of damaging the bond Dierdre and I shared. I did not recognize how badly shaken the bond already had become if we effectively could not get it on with relish. Though it took four years for us to see that our not fucking had something to do with our not communicating, our resistance finally wore out. That is when we called it quits. Could this marriage have been saved? I think not. I think we both needed to move on, to grow up in different ways; and I have always honored us jointly and severally for our willingness to go to the mat, and then to say uncle from the heart.

b. Matings with Remarkable Men

I've been in other steamrooms where a person's simple presence implied that he was looking to get laid: where if you wore a towel at all its chief purpose was to wipe your brow, your hands, and your crotch much later on. On one of those occasions, merely months before I started seeing Dierdre, I led a gentle, silent man to a wide, vacant mattress in a red-lit, doorless alcove in a warren of erotica, and vanished in a visible embrace that lasted for hours.

In the days before AIDS, in the venue of the baths, fucks were frequently quick and dirty. Partners were strangers, and the stranger the better. So it came as a surprise to both of us to find a transient meeting of the heart, mind, and spirit, as well as of the groin, and we reveled in our good fortune as we reveled in each other's arms. This nameless being, his mustached face another faded recollection I would never recognize, touched me and I cared for him; we met and moved and parted virtually without a word, encountering a realm of spirit in pure giving. For the duration of our coming together in the seediest circumstances, we were lovers in the noblest ways. And while we were buried in each other's eyes and mouths and asses other people passed and tried to join us. Of course we shunned them. But I could not prevent my foot from cocking repeatedly in the hand of one man as he acceded to our need and started on his way, and he came back again and again, confused as I was by the gesture.

c. The Unconscionable Treachery of Fate

Justine and I have always had great sex, from the affair we were in the midst of when I started to see Dierdre to this morning's erotic aerobics. Back then she was married and I did not even consider whether there might be something more than a great good time to be had from our hours in the sack. So we climbed out of bed one evening and went to dinner and there I told her I was in love. Then we went to a party Dierdre had organized, and when, quite drunk, I took Justine home and asked her to spend the night, she graciously declined.

We met again last year, much water gone under many a bridge, and Justine, divorced, said she had always been in love with me. Over some months she engaged me almost against my will in a relationship more profound than an affair. I think sometimes that if she persists in breaking off with me I will let her go, relieved to be free of the tumult she engenders in my life; and yet I know I would regret the loss and miss her, and each of the half-dozen times she has abandoned hope and left me I have gone to her with the intuitive, not rational, intention to repair whatever damage we had made.

Since we started to see each other again Justine has told me that in our old days I was very dominant in sex and that she had liked that then, but that this time I am both gentler and more malleable, which gives her the freedom also to explore us both and to be dominant from time to time. Now I remember the sight of her with her ankles behind her ears, her body twitching beneath me; and I remember being bound hand and foot while her hands and mouth made me tremble and cry out. I have not said a word to her about surrender or even God. Though I count myself a very lucky guy all told in my life, nothing has ever turned out as I expected anyway.

Plaisir d'Amour:
My Justine, Part Three

The courtship of animals is by no means so simple and short an affair as might be thought. – Charles Darwin, Sexual Selection

ONE: ONE FROM THE HEART

On the phone Justine said it felt like an amputation, and in a way it feels like that to me as well. I have spent some part of every free evening since that day we parted a couple of weeks ago fretting with my loneliness and loss, thrusting my awareness like a tongue into the cavity of my emptiness to test the presence of its pain. All day Sunday I lay reading and dozing and musing about what could have been, what should have been, what would have been, and what was and is. I guess her anguish to be more encompassing than mine, as these things can be reckoned, because she has always been the more committed of us two. Even so, grief spreads out in me like an ice crystal, marbling my emotions and making me feel tired, weak, and vulnerable to everything except love. To love – to romantic, erotic love – I am today invulnerable. The bonds that tied are still too far from healed for me to be available for any close connections of this sort.

She phoned the next day in anger, to call me a bastard as if I had willfully toyed with her affections because, though I tried to give her what she wanted, I could not return her love in kind. And I cannot: the desperation of her need seems a bottomless well to me, and I know for myself, from having been on the other side of a similar conundrum years ago, that no one can satisfy that hunger but herself; and that as long as it is omnivorously present we can never love as equals; and that mutually satisfying, mutually strengthening, mutually enlightening love can only take place between equals. Not only can the power of love not reside with just one of two partners, but when love is overlaid with need it is need, not love, that will be served. For nine months we have tried to serve the love, and her need for what I could not give, and mine to be free of her demand, bore misery that wore us down.

On the phone I let her dump her anger, not for the first time but perhaps for the last: while I am glad she is not beating herself up as she has done so often, I do not accept the blame nor do I care to be abused. After the call, I took my sad and sorry lonesome self to a late night movie diversion where women with long legs sucked off men with long cocks to feed the fantasies of fools like me.

That night I looked at my own life in the celluloid light filled with images of wet thighs, shooting gism, tits and ass and cock-cleaved cunts. They seemed somehow to be the same to me: fantastic thoughts and fantasy images, grand illusions and self-delusion, surreptitious masturbation in the blue-lit cinema of the mind. I wanted to hold Justine and tell her that when she licked my nipples the way she used to do my whole body went into electric spasms; that the flame of love burned bright between us when she held my cock and lapped it like a torch; that I could have more pleasure nibbling on her clitoris while she shuddered till her hair shook loose than I had in my own orgasms; and that to fuck with her was to take me out of time, sometimes, to where I could forget myself. As one hero's cock slid in and out between his heroine's hungry lips I thought of Justine whose body in love spoke in infinite tongues with mine. The memory of her face in orgasm made me feel a fraud in the fake-erotic dark, and I left the theatre to walk the flaccid midnight streets.

Two: Cutting Through Sexual Materialism

I feel as if I'll never fuck again. One component of the depression that has accompanied my separation from Justine is that I do not care for much. Awakening in the grey or sun-lit mornings I find neither purpose nor penis hard. My heart is low and I do not care to get it up. Even the lovely girl in the low-slung bathing suit who shared the steam room with me at the gym this afternoon, where I went when I could not force myself to write, excited in me only memories of excitement. I noted appreciatively but abstractly, without appetite, her sculpted head, her graceful back, the firm, fine lines of her legs. Often in the past I fled to sex from pain: I have known good whores to dull the edge of a broken love affair. But this time I've chosen loneliness, apart from the slightest simulacrum of that which by convention we call "making love."

In "Sex and Existence," Adrian Van Kamm clarifies the existential relationship between the self and its physical form:

> *Many people are inclined to perceive the I and the body as two seprate entities. In reality, however, there is no separation between me and my body. I am an embodied consciousness, a subject that is incarnated.... I am neither a disembodied self nor a mechanical organism, but a living unity, a body permeated by self.*

So it is that my body with its shoulders bowed, its belly slack, its penis hanging uninspired, the heavy-hearted threnody every part of my corpus sings, expresses exactly my sad soul's sorry state. My body is depressed not just *because* I am depressed; my body is depressed *as* I am depressed. My body tells me the state of my soul, if I need to ask: my body is my spirit in the flesh, a perfect biofeedback register. I is, my body am, we are *down*. It is no wonder I don't want to fuck. Van Kamm:

> *The sexual dimension of our life is not isolated from the whole of our existence or from the other dimensions of our life. On the contrary, the orientation of our sexuality is intimately connected with the orientation of our existence as a whole.*

And this means moment by moment, as well as in the broader scheme of things. Sex is not only the core and metaphorical dilemma of being human, it is the clearest path to learning the body's truths, and thence the truths of the soul: slack cock, slack heart; slack heart, slack spirit. "When you were born [conceived]," Bagwan Shree Rajneesh proposes, "two sex cells met and your being was created, your body was created. These two sex cells are everywhere in your body. They have multiplied and multiplied and multiplied, but your basic unit remains the sex cell."

I would not try to demonstrate its logic in so short a meditation as this one is, but I am willing to take the position that sexual and spiritual experiences can be identical; and even if my premise fails, in any case they have the body in common. I have never known a person to have sex without a body, as I have never known someone to have an out-of-body experience without a body to have it out of. After the fall it always seems that there will never be another lover, but the time comes 'round. I will feel like loving once again, and I will feel like fucking once again. I'll know when my soul is ready for the encounter because my heart will rise up, and my cock will crow.

THREE: THE DESCENT OF MAN

This evening Justine called to ask if it was me she saw in a car like mine, in a neighborhood I frequent, with a shaggy-haired blonde beside me. "I know it's presumptuous of me to ask," she said, "but it shook me." I agreed it was presumptuous, and said it was not me. We talked about our relationship, like good Californians of the Aquarian Age. I told her I had felt sad about the way our separation seemed to be coming down, and that while I was glad she was getting her anger out, I did not feel I was the bad guy. She said she knew I was not. I grew misty-eyed. She asked if I would come over for a drink. Her naked body took form in my mind's eye, and I longed to be with her – or at least, with it. And then I thought one amputation was enough. I declined.

Notes

Adrian Van Kamm, "Sex and Existence," from Lawrence, N. and O'Connor, D. (eds), Readings in Existential Phenomenology. *Englewood Cliffs, NJ: Prentice-Hall, 1967, pp 227 - 242; originally published in the* Review of Existential Psychology and Psychiatry, *Vol III, No. 2, Spring, 1963.*

Incubus

ONE

The summer sun has set already. Its fading light, reflected off high scattered clouds, shines bronze and gold and burgundy on your mottled skin. You stand before me naked, limp as you can go, head fallen, eyes closed, and breath gone slow, fingers now unclenching one by one without relinquishing their hold on the white ash bar suspended just six inches above your head. Your wrists remain cuffed to it, and your ankles, kept apart by a similar bar, are cuffed to thick ringbolts sunk deeply into the woodwork of the archway framing you.

From the floor I contemplate what I have done to you: my eyes connect the dots, the purple starburst flares I've bitten and sucked in flagrant arcs down the sides of your neck, across your chest, upon the hillocks of your breasts, under your arms, and back and forth across your belly to meet in a single snakeline down to your bare pubis, then apart again as if to end in livid whorls along the insides of both thighs but with trailers that terminate, I know, in a final pair of fountains on the cheeks of your ass. Here on your belly is a drop of blood I catch with my tongue before it streaks: you don't even shiver at my touch. You stopped crying an hour ago, when I had barely reached your breasts. Your muscles all went slack, you wet and soiled yourself, surrendered absolutely. Now I smell you, your waters, your sweat. The sounds of nesting birds filter through the walls and windows;

somewhere there is traffic. We will see these marks all week and beyond.

I release your legs first, rub your ankles, make you walk in place. You are hardly conscious but you take direction as you always do from me. One foot comes up till the toes are in the air then settles back on the polished wooden floor, damp with your urine and excrement. Then the second foot. You keep shambling while I stand and release your arms, wrapping them around my neck, holding you close to me, skin to skin.

I lift and carry you to the huge old claw-foot tub where I ran a scalding bath with jasmine petals before we began. The bath's cooled off now to slightly more than baby-bottle warm. Your head is lolling on my chest. A dozen candle-flames reflected in three walls of mirrors light my way. I climb into the sweetly-scented water and lean back with you buoyant in my arms. I reach my left foot up to turn a trickle of hot water on, settle my neck into the air pillow velcroed at my back, and start to sing your favorite lullaby.

Two

Can any image gladden my heart more swiftly and completely than the sight of my darling girl kneeling, naked, face to the floor, arms stretched out before her crossed at the wrists, hands palms down, honeyed hair in gentle disarray sheltering her face?

I close the door behind me quietly and lock it, pocketing the inside key. I drape my jacket on the chair nearby, knowing you'll attend to it when I'm ready. I walk around you slowly, savoring the sight of your hips high in the air, your legs spread far enough apart to give me access if I choose to take you from behind right now, both entries washed, shorn of even their finest hairs, and smoothly oiled. Your thighs quiver as I brush one finger lightly up your cleft and over the little golden heart-shaped padlock that holds together the ruby-eyed ouroboros rings with which I pierced your labia; they relax as my finger comes to rest on your fawning hole that puckers up Rimbaldian at my touch like a mouth that's begging to be kissed, and then recedes. You've pumiced your feet and softened them with cream and left all color off their nails as I instructed you to do. Leaning forward as you are your breasts seem at rest, nipples nearly brushing the white rug beneath you.

I sit beside my jacket and place one booted foot before you. You lift your head just enough to reach me and you kiss, lips and tongue embracing me from toe to arch to instep. That's all I require for the moment, for it's all that you require to make your body shake and your hips pump forward and back while a noise between a gasp and a moan escapes your pulsing throat. I put two fingers beneath your chin and raise your precious face. Your eyes are filled with tears, your pouting lips are trembling. By the pressure of my fingers I pull you to your knees. You clasp your hands behind your back. I bring my mouth to yours. You open softly, enfold me with your lips. You lick and suck my tongue deliberately, as if it were a baby's penis, though your whole face is hungry. I place your arms around my waist, hug you and let you hug me back. I kiss you harder and with one long sigh you open your throat and start to whimper, still sucking on my tongue.

From my pocket I take a strip of white leather whose silver buckle rolls free in the air. I let the collar touch your face and feel you writhe in my hands. The noises in your throat are taking on the form of words. I know what they say, and why: Please, they say; they say please please please please please. Please let me wear your collar. Please put your collar on me. Please remind me that you are my Master. Please let me know that I belong to you. Please let me know that I am your possession. Please let me know again you care for what I give you. Please show me over and over. Please please please please please.

I stop kissing you and hold the collar to your lips. You move toward it as if it were a benediction, and when I take it from your mouth you bend your head like a supplicant. I wrap the collar closely around your neck. I shut the buckle and your body grows tense. I snap the lock and you cry out, quake, and slump in my arms, weeping, released. When you look up at me your face glows as if you've seen an angel reflecting your angelic light.

T HREE

Darling, darling, darling girl, you are the girl of my golden dreams, molded out of molten flesh, hot and liquid with your own unique desires, given forever into my keeping. Slight and delicate like some reluctant spring flower, you drape and waft your limbs as you move, as if they're lacey petals drifting in a summer breeze. Your brow is far too smooth for a grown-up's face, your huge hazel eyes are set too wide apart between high cheekbones, your sculpted nose is faintly rounded, your bee-stung lips are full and actually scarlet. Yet, all put together beneath your long, waved golden hair they form a sad little-girl's face that always makes me want to rescue you from your own lost life, and makes me want to cry for mine. This, perhaps, is why I'm more patient with you than I've ever been with anybody else.

Still, I treat your body like an adult woman's body. Your ass is shaped like a lilac leaf, so that from a certain angle, when I bend you face-forward over the back of the couch or the hood of a car, it resembles little so much as a valentine that beckons me. Your smoothly pouting pussy is round and full and shaved every day to keep it fresh for pinching with my fingers, my lips, my teeth. Your inner labia lap from your body like little tongues, locked together with three snakes. I pierced your pale pink nipples as well, and trained them to ache whenever I remove the rings I had made especially for them, with my initials acid-etched in twined relief on their inner surfaces, and to ache as well for the fine silver chains I keep in a blue velvet box that are intended to do nothing but link your nipple rings to the snakes below. The stark white spiral brand on your right buttock is also mine, and the heart-shaped locket depending from the silver choker welded around your neck, which is inscribed,

Property of
Sir James
If found please
telephone
(415) 000-0000
Reward

During the week you go to work and come home, just like millions of other young women. But when you dress each workday morning you put on clothing and jewelry I have selected to show off your beauty without exciting familiarity. Then you set your bag beside the front door, and with your head up, your eyes cast down, your hands held patiently behind your back, you wait obediently on your knees for me to approve of the way your hair is brushed, and how you have applied the eye shadow, liner, mascara, blush, and lipstick that complete your presentation. My approval is nearly rote by now, after three years of practice and discipline, but I retain the ritual as a reminder to us both that approval is my right, and as a transparent excuse to touch your cheek before you leave the house, and to look into your deep eyes and reassure you that you are my most prized possession: a treasure beyond measure or price to me.

OUR

Our life together is focused on me. Your job is dedicated devotion and service: you attend and you minister, you wait, you obey, you please. I make your gift meaningful by guiding and containing what you bring. But you could not serve me if I would not be served, and I could not care for you if you would not find here benefit for yourself: to take your pleasure in my pleasure, to study my desires and make them yours, to place yourself without question in my trust, to learn what I say you shall learn, to do as I say you shall do, to be as I say you shall be, to the best of your ability. If our life were not so sexual, you might be the chela in some esoteric tradition and I, of course, the Master. Our focus on me is a ruse. We *are* monks in an esoteric tradition. That is how much I learn from you.

IVE

I walk down the red and black-lit hall with my pet in tow. Your soft white leather collar is closed with a fine filigreed silver lock, as are the white leather cuffs that hold your wrists and ankles. Locked silver chains attach the cuffs to silver rings sewn into the small white leather girdle that completes your dress; their brevity keeps your movements circumspect. I hold the loop of the white leather leash I have clipped to the collar ring so I can feel the gentle tension as you seek to maintain your place two steps behind me.

We turn a corner and find ourselves face to face with a wall of mirror we all but fall into. I stop so quickly you nearly falter, but you catch yourself and come to rest behind me. After a minute I step to the side and gesture toward our *döppelgänger* images.

"Look, pet: what do you see?"

"I see my Master, Sir, with his pet girl on his leash, Sir."

I nod, bemused. We make such a pretty picture, both of us all in white, I want to watch us to see what we might do. In a moment the Master turns and pulls on his leash a little bit, and his pet takes two small barefoot steps to stand before him. He lifts her face with three fingers and smiles at her kindly. She smiles back and her body trembles visibly. He pulls her the last brief inches toward him; tenderly he kisses her mouth. She gasps and sighs and obeys his hand that is now on her back, moving forward into his embrace. After he releases her she burrows her head into the hollow of his chest and sighs and closes her eyes.

IX

On weekends you may not dress. I like to decorate you instead, in ribbons and bows and smatterings of lace, or sometimes in dozens of little techno-clothespins. I like to watch the brightly-colored bits of plastic jiggle while you fetch my coffee or make my bed. I'm amused when you grimace every now and then, or whimper as some piece of pillow case catches on the lip of a pin. Every time you look at me with your wide, round, scared-doe eyes I know you want to plead with me to take the clothespins off, Oh, Master *please*! But I also know you love to suffer for me, and to obey: at heart you are a very good girl. And I know you know there'd be no point in asking. I know how long you can last without damage, and so you continue happily with your chores.

At some point along the way today I start to fondle you and make you squirm. I know you get excited best this way. Your breath grows short and shallow, perspiration spots your upper lip and forehead, your thighs grow slippery with your own desire, and your lower lips swell up until I want to bite them open, setting free the blood that wants to flow. Instead I keep my hands on you and do not let you stop your chores. Now and then a tremor runs through you, but you do not come, although I know you're on the edge. You do not have permission to come yet, and it will be hours before I give you that. That this permission is mine to grant or withhold – that you let me have this control over so deep and intimate and central a part of you – is part of what makes you so dear to my heart. You give me every greatest boon that I could want. You give me every portion of yourself that I desire. You capture me with your endless gift.

Jason's Cock

What I love most about Jason's cock is not its size but its grace, in every sense. I like to lie with my cheek on his belly and introduce myself to it over and over again, getting to know it for the first time every time, brushing it over my eyes, my cheeks, my nose, my mouth, trailing it down my throat inside and out. It always stands up for me like a sentinel, ready to serve, eager to please. The skin is soft and smooth as a tropical breeze signaling monsoons in days to come. It darkens and flushes, pales, darkens and flushes again as if it were a special landscape of flesh the clouds pass over on their way to rain. It smells like a summer beach at sunset after a long day of lying in hot sand anticipating everything forbidden. It pulses slowly with the steady beat of his life and sometimes with a less steady beat of its own, and if I press it with my finger underneath his balls it dances like a tap dog and his balls begin to steal away as if they're tip-toeing out the door at midnight when they promised to stay home at ten, and if I rest my ear against his sac I can hear the single odd-nailed floorboard creak with almost every other step.

The way it arches like a well-strung bow brings back the fantasies I used to have of sucking cock when I was still too young to have really tried. I thought I'd find another boy who'd somehow be staying in a house nearby when we were on vacation at the lake in Michigan. I'd see him on the beach one day, and even though we wouldn't say a word I'd know that he'd seen me as well. Dusk would fall, and then full night. My family would go to sleep and I'd go out for a moonlight walk. The air would still be warm from the day, and the lake would be so flat the moon and her entire history would lie across its missing ripples like silver two-dimensional apples. There would still be frogs and crickets in those days, fireflies would glitter like tiny spotlights caught on distant tinsel tassels, the grass above the sand would be wet with early dew. I would have no way to know that he was there and still I'd walk along the grass and underneath a tree right into his arms and we would kiss until we fell down from the weight of memory, knowing already how our lives would fit. Somehow our clothes just disappeared, and I made him cry out with desire as I milked him with my mouth but took myself away before he came and made him stop, and made him count from ten to one aloud and slowly before I swallowed his balls and let them try to slip from between my thinly parted lips, ran my tongue like a swift snake down his root to where it disappeared inside his body, and licked him where the hot lake had not dried yet. I tongue his fawn-brown pucker and come back in a swallow to this graceful instrument that looks now like a stretching cat caught in a moment it cannot relieve.

Jason is so wet I could fuck myself on him without any lube, but I'm not nearly ready to let him come so close to coming. I have only just begun to worship, I have just begun to let my tongue get slippery in all that moisture, pushing it into the little hole that opens and opens and opens for me to fuck it but is still too small, so I suck him up instead and feel his head get harder and hotter and I know he's ready so I slide him out from between my tightened lips and back away again just as I did with the boy at the lake, and watch him throb before my eyes enfolded now in nothing but this wind I've whipped up with my breath to blow on him, to cool him down, to slow his movement that he wants and needs and thinks is inevitable, letting him show me now how much he's learned because he knows he doesn't have permission yet I haven't said *good boy now you can come* I haven't finished yet with Jason's cock. There is this little line, this little crimp of pleated skin below his head in front that leads me down to where his hard soft shaft is so translucent I imagine I can see the muscle filling and emptying, this little line that leads me away from his small hole and down the thick blue vein I want to bite into so I can drink his hidden blood while he comes, and so I nibble now a little letting Jason know that I have teeth and that I am not using them, not yet, not as fully as I could, and when he shakes so hard his thighs and belly tremble but he still does not come then I know that he has understood.

This other vein that runs along the side reminds me more of rope and so remembering the first boy I ever tied to my bed I lick that rope on Jason while he tries to keep from screaming. The boy was probably a virgin, and he let on that he was straight. I brought him home on the pretense that he'd like to see the black and yellow butterfly I'd chloroformed and pinned to a white board under glass. He was not the kind of boy who pulled the wings off flies but I was. I showed him the butterfly but made him beg to see it first, and when he'd begged me hard enough I told him he could only see it if he took off his shirt, and then his pants, and then all his clothes. He was obviously scared and just as obviously excited, his pants when I told him about the shirt were standing out and dark with his wet precum. Then he was naked in my bedroom with just a few tan pubic hairs and a cock very much like Jason's only younger, curved and graceful as a sonatina, so I showed him the butterfly and stood behind him pressing up against his ass while he examined every minute vein and curl on the butterfly's wing as if he were a fascinated lepidopterist who did not even notice he was naked in my gaze. I put my arms around him to show him what the butterfly looked like upside down and sideways, and worked my way up his belly to his tits with one hand while I worked my own pants down and off rubbing my dick against his butt as hard and round as a 12-year-old baking bowl. That was the day I learned I didn't have to come if I didn't want to because I made myself stop so what we were doing could go on into the afternoon.

He turned to face me when I was naked too and I kissed him, took the butterfly away and set it on my dresser where it wouldn't get hurt, then took his arms in my two hands and pushed them behind him and held them there while I hugged him to me and kissed him the way I wanted to kiss the boy on the beach beside the lake at night, only this one was alive and kissed me back. I pushed him backwards toward the bed and pushed him down on his back and stood over him astonished at what God had suddenly given me, as I am astonished now rubbing Jason's sweet cock up and down with my hungry tongue as fast as I can move my head while his hips buck up and down shoving his dick into space searching for relief while his balls roll free. I take those fat nuggets in my empty hand and slowly slowly slowly start to squeeze them ever so slightly gently but more and more firmly, painfully, harder, press them because he knows I want to burst their bloody juices in my hand, and I work my tongue around the head of his cock again and again while he slaps at the bed, at his own thigh, and pinch it just exactly underneath the head front and back anytime I think he's getting too close for my own comfort, slow him down and speed him up at once, which is what I did to the boy on my childhood bed.

I smiled at him as if I knew what I was doing, took the clothesline I'd been saving for what I didn't know till then, and tied a noose around his balls and tied them tightly to his ankles so he had to bend his knees and looked at me with fear that was almost horror and made me want to laugh. I tied his hands together to the bedpost then and said I wanted to watch him come. I spit in my hand and greased his ass and fucked him while I pulled him off and just kept fucking him while his ass rings squeezed my dick and he gushed all over the sheet and when he cried because he didn't know what else to do I came as well, came up his ass and lost my dick in him and lost myself. Later I untied him except for the noose on his balls and the rope I had attached to them that I held like a leash while he looked up at me like a happy puppy and fell asleep in my arms until my mother called up the stairs that it was dinner time. I got him up in the early evening light and we got dressed, he kissed me and went home alone, and I never even saw him in school again.

Jason, on the other hand, will never leave because I never let him come until he's passed the point of wanting to. I like it when he cries because he's just so full he cannot stand to have me near his dick and I don't even want to pause to breathe, I want to drink the smell and sound and taste and sight and feel of him down into me until he fills me up which he can never do and so it's easy for me to keep him on the edge as long as I want and he knows it is my right to do it, my right to command him to come or command him not to come and let him sleep with his blue balls for a month, but I have never been pointlessly mean, I just like him to know who's boss and that is what he begs me for, crawling down the corridor on his knees and manacled hands some days after I've been lunching on his straining cock while the sun moved gradually across the patient sky, dragging his shackled ankles chained to his steel-collared balls from the kitchen where I've sent him for a glass of water just because I can and back into the living room where I'm leaning against the far arm of the couch watching traffic in the street two floors below.

The woman who lives across the narrow courtyard, old enough to be his mother, is standing in her window the way she's done for weeks when I come into the living room bare-assed, I think she thinks she's hidden by her lacy drapery and that I can't see she's got her own hand up her skirt I know she'll have off long before I'm done with Jason crawling toward me in his chains, bringing with him not only the glass of water but also his pretty penis dick-a-dangle heavy hot-hung hook of hulking manflesh ramrod pigtool Lenny Bruce's thick fuckin' pile-drivin' fist at the end of a baby's arm o! so sweet and graceful cock I want to rip it from his body and carry it with me in my mouth next to my heart take it out and look at it on the subway suck on it and show it off, honey cock I dream about from time to time like a blimp taking up my entire sky, like a love fat baby I rock in my arms, like a stag I run down and mount, like the whole loved life that Jason reminds me is here before it's too late and gone.

No one else saw the stag, they were off chasing some other forest thing, and I was too young to know that killing it would haunt me and I didn't run it down I shot it blam between the eyes the first and only time I shot the rifle Dad had given me and it fell backwards as if some atomic blast had knocked it over not a little piece of lead that happened to find its way across a chasm of experience. By the time I reached its side its eyes were fluttering but it was still alive and looked at me. I had never been so hard in all my life and I forgot the other people in the woods, dropped my rifle, dropped my pants, and sank myself into it while it died. The spirit of a god passed out from between its lips in a rushing gasp of flight, its eyes went empty and we were nothing else but flesh together except that I was still alive. I climbed off and pulled up my pants before I got too scared to stay and no one ever knew I killed the stag, they'd all shot another deer and that was all they cared about, soon we all went home and soon thereafter I threw away the gun.

Jason is a little like a stag sometimes in his muscles and his brow but he is docile now because I have his balls wrapped up so tightly in my fist and I am looking murder in his eyes, I bare my teeth he knows I want to kill him with my dick because I cannot stand how much I love him, I look at his penis pleading for release but he's stopped bucking, he's stopped moving he has stopped believing altogether I will let him have relief and only tears are rolling down his cheeks which means I think the time has come. I pull his balls and punch him with the hand I hold them in until he yells so loudly that the woman whose skirt is gone is startled, and I take his whole cock down my throat and swallow it again and again until he starts to beg again and call me *Sir* and *Sir* and *Sir please Sir please ow ow ow Sir please Sir please Sir please may I come* and I say word by word as I bring him all the way out of my mouth, *On the count of three you may come, yes, you may come, yes, one, two, three* and he shouts and cries and screams and my face and throat are wet-hot and spunky and poor Jason shivers and shakes like a dying old jalopy and comes some more and finally starts calming down and bends himself into a little ball and commences sobbing in my arms. When he's fully quiet and starting to doze I turn him softly on his belly and use his own gism and my own spit as lube, settle myself deep in his ass and pull up gently on his hair. He raises his ass to meet me as I move, and starts to move himself up and down for me while I ride on his hipbones and watch his hole darken as he takes me in, then pink up as he lets me out, darken and pink, darken and pink. I remember the first time that I fucked Jason and how I will fuck him again and again just as long as forever, knowing I will never stop until I have done the impossible and satisfied myself with the grace of his cock in every sense. I ride and I ride and I ride, holding myself in check until he's rasping and shoving himself back on me, clawing at the sheets and I can feel his asshole twitch, and then at last at last I let myself go.

Trust

The stone floor turned cold beneath my naked feet and I felt the great relief of knowing that if I had ever had a chance to turn back, that chance was surely lost by now. The air itself became cold, and then a frigid gust of wind nearly sent me sprawling. I recovered with difficulty because the shackles that held my wrists were tightly chained behind my back, and the shackles that bound my ankles were also chained and hobbled me, and the hand that held the chain leash locked to the collar around my neck pulled me along on this blindfold journey even as the icy wind whipped my bare skin and the floor itself turned to pellets of ice and gravel, freezing and cutting sharp.

Then we were out of the wind, but the cold remained, as if we were walking now along an outdoor corridor between two walls; the floor here was a greasy pad, like a plastic carpet years of muddy boots had trod to a slick. The gloved hand covered my face and stopped me as the leash went slack. The hand slid down my covered eyes, my cheeks, my lips, and lifted up my chin. It turned my face to the left and right, then carefully pinched shut my nose and clamped my mouth closed. After my brain began to whirl, and when my lungs began to heave inside my chest, I still had not moved my head or arms, or tried in any way to escape the soft caress that moved now from my face. As air rushed into me I gasped and sought the glove again with my mouth. It slapped me across the cheek and I withdrew, chastened; then in a moment it fluttered over my chest as if searching for my living heart. Its fingers spread and rested on my breast and lightly pushed me back.

The march went on. The ground was briefly snow, so cold it squeaked. Then I was thrust into an embrace of sudden warmth, as if the air itself had reached out and taken me. I almost fell again, but again the gloved hand caught me, and I started to shiver from the change from cold to warm, and to shiver with gratitude for the hand I longed to kiss. The floor was carpeted, soft, warm, and dry. My feet ached but they were not numb. The hand pressed me gently to my knees. I heard a scurry at my back, then I was left with silence.

✦✦

TRUST

the advertisement had read,

> YOU WILL BE REQUIRED TO GIVE EVERYTHING BEFORE KNOWING IF YOU WILL RECEIVE ANYTHING. Special man sought by special woman. Absolute possession non-negotiable. You give all, I take all. Your life in my hands or do not write. Box. City.

What the ad called for was far beyond the picnic flings She had long since given me permission to enjoy: beyond the play parties where we watched the new ones at their whips, beyond the idle curiosities concerning this one's skill and that one's heart, beyond the formal research I'd conducted for my Ph.D. about the methods certain kinds of women use to ply their trade. I was not ignorant. I could read the barely coded message: this was a Goddess's invitation to eternity.

My genitals tingled and my face flushed hot: I wanted to vanish into the unknown She. Yet, as the locked gold ring that pierced my scrotum testified, I was property already. I had given myself to Her, who had known me at first sight, and I had no rights left to give away. I was only loose as a privilege, because I had proved myself trustworthy over time. Then why did I, already owned by the Goddess of my heart's desire, answer a come-on that I knew had to be real?

Say I was hungry. Say I was desperate. Say I felt I had no choice because I had to be taken or I would break and She had been unable to take me for years. Say I felt abandoned by Her own internal processes. Say I felt hurt, angry, frightened, and alone. Say I thought

I was a novelist, who could concoct an exciting escape on the very last page, and ride off into a sequel with my hat in my hand and my heart on my sleeve. Say I was desire caught by the tail. Say I wanted Her attention. Say mine was a gesture of hope as much as of despair. Say I was fulfilling my archetype, and making sure the world would still have winter. Say I was the same as any of the Goddess's other failed consorts. Say I was a fool.

A trained slave is not lightly turned away by a Mistress who desires service, a Goddess who demands to be adored, or a sadist whose heart is lifted up by cries of willing agony. Employed, educated, gentle, and polite, capable of thinking for himself, able to top the rest of your stable if you wish, a pansexual lesbian-identified whipmaster who prefers without question to kneel before the woman who holds him in thrall, to submit to Her power, to surrender to Her will – She answered back, of course.

But She did not tell me what the test would be: only where to show up, and when. So I had gone to the vacant house three hours after sunset, found the solitary mattress in the hollow room, undressed and left my clothing in the waiting box, lain down upon my belly with my face to the window wall, and waited.

Perhaps I dozed, exhausted from tension and strain; perhaps I simply disappeared and stayed connected with my body by some silver thread; perhaps my very life was drugged. All at once I knew I was alone no longer. A soundless presence wakened all my senses. I made myself lie still even though my eyes had opened wide and my heart was beating so hard I thought my body must be shaking with its rhythm.

For the first time the gloved hands touched my face, wrapping and sealing the blindfold in place. They lifted me to my knees and shackled me and collared me. They let me feel the length of chain across my lips. They let me feel the fitting of the leash into the collar ring, and let me hear the lock snap shut. They stood me on my feet, and footsteps slowly circled me. The gloved hands felt my head, my arms, my chest, my back, my belly, my balls, my ass, my legs; the leash went taut, and, trained, I followed it.

＊＊

In the room where I'd been left the silence took on voices. First the susurrations of the air disturbed somewhere, then the air itself, and finally the pounding of another heart caught in the vortex between the possibilities of terror and the possibilities of ecstasy; the soft caress of supple leather on live skin, the snapping tendons of a bending knee, the song of chain links touching one another, the cats-paw pacing and circling; then all movement slipped away.

Time. Time. Time in darkness loses duration. Time in silence loses its shape. In the time we had someone must have felt me.

"Who are you?" was followed by a wish of whip and a startled cry that told me we were three at least: myself, the punished one who had dared to speak, and our guardian.

Hours of darkness, days of silence may have passed in minutes. Twice more there was movement as of people coming or going.

The gloved hand rested on my shoulder. "After I touch you," came a loud stage whisper, "you may stand, lie down, or stretch your body any way you like within the confines of your bondage. When I touch you a second time return to your knees. A bowl of water will be placed in front of you. You may bend to drink from it, after which it will be removed."

The hand released me and I fell to the floor. I rolled and bent and pressed my tired muscles against my bonds. Before I could begin to stand the gloved hand touched my back. I knelt again, blood rushing through my veins. I bent forward and my face met a metal bowl. I lapped and sucked and wet my face drinking all the water I could; panting, then, I knelt down. Sounds told me the activity was being repeated in all the other quarters of the room. Finally we were still again.

"You are all Scheherazade," the voice that whispered told us. "It lies with you to keep your Queen amused. When I touch you, you are to tell a single story of an encounter you enjoyed with a Mistress, a Goddess, a Priestess, or a Queen, or with any other woman whose sexual and spiritual power you venerated or wished to venerate. You may not revise your story, nor may you tell two tales. You may ask no questions."

I waited for the hand, expecting to be first, and then I heard, in a halting voice, a man across the room commence.

"I arrived at X's home," he said, "as I had been instructed to do: at 10:30 in the morning, with a picnic lunch and a full tank of gas in the car, and wearing button-front pants over a posing strap. X admitted me and instructed me to wait on my knees in front of Her chair. In a few minutes She returned, put on some music, sat, and instructed me to remove Her slippers and kiss Her feet. After I had complied to Her satisfaction X told me to stand in the center of the room and strip to my posing strap and then to present myself to Her. I am not young or muscled, nor am I a graceful dancer, so I was chagrined; but of course I did as I was told.

"When I finished I was on my knees and arms before X, with my face on the floor and my wrists crossed as if bound at Her feet. X pushed my face with Her toe and told me to repeat while looking into Her eyes that I would respect and obey Her wishes and commands. She collared me and had me turn around and tied my hands together, then had me turn back to face Her. She told me She wanted to visit a friend of Hers in D_____ for the next few days, and that my job would be to drive Her there and then to return to N_____ alone.

"X said that before we left She wanted to take me down a bit. She read a couple of lines to me from a letter I had written at Her instruction. The lines concerned the hope I held dear that She would truly like commanding me, and the value I placed on the rights of Her status, including the right to cause me pain. I had also written that a right not exercised might be open to question. She said She disagreed with that surmise, but that Her disagreement would not prevent Her from pleasing Herself by hurting me. She removed my posing strap and had me lie on my back, then took my balls in Her hand. She experimented with varying degrees of pressure, slapping my balls with Her hands, stepping on them with Her bare feet, and squeezing them with increasing pressure until I was gasping and fighting to keep my place. Her eyes shone.

"I lost track of time but I did not want Her to stop; I felt taken and possessed; I was grateful; I wanted to worship Her in gratitude, to be used by Her, to do something for Her, to give Her more of me, to give Her anything. After a while She released me and my body convulsed. When I quieted down She held Her hand to my face and said, 'This is the hand that hurt you,' and allowed me to kiss that hand.

"X put a collar on my balls – a small stretcher with a D-ring attached – untied my hands, and told me to dress, leaving off the posing strap and leaving the buttons to my pants open, then to wait for Her at my place. Before we left She attached a short leash to the collar around my balls. The leash came out through the button fly and could be dropped down the leg of my pants, tucked into my pocket, or simply hooked over my belt if X wished to be discreet, as She did leaving Her apartment and driving on the city streets.

"X gave me instructions for leaving town. On one occasion I made a wrong turn and She asked how long my error would delay us. I said it would cost us about five minutes. When we left major traffic She opened my pants. During the drive She played with the leash from time to time, tightening and relaxing the tension, yet reminding me to pay attention to the road.

"We stopped for lunch on a hill overlooking the ocean. X closed my pants with the leash and went for a short walk while I spread a large towel for ground cover and laid out the food. When She returned She told me what to put on Her plate and in Her cup, and had me present Her lunch to Her as an offering; She ate and allowed me to eat.

"She spoke about the day and asked me questions, so I was feeling expansive in Her presence, and when a young couple walked past I did not realize I was talking too loudly to please X. She made me kneel, pulled down my pants, and spanked me loudly enough for the couple to hear. Then She explained my transgression, and my speech became more docile.

"X explored our hill some more while I packed up the car, then we drove on. Her friend lived in a small semi-rural home with a large wooded back yard. X had me carry Her bags to the house and wait in the hallway while She visited with Her friend. After an hour or so X returned with a cane in one hand and led me out the back door into the woods.

"When X found a spot She liked She told me to put my hands up. She tied my wrists and ankles to a tree, pulled down my pants, and looped the leash over a branch and snapped it back on itself. When I was secured She asked me if the number five meant anything to me, and when I said No, She said She would therefore cane me five times instead of once for each of the five minutes I had cost us by making a wrong turn. She pointed out that She could, if She wanted, cane me five times for each of the 300 seconds we had lost, but She wanted to spend more time with Her friend.

"I had not sought to be punished – I do not try to misbehave as a rule – but I was thrilled that X would punish me, and thrilled that

She would do so with the cane: I knew the way She used it I would bear the marks for several days.

"X gave me no warm-up and was not delicate. I did not cry but I could not keep entirely quiet. After the twenty-fifth stroke She examined and petted my welted and stinging buttocks. She said She liked to hear me whimper. She said someday She would like to take me far enough away from other people that She could hurt me and make me cry at Her leisure all day and night. She released me from the tree, pushed me to the ground, and put Her boot against my mouth, which She knew I did not like. When I kissed it as I knew She wanted me to do She let me hold Her legs while I shuddered over and over again. Finally She said that it was time for me to leave.

"X told me She was pleased with me and that I had done my job well, but said She was not going to let me come because She was not ready to let go of me. I bowed my head and She removed the collar from my neck. As I kissed the collar and I kissed Her hand I felt terribly sad. She held my balls gently as She removed the leash, then gave them one last squeeze and told me I was to leave the collar on my balls and not masturbate at least till I reached home. I dressed and left and did as She said."

The whisper said, "That was a long encounter."

"Yes – "

"Silence. You were not invited to speak."

In a minute another voice began.

"T always liked personal service," he said. "Sometimes She liked household service, and She often liked to tease me with Her body. She liked me to brush Her hair, for instance – especially while several buttons on Her shirt were open and Her breasts were visible – and to rub lotion into Her feet and legs while She wore a skirt with no underwear. Several times She had me hold and massage Her breasts, though She never told me to kiss them and I would never have done so uninvited.

"One day She greeted me wearing only mules and a lacy black peignoir. After having me undress She had me crawl after Her and repeatedly kiss her feet while She walked me around Her living room on a collar and leash. She stopped in front of a full-length mirror and studied our images for several minutes while I kept my mouth to her toes and insteps, then She instructed me to look at the mirror as well. The sight of T standing above me, holding the leash attached to the collar around my neck while I knelt naked at Her feet to which I had just been making love filled me with serenity. I smiled up at Her. 'Very good,' She said.

"T led me to a make-shift altar, showed me Her supplies, and told me to do a small incense-and-candle ritual while I knelt beside Her. Afterwards She told me to remove Her gown and to tell Her about it psychically, and what She could do to make it Hers, since She had acquired it from someone else recently. I told Her it felt friendly to me, and I would only sage it and wash it and sleep with it. She nodded, and stepped out of Her mules.

"Entirely naked She sat in Her chair and had me bring to Her a bowl of water in which rose petals were floating. She instructed me to use my hand to bathe Her with the water: first Her face, then Her breasts, then Her underarms, then Her vulva; then, with tissue paper She gave me after She stood up and turned around, Her anus. My penis had grown partially erect, and when She turned back to face me and saw it She took up a crop and stroked me with its flap. 'Are you glad to see me?' She asked. 'Yes, Mistress,' I replied, growing harder. She slapped my penis with Her crop repeatedly, while I cringed. 'You don't have permission,' She said quite seriously.

"T moved to sit in a chair whose cane seat was torn open. She tied a rope around my balls and told me to lie on my back under the seat; She sat on the chair resting Her feet on my belly and told me to lick and kiss Her thighs and buttocks but not to touch Her crotch, and to masturbate for Her but to let Her know when I was close to coming.

"It was very hard for me not to kiss where I had been forbidden. I longed to touch, to smell, to taste, and my longing increased my excitement. Each time I said I was nearing orgasm T pulled hard on the rope while holding me down with Her feet, and warned me not to come. Several times I was able to stop, but at last I failed and came despite myself. She laughed and said, You must learn to control yourself: turn over. Then She spanked and cropped me while I begged Her to stop. At one point when I pleaded especially hard I thought She came, but I never really knew."

The whisper asked, "How did you psychometrize the gown?"

"I examined its aura and followed the cords that ran to and from its history and its future, Ma'am."

Almost immediately the third man began.

"F was impatient watching me undress. She wanted me to fold my clothes and pile them on the floor beside Her couch, but She was tapping Her boot with a cane and I was trying to hurry for Her, so it took me three tries before She found the pile neat enough. Then She told me to kneel in the middle of the room on my hands and knees, keeping my eyes to the floor. She fixed a chain around my neck, then told me to turn over on my back and cuffed my feet and hands. She attached the collar and cuffs to a few ringbolts in Her walls with other chains that were all long enough to leave me some freedom of movement. And She attached everything with real locks, whose real keys She wore on a ring around Her neck. When I was thoroughly locked up She took my clothes out of the room and put them I knew not where.

"F was gone for several minutes. When She returned She strolled around me, pulling at the hair on my head and all over my body. Whenever I flinched or gasped She narrowed Her focus and pulled harder and more slowly. After a while She left off the hairs and pinched my nipples between Her fingers and Her nails. She started softly and built the sensation until I was almost pleading for mercy. She observed that She could cause quite a lot of pain without using anything but Her hands, and She was right.

"She nestled my ass and head in a couple of towels, held a small jar before my eyes, then passed it underneath my nose. It was piss. Some people want it from the source, She said, but you have to earn that. Would you like to earn that? I said Yes. She filled the hollow of my navel with the piss, and using Her finger painted my nostrils and lips with it, then poured some on my genitals. How would you earn it from me? She asked as She took the jar away; you smell like piss. She dropped a squeeze bottle and a cloth on my belly and said, Clean yourself up. The bottle contained alcohol. I mopped and swabbed myself.

"F removed all the towels and bottles and told me to get back up on all fours. Then She resumed Her stroll, prodding me as She went with the tip of the cane She carried or with the toe of Her boot; She pushed my head down with Her foot till my face was on the floor, then tapped my ass with Her cane. 'Spread your cheeks,' She ordered, and I opened my ass for Her. She put on a latex glove and lubed me, then slowly inserted a finger into my anus, maybe two. I was relieved as She moved in and out, and felt around inside my rectum, that I had given myself an enema before I visited Her. 'Some hate it,' She said,' and some long for it; which are you?' I thought She meant submission, and I whispered that I longed for it. She did not mean submission: She straddled me from behind and lubed me some more, then fucked me with a strap-on dildo, caning me now and then as if She were riding me.

"When She was through fucking me She told me to turn over on my back again. 'You are hopeless,' She said: 'you can't fold your clothes in a neat pile, you don't know how to earn your drink from the source, and you are not the least fun to ride.' She left the room and returned with my clothes, which She set down on the couch, still in a neat pile. She shortened the chains so that my limbs were spread and I was widely and helplessly exposed. Then She whipped my inner thighs and cock and balls with a whip that was soft but not light. When I started to complain She put my own underpants in my mouth, and whipped me some more.

"The telephone rang, and to my surprise F answered it. When She hung up She said, 'My slave is coming over and she really does not like men so I'm going to spare you both.' She unlocked all my bonds including the collar, told me to get dressed, had me crawl to the door and kiss Her boots, then sent me on my way."

"What did you enjoy about that encounter?"

"That She was in control, Ma'am."

The hand on my shoulder startled me. I had been listening to the other mens' stories, and had not planned out anything to say. I was still frightened that I had come, but I knew that this was not the time to fabricate, and so I told the true story of my recent life.

I said, "When S was first training me I enjoyed *every* encounter, partly because we were newly in love and partly because everything was a scene. Sometimes She had me undress at the foot of Her stairs as soon as I arrived, and crawl up to kiss Her feet. Sometimes She waited to collar me until after we had kissed hello. She was always Ma'am or Mistress to me except when public life made overt role inappropriate or too difficult for me to sustain, then the metaphysical leash was stretched; but I wore Her cock collar underneath my clothes for months at a time at work and at play, and removed it with permission only to bathe; and I still wear Her ring in my balls today, as you can see.

"I was rarely dressed when we were alone except in the decorations She liked most. I found enormous joy passing a mirror in Her home and seeing one collar around my neck, another around my cock and balls, cuffs around my wrists and ankles, and sometimes collars attached to one another by the chains She liked to have me wear. She trained me kindly but relentlessly in part because She was relentless, and in part because I wanted so deeply to be trained.

"In those mornings with S, even when I slept in chains, I usually had permission to get up, go to the bathroom, drink water, and prepare breakfast. I brought Her breakfast in bed for more than a year of weekends when circumstances, not reluctance, changed our habits. I made Her dinner most weekend nights as well, cleared the meals, and washed the dishes. I watered Her plants, collected Her garbage, made Her bed, hung out Her laundry, and helped Her organize Her piles of paperwork. I learned to serve my Mistress in Her personal sphere because I was Her consort and She needed service there, where She would not allow Her public houseboys.

"S trained me to Her leash both standing and crawling; She trained me to bring and to present Her glass of wine; She trained me to the mantra I discovered on my own – 'What *She* wants' – and She trained me to submit and then surrender, which was what I wanted all along. She hung me up and spread me out and whipped me for the fun of it. She threw me in the sling and fucked me. She shaved my balls and ass regularly, not only to keep me more accessible, but also to take from me a symbol of adulthood and the independence that comes with it. She pierced my penis and scrotum despite my needle terror, and gave me photographs of the needles sticking through me to contemplate what I was willing to give up for Her. Later She put Her gold ring in my scrotum to claim me in a ritual before 13 witnesses. She had me kneel and sit and lie beneath Her and eat Her through multiple multiple orgasms. She tied a leash around my balls to take me into Her at Her pace. She taught me to ask before I came. On the rare occasions I was willfully disobedient She punished me cleanly and when I got too toppy for Her taste She simply said, 'Kneel,' and kneel I did. She was gentle with my accidental failures and gentle with my limits, and I eagerly became Her devoted slave and Her private exhibitionist.

"S trained me as Her slave, and when She fell ill I cared for Her as Her slave – and as Her lover, baby, daddy, wife, childhood sweetheart, student, teacher, best friend, and more. In Her recuperation most of my parts remain active with most of Hers, but Her slave can only wait. My Mistress is on a long journey and does not know when or to what extent She will finally come home. And though I am a complex man with other features to my erotic life, I still yearn to be collared and leashed, to be humbled, hurt, and controlled by a woman who knows Her own erotic power, and who both wants to take and is capable of holding what I have to give.

"Perhaps I should not have answered the advertisement, since I cannot place my life in anyone else's hands, nor can I become another's property, for I am Hers. Instead I offer what I can of myself to a Keeper to contain me: a Domina or Priestess capable of caring for my Mistress's property in Her absence, who will return me to Her when She is ready.

"I do not know what kind of service or worship You require, nor do I know if You will want to use me as I need to be used, or to hold me in my Mistress's name. But if my limits are acceptable to you then I am willing to find out. I am willing to learn to serve You and please You to the best of my ability, and chiefly what I ask besides the right to serve, please, and adore is to be taken: psychologically and physically, kindly but strictly, gently but far. I do not wish to struggle with my Domina. I want to give up, I need to surrender to a woman who can hold me and take what She wants from me in doing so. In that way I can be, and give from, who I most centrally am."

"You take a great risk," the whisper said after a very long time. "What if I chose to keep you, and your Mistress be damned? How would She ever find you?"

Before I might have spoken I was lifted to my feet and trussed against a wall. The shackles on my wrists and legs were swiftly opened and as swiftly locked again, this time spread apart. The leash on the collar was also made secure, tightly chained to the wall behind me. Another ring was locked around my balls and pulled down, locked to the floor between my feet.

I heard movement all around me, and when it subsided the gloved hand took my blindfold off. The room was almost dark, yet to my eyes, which had been hidden from all light for so long, sight was only blurry; and as the images slowly evened out, She took on a growing definition. She knew the room, and knew exactly the moment when the last little lingering doubt would have passed, and when I would know Her as surely as I knew that from that breath forward every breath I took would be a gesture of Her own generosity.

"Lucky for you, you made your position well known, boy," my Mistress said, "and explained why you applied for this position at all. But didn't you also know better? Someone else might really have kept you against your will and mine. Almost as bad, considering that you are property, don't you think your response was designed to lead on whoever the woman might have been, whose advertisement drew you? Be careful how you answer," She said as I opened my mouth. "I have returned, and you are in no position to win but mine."

A gentle motor began to hum and the little section of floor between my feet where my balls were chained slowly started to sink beneath the surface of the carpet. I felt the tug as my scrotum grew taut, and my Mistress took Her Athame from the altar beside Her and silently cast a circle with me at its center. She held the blade to the light so I could see its edge, and stood in front of me. Gently She touched the base of my throat with the tip of the blade, and ran the knife quickly down my chest and belly, stopping when She reached my hardening penis. A fine dark line of blood followed in the knife blade's wake.

"Very well," my Mistress said, "I accept your application. You will be required to give everything before knowing if you will receive anything. Trust."

Light

Look! They've brought the virgin out and
shot her. That'll teach the twit
to wear my fancy dress, or to make light of it.
Who's next? Who else will say
my dick's a maypole, or the starry night's
an epileptic seizure?
Do you think I'm listening?
No god, no goddess – just for this one moment me
and you, so much like human animals we fool ourselves –
And in that moment I am the virgin
you are the dress and everything,
everything makes light.

James Williams's writings have been published in magazines such as *Advocate Men, Attitude, Black Sheets, Blue Food, International Leatherman, Paramour, Sandmutopia Guardian,* and *Spectator;* online in *Mind Caviar, Suspect Thoughts,* and *Velvet Mafia;* and in anthologies such as *Best American Erotica of 1995,* edited by Susie Bright (Simon & Schuster), *Best American Erotica of 2001,* edited by Susie Bright (Simon & Schuster), *Best American Erotica of 2003,* edited by Susie Bright (Simon & Schuster), *Best Gay Erotica of* 2002, edited by Richard LaBonté, *Best S/M Erotica: Extreme Stories of Extreme Sex,* edited by M. Christian and Simon Sheppard (Venus Book Club, 2002; Black Books, 2003), *Bitch Goddess,* edited by Pat Califia and Drew Campbell (Greenery Press), *Doing It for Daddy,* edited by Pat Califia (Alyson Publications), *My Biggest O,* edited by Jack Hart (Alyson Publications), *Rough Stuff 2,* edited by M. Christian and Simon Sheppard (Black Books), and *SM Futures* and *SM Visions,* both edited by Cecilia Tan (Richard Kasek Books and Circlet Press). He was the subject of profile interviews in *Different Loving,* by Gloria Brame, Will Brame, and Jon Jacobs (Villard), and *Sex: An Oral History,* by Harry Maurer (Viking). He lives in San Francisco.

Other Books from Greenery Press

General Sexuality

Big Big Love: A Sourcebook on Sex for People of Size and Those Who Love Them
Hanne Blank $15.95

The Bride Wore Black Leather... And He Looked Fabulous!
Andrew Campbell $11.95

The Ethical Slut: A Guide to Infinite Sexual Possibilities
Dossie Easton & Catherine A. Liszt $16.95

A Hand in the Bush: The Fine Art of Vaginal Fisting
Deborah Addington $13.95

Health Care Without Shame: A Handbook for the Sexually Diverse and Their Caregivers
Charles Moser, Ph.D., M.D. $11.95

Look Into My Eyes: How to Use Hypnosis to Bring Out the Best in Your Sex Life
Peter Masters $16.95

Phone Sex: Oral Thrills and Aural Skills
Miranda Austin $15.95

Sex Disasters... And How to Survive Them
C. Moser, Ph.D., M.D. and J. Hardy $16.95

Turning Pro: A Guide to Sex Work for the Ambitious and the Intrigued
Magdalene Meretrix $16.95

When Someone You Love Is Kinky
Dossie Easton & Catherine A. Liszt $15.95

BDSM/Kink

The Bullwhip Book
Andrew Conway $11.95

The Compleat Spanker
Lady Green $12.95

Family Jewels: A Guide to Male Genital Play and Torment
Hardy Haberman $12.95

Flogging
Joseph W. Bean $11.95

Jay Wiseman's Erotic Bondage Handbook
Jay Wiseman $16.95

KinkyCrafts: 99 Do-It-Yourself S/M Toys
Lady Green $16.95

The Loving Dominant
John Warren $16.95

Miss Abernathy's Concise Slave Training Manual
Christina Abernathy $12.95

The Mistress Manual: The Good Girl's Guide to Female Dominance
Mistress Lorelei $16.95

The Seductive Art of Japanese Bondage
Midori, photographed by Craig Morey $27.95

The Sexually Dominant Woman: A Workbook for Nervous Beginners
Lady Green $11.95

SM 101: A Realistic Introduction
Jay Wiseman $24.95

Fiction

The 43rd Mistress: A Sensual Odyssey
Grant Antrews $11.95

Haughty Spirit
Sharon Green $11.95

Love, Sal: letters from a boy in The City
Sal Iacopelli, ill. Phil Foglio $13.95

Murder At Roissy
John Warren $15.95

The Warrior Within
Sharon Green $11.95

The Warrior Enchained
Sharon Green $11.95

Please include $3 for first book and $1 for each additional book with your order to cover shipping and handling costs, plus $10 for overseas orders. VISA/MC accepted. Order from:

greenery press
3403 Piedmont Ave. #301, Oakland, CA 94611
toll-free 888/944-4434 http://www.greenerypress.com